Under the Ginkgo Tree

Sherry Slover Patterson

For:

Ashley Patterson Jones, Jamie Patterson,
AJ Patterson, Carter Jones, Leah Jones, and Lily Patterson

So that they may remember the courage and sacrifice
for freedom made by their grandparents
and great-grandparents

In memory of:

Nora Ethel Coggins Brantley, Thomas Wesley Brantley,
Kathleen Marguerite Brantley Slover, Walter Calvin
Slover, Robert Burgess Brantley, Roger Wesley Brantley,
Doris Dean Brantley Rice Johnson, James Cantrell Rice,
and
Eugene Fields Brantley

In honor of:

Evelyn Lou Brantley Kelly, my Aunt Evo

Foreword

This story is loosely based on my mother's family during the Second World War. Historical facts are accurate, and some events are real. But most of it is how I imagined the lives of my mother, her two sisters, and their mother during those difficult days.

Although some characters, events, information, and places in this book are actual and factual, every means possible has been utilized to acquire permissions for their use. These are recollections, diary/journal entries, shared with the author, and the author's point of view and should not be taken in any other context. All character interactions and dialogue are products of the author's imagination.

1941 January 10
Kathleen
Nazis in Paris

Shredding bits of notebook paper, I squeeze them into tight little balls and line them up like tiny soldiers in the pencil slot on the front of my desk.

The teacher's voice is background noise. My head is in German-occupied Paris. Bombs falling on the City of Lights. Parisians fleeing. Hammering boots tramping under the *Arc de Triumph* down the *Champs-Elysees* to the Seine and *Tour Eiffel*. People cowering in their apartments and peeking out of doors. Hitler, his smug self, touring the city's treasures. Striding through the Louvre. A sacrilege! Ugliness gazing upon the perfect beauty of Mona Lisa, Venus de Milo....

"Kathleen! Faites-vous attention!"

Heat rises on my cheeks, and I twist a curl at the nape of my neck. I have no idea what the teacher said. *"Pardon. Répétez s'il vous plait, Mademoiselle Whitehead."*

A sharp punch stabs my shoulder, and Tommy Bruce waves his pencil in my face. And then, loud so the whole class can hear, "Frenchwoman slipped up!"

" Kathleen, Où est le papier?"

" Um......c'est sur la table, Mademoiselle."

"Très bon!"

I love French and try to speak it well, but I am an irritation to my lazy high school classmates. Mademoiselle continues quizzing the class. Responses are mostly blank stares or mispronounced phrases.

I escape my embarrassment by retreating again into images of elegant Paris. The tower rising above blossoming cherry trees along the Seine. I'm in a boat drifting under the ancient bridges. The arm of a handsome Frenchman is draped around my shoulders. Looking up at the magnificent rose window and flying buttresses of *Notre Dame de Paris*.

1

Pausing at a street side cafe for onion soup and a glass of wine. No! Not wine! My family are Baptists, and we don't touch alcohol.

I am speaking fluent French, and my man reaches for my hand and calls me *Marguerite*. I hated my name Kathleen Marguerite until Mademoiselle had us research to see if our names had French origins. I love, love that part of my name is French!

Laughter fills the classroom as Tommy garbles, "Me parless Frenchy."

Mademoiselle corrects him. "Tommy, it's '*Je parle francais*.' Please try again."

I fantasize about Paris almost every day. But now the scene is ruined by last summer's events. Mrs. Brigman, my history teacher, said the French just rolled over and played dead and let the Nazis have the whole dang country.

Will I ever go to Paris or has my dream perished under the dust of Nazi boots?

1941 January 11
Kathleen
Frost Flowers

Evo and I rest our elbows on the window sill, our eyes studying the "frost flowers" blooming on the panes. That's what Charlotte Bronte called icy accumulations in *Jane Eyre* that we are reading in English class. I can't pull my gaze from swirling flakes that blanket dirty ground and bare limbs.

Just as Evo is scratching her name in the frost, Mama taps me on the shoulder. "Kathleen! You better get ready for school! And Evelyn Lou, you aren't even dressed yet! Get a' moving, girls!"

Evo begs, "Mama, can't I stay and play in the snow? The kids across the street are making a snowman. I bet their mamas are letting them stay home."

"No, you may not!"

My sister's lips poke out in an ugly pout. She storms to the bedroom.

Pulling on my shabby boots and bundling into my coat and scarf, I can't find my heavy gloves. "Doris, may I borrow your gloves, the furry ones? You won't need them in your warm car."

She's plopped on the couch with the latest *Glamour Magazine.* "No, Kathleen, you'll get them dirty and suede doesn't wash." She flips a page. She only thinks of herself and her fancy clothing.

"Thanks for nothing, Doris! Enjoy your toasty ride to work." Grabbing my book satchel, I'm out the front door as Mama warns, "Be particular, you hear!"

It is quiet. Lovely. But I'm freezing as I make my way down the four blocks to the school. My face is stiff with cold. I should have brought an extra scarf. Pushing my satchel under my arm, I stuff bare hands into my pockets. The snow is falling harder and faster, and I can barely make out the cupola atop the school.

At last, in the shelter of homeroom, I shed my coat. Dang it! Tommy Bruce is already here. "Frenchwoman," he calls me, yet again. Heads turn and stare. I tremble and blush. I want to pull my coat over my head and disappear. I plop into my desk and escape to Paris.

It's snowing there, too. My French boyfriend and I are strolling by the Seine. Falling snow disappearing into the water. He brushes flakes from my face and warms my hands in his. The Germans are not part of this scene because in my dream they never took over my city.

My life here is boring. Nothing beautiful or exciting. I want to go to the University of North Carolina, major in French, and move to Paris. I'd be a translator or secretary. But I'll probably never leave Fayetteville, North Carolina, unless I marry a soldier who will take me back to his home after his service is over. Having him go to war is not part of my plan.

"Hey, Kathleen! Lemme see your French homework. I just need to fill in a couple of verbs." What Tommy really wants is to copy the whole thing. I turn my head to the window.

Boys! I'm sick and tired of fickle ones who ask me out and nothing comes of it. And the two timers like Robert. I thought he liked me, and I certainly liked him. I haven't heard from him since before Christmas, and Doris saw him on Hay Street with another girl. I think she enjoyed telling me. As they say, "Ashes to ashes, dust to dust, show me a boy that a girl can trust."

Doris and I date many boys from nearby Fort Bragg. Most are very mannerly and respectful, but some of them only want "you know what." I like some kissing and cuddling, but that is where I draw the line. If one tries to go further, I show him the door. I am not going there until I

4

marry, which I am in no hurry to do since I am only sixteen.

The bell rings. Students spill out doors into the chaos of the hallway. My best friend Betty Sue catches up with me.

"Kat, I went to the soda shoppe with Tom Adams, but it was boring, boring. He just jabbered on about football."

"Yep. That's the way with high school boys. The soldiers are far more interesting. See you after school, Betty Sue."

There is no shortage of soldiers to date. Fort Bragg has more and more stationed there since the beginning of the war in Europe. They come Fayetteville on the weekends to go to the movies, USO, or restaurants. And of course, they are looking for girls.

I settle into math class, but teacher doesn't begin class. She's grading papers. Students start chattering. After a few empty minutes, I pull out the little notebook I carry in my purse in case I get inspired to write a poem. I love words and the magic can happen when you put them together.

My poems aren't good, nothing like my favorite Edna St Vincent Millay. But writing soothes me when I'm nervous and helps me vent my emotions. I never share secret feelings, except with Betty Sue. She doesn't laugh at my poems as I'm sure Doris would. I open the notebook and read what I started last night:

> *Who?*
> *There is someone I haven't met*
> *Who flashes a smile so rare*
> *That brings light to his eyes*
> *And gold to his sea of wavy hair.*
> *This one who, when he speaks*
> *Writes a book with his words*
> *True, honest...*

"Ok, class. Settle down and get out your books."
Back to reality, Kathleen. I close my notebook and tuck it in my purse.

By the time I leave school, the snow has stopped, and the sun is out. All the beauty gone. Just the plain old dingy Roberson street, slushy under my feet.

1941 January 11
Evo
Janie Ringo

I can't wait to get out of this school and meet Edna and play in the snow. I hope there will be enough to make a snowman and have a good snowball fight!

Miss Smith is carrying on about multiplying fractions. And I don't care. "Evelyn Brantley! Stop staring out the window! Pay attention!"

Oh, shoot! It is slowing down. No nine year old should be made to sit through this boring stuff when she could be out there having fun.

At least, I can look forward to last period when Mrs. Hall will surely read us a story in English class. The last one she read was the entire *Adventures of Huckleberry Finn*. I loved it all, but especially the part where Huck pretends to be a girl to hide from his Pap. Huck's father was mean and worthless, not like my sweet and kind Daddy. I miss him so much. Why did he have to get sick and die?

I love reading, but I also like stories on the radio. There's a new one called *Inner Sanctum*. Scary, with mysterious squeaking doors and ghosts. I adore stories. I feel like I am sneaking into somebody else's life. I can see it all in my head.

Dang! Drat! Dang! The snow has stopped, and the sun is shining!

School has let out, and I'm headed home. I try to make a snowball, but it melts in my gloves. I wish I had a nickel for some candy at Gibson's Grocery. I'm going to stop at Janie Ringo's house. She will surely give me a cookie, and I can play with her little children Rex and Abby.

Janie Ringo isn't her real name, at least not the

Ringo part. She comes to our house to help, especially when Mama is laid up with a kidney stone. She sings while she works. Sometimes "Ring, Ring de Banjo." That's where the Ringo part came from.

Doris says I shouldn't be going to Janie's house since she is a Negro. I don't care what the high and mighty Doris thinks. I like Janie and Abby and Rex. They are fun and happy. I just won't tell Doris. She would make a stink about it and make me cry.

Just past Gibson's Grocery, I hear "Hey, Evo!" I turn as a soggy snow/mud ball smacks me in the face. It's that pesky Frankie Kelly who works at the store as a delivery boy after school.

"I will get you back, Frankie Kelly!" I run to the safety of Janie's porch. She opens the door and shoos me in.

Janie can't stop laughing, and her big belly shakes. "Lord child, your face is half white and half black and dripping! Let me clean you up." Pulling me into the kitchen, she wipes my face. First with her apron and then with a warm cloth from the sink. "You gonna have to stop letting that Frankie boy mess with you and fight back. I gon' tell his Mama."

"Please don't do that, Janie. She'll tan his hide, and then he will be mad at me."

Janie gives me and her little ones cookies and glasses of cold, sweet milk. We're munching and slurping when Janie says, "Miss Evelyn, ain't you got your piano lesson today with Mrs. Loy?"

I almost choke on my cookie. I'm supposed to go to Mrs. Loy's right from school.

"Thanks for the cookie, Janie. Bye, Abby and Rex." I grab my coat and bolt out the door, running to make Mrs. Loy's not too, too late. I hope I don't run into Frankie again.

1941 January 15
Ethel
My Girls

Doris and Kathleen go out almost every night with some local boys, but mainly with soldiers. Boys come to our house to sing around our piano or play games with the girls and the rest of the family. We are renting a room to Sgt. Mike White and his wife Linda, nice folks. They are so cute together. Mike is so very tall that Linda looks like a midget next to him. They often join in the fun.

I worry about Kathleen going out so much, as she is fixing to finish her senior year and needs to tend to her studies. But she's smart and continues to make top grades. She should go to college, but we can't afford it. She has some highfalutin plans, but probably the best she will be able to do is to get a job to pay tuition at Worth Business College. With all the eligible young men crossing her path, I reckon she will most likely marry one. I hope that she won't pick a soldier because we will probably get into the war. And off will go the boys and husbands and sons.

Doris, at twenty-one, is a flirt and tosses off boys when better ones come along. She wasn't interested in studies and couldn't wait to graduate and do whatever she wanted. Kathleen often did her homework for her! No interest in college or any other kind of further training. She's "miss personality plus" as front desk clerk at Verne's Tailor Shop at Fort Bragg. She is attending "the college of young men" and majoring in fashion! Every spare dime she gets goes to new clothes or makeup.

Of course, all the children do help with part of their salaries for our expenses like food, rent, and light bills. Thank goodness for that because we would never be able to make it.

With my Wesley dying with leukemia just two years ago, things have been tough. I was lucky that I could sew and work part time at JC Penny's doing alterations. This was not enough, so we have had several sets of roomers. Very crowded in this house. The roomers taking the front bedroom. The boys, fifteen-year-old Gene and nineteen-year-old Roger, are in the middle bedroom. The girls are in the back one. I sleep in the little room we added on behind the kitchen. Buck, who is twenty-four, has an apartment with his new wife Pauline Dees.

Evelyn is too young at nine for all of this boy stuff, thank goodness. Her free time is spent skedaddling up the hill to play with her friend Edna. They go to the woods near Edna's house to do who knows what and share whatever secrets nine year olds share.

She comes home with scratches and bruises and tears in her clothes. Last fall, she was climbing a fence and tore a big hole in the blue corduroy jumper I had just made her. I had told her to change out of her school clothes before she dashed out to Edna. But she was in too much of a hurry. I tanned her hide good for that one, but she did not cry. Just like her, tough and proud.

1941 February 14
Kathleen
Mr. Rochester

It's Valentine's Day which means nothing to me as I have no beau or expectation of receiving any greeting from anyone. Except Mama, of course, who will have cookies or a cake when we all get home tonight.

Just a plain ol' school day except that I ordered my class ring. I plunked down a whole fifteen dollars which amounts to almost two months of my salary at the Candy Kitchen! When I found out how much the ring would cost, I told Mama I was not going to get one. She would not hear of it. She said I had worked hard and I should have the ring as a symbol of my achievement. Oh, and I made ninety-eight on my French test, the highest grade in the class. I just missed one verb conjugation.

Betty Sue and I are going on a double date tonight with two boys Doris dragged to the house last Saturday for card playing. I don't particularly care for either of them, but going out on a floppy date is better than sitting home.

That Doris is shameless in the way she flirts with the soldiers who come into the tailor shop. She just keeps collecting them and inviting them home and then she takes her pick. Sometimes she even stands one up if someone better comes along. In that case we turn them away, or if they look real down faced, we might invite them in. Once or twice I have gone out with one. Mama keeps talking to Doris about how rude this is, but it does no good. She might as well be talking to the fence post.

After school, I am going right to the Candy Kitchen for a couple of hours. I hate that job. It is hot with all the sweet concoctions boiling away on the stoves. When Janie Ringo's big, strong husband Sam pours the candy out onto the marble slab, it's my job to watch and decide when it's cool enough to cut into squares. If I do it too soon, I have a gooey mess. If I wait too long, it's too hard to cut. Then, I wrap the squares in paper and start the whole thing all over again. It is a mindless task which I will never have to do again once I graduate, get my business degree, and get a real job.

When I get home after the date, I will have to read a few chapters of *Jane Eyre* for English class. I hope that somehow sweet and selfless Jane will get together with the strange and moody Mr. Rochester. And the story will turn from dark to happy, just like I want my life to do.

1941 February 16
Kathleen
"Button Your Pants Up"

Doris, Evo, and I walked to First Baptist church on the corner of Anderson and Olds downtown this morning. Olds is an appropriate name for the location because the towering brick building is ancient, built around 1910. But the people there are nice, and the minister is kind. This morning he prayed for all the people in the European war. It scares me when that war is mentioned.

Soldiers tell us about their training at Fort Bragg, and that upsets me too as it seems they are getting ready for something. My oldest brother Buck says that our military needs to be prepared just in case. He believes we are so far away that the war should not affect us. I am not so sure.

In the afternoon Betty Sue and I went to Fort Bragg to see a play with Raeford and Worth. There's a talented group of soldier actors that put on a play occasionally. Well, we never made it there as Raeford's car ran out of gas on Bragg Boulevard. He had to walk two miles back toward town to find a station open since it was Sunday. Betty Sue and I and Worth waited in the car. It was cold and boring. Of course, when Raeford got back with the gas, which he said had cost him a whole twelve cents a gallon, we had missed the start of the play. We just came back to the house and talked a while before the boys had to leave and get back to base.

After supper, I went to Baptist Young People's Union, better known as BYPU. Everyone calls it "Button Your Pants Up," but not in front of the leaders. It's fun because there's refreshments and games after the program. Mama does not like the playing of any games on Sunday because she firmly believes the Sabbath should be reserved for quiet, reflection, and rest. She says God rested on the seventh day after creating the world, so we should too. She does not know how rowdy BYPU gets, or she wouldn't let me go.

Before bed, I wrote a letter to my Canadian pen pal Marjorie. Mademoiselle Whitehead got the class involved in an exchange between French and English speakers. It's hard as none of us in the class is fluent. But it's easier to write than speak since you can look things up. Marj writes in English, and I write back in French. Of course, she's confident in both languages. She is so kind even though my French is poor. She corrects me gently, so I can learn. I never need to correct her English.

Marj wrote that their high schools are ending their term after Easter to allow teens to work on farms or in munitions factories. Canada is independent from the British Empire, but the two share George VI as their monarch. The country didn't have to help England in the war, but they wanted to.

Poor England! German blitz bombs falling on them all the time. They need help. I hope we won't have to be that help.

1941 March 20
Doris
Jimmie Rice

It's depressingly slow this afternoon in the shop. Four-fifteen, as the minutes tick away toward five o'clock when I can go home and wait for my handsome date. He came in at noon to leave his uniform trousers to be altered for a tighter waist fit. His name is Walter Slover, and he is a first sergeant. I like dating men with higher rank who are older than some of the silly privates. He talked funny like he was from up north. Anyway, he is coming by the house at six-thirty. I must get home in time to doll up a bit and change into my new green dress.

I'm starting to count the cash drawer. I want to be ready to make a dash for my car at five sharp. The irritating bell tingles at the door.

In walks heaven, topped by the blondest hair outside of a dye job at Little Bit's Beauty Parlor. His wavy hair shines in the afternoon sunlight. My heart is beating faster, and my palms are sweaty as he walks directly toward me, blue eyes looking right into mine. He smiles, stops at the counter, puts both hands on it and leans in.

"May I help you?" I squeak out over the pounding of my heart.

"Oh, yes, I hope so. I've walked by this door about four times, admiring your deep brown curls which look just like Vivien Leigh's, Miss Scarlett O'Hara in *Gone with the Wind*. Except you are much prettier. I had to keep coming by to make sure you were real and not part of a movie poster."

Oh, my! I'm so taken aback that I am speechless. He is flirting to the nth degree. I'm usually able to flirt back, but the directness of his gaze leaves me feeling like a silly, gutless girl.

"Well, thank you. You look pretty good, yourself." *I can't believe I actually said that.*

"Well, Miss Luscious Curls, I am Corporal James Cantrell Rice, your admirer. Do you have a name?"

"Doris Brantley."

"Well, Miss Brantley, you are going to accompany me tonight to the USO dance in Fayetteville. I have a car, and I'll pick you up at eighteen hundred hours." He shows off with military time, like I wouldn't know he means six o'clock.

I muster up my courage. "Wait, I haven't even said I'll go with you!"

"Of course, you will accompany me. I offered an invitation that you can't pass up because I can guarantee that you'll have the time of your life. I'm a superb dancer, and it was meant for us to be together tonight. You see, I believe in fate. I think everything that happens was meant to be. So, there you are. This is our time, and it can't be altered by your refusing me."

"That's poppycock. I don't believe a word you just said. A person creates his or her own fate. I didn't get this good job by sitting around waiting for something to happen. After high school, I got myself out here to answer an ad in *The Fayetteville Observer*. I dressed up and took the bus to this tailor shop. I made a good impression on Verne because I was straightforward and organized. I have worked here two years and saved enough to buy an old, but reliable car. All of that was not fate; I made it happen!" *Why did I say all that? I sounded like a preacher.*

"Well, I don't know about that, but I can certainly see that you're flirting with me because the proof is in your eyes and the bit of blushing on your cheeks."

"I am most certainly not blushing. It is my rouge."

"Hmm, there was no rouge or blush or whatever you want to call it when I first walked in. Please go with me tonight. I am a lonely airman training hard every day and in need of some fun. Even though you are strikingly beautiful, you look a little weary with your job and could use a jolly evening with the best dancer in all of Fort Bragg."

I'm overwhelmed by his good looks and nerve, and I hear myself saying, "Ok." *I am not even sure this came out of my mouth, or that I was just thinking it.*

"Great! What is your address?"

"229 Roberson Street near the high school."

"Wonderful! I will see you at eighteen hundred hours, sharp." With that he turns on his heels and strides out of Verne's. The bell jingle is now cheerful.

Well, Doris, you have certainly surprised yourself. I'm both excited and nervous about this date. Never have I met a man who overwhelmed me so quickly. And … he is a dreamboat!

Yikes! My memory jolts. I'm supposed to go out with that Walter fellow at six-thirty! I didn't even think of it after Jimmie Rice slid so smoothly into my day. Oh well. I will have left with Jimmie at six before Walter shows up. Whew, am I ever glad I didn't make the two dates at the same time! Kathleen, Mama, and Evelyn will make up a story for me like maybe I had to work late or visit a sick friend. Mama will be mad as a wet hen, but she will get over it.

And I will be out with the handsome and charming Jimmie Rice.

1941 March 20
Doris
Gentleman Caller

I'm barely home and dressed when Mama sticks her head in the bedroom door. "There is a gentleman caller asking for you in the front room." I wish she wouldn't say "gentleman caller," but I don't have time to argue with her about that outdated phrase.

It's only five forty-five. Jimmie is early. That's good because now there is no chance we will run in to Walter. Unless he comes way earlier than the six-thirty we arranged!

I raise my eyebrows, drop my jaw, and my mouth forms an O as I press the curler to my lashes. And a final touch of lipstick which I blot on a Kleenex. I stand and look at myself in the dresser mirror. Hmmm. I look pretty good in my slim green dress and heels. I turn a bit and check to see if the seams in my nylons are straight. Yep. I read that the girls in England can't get nylons because the fabric is used for parachutes, and they draw fake seam lines right on their bare legs with chalk. What a bother that would be!

Gads! I have a paralyzing thought. What if the caller is Walter and not Jimmie! I peep around the corner and see Jimmie's blonde hair and breathe a sigh of relief. Whew! My heart starts to beat faster like it did when I saw Jimmie in the shop. I step out of the bedroom and into the dining room. Just as I see him and he sees me, I bang my foot on the piano leg.

"Gee, Doris. You are in a hurry to see me. Did you hurt yourself?"

"No. Just a little bump. I'm fine."

"Don't you want me to look at your foot and maybe massage it a bit? We don't want a bum foot to interfere with our dancing, do we?"

I don't reply to this. The nerve of him to suggest something even mildly intimate when I hardly know him!

"No thank you. Shall we go now?" *Better get out of here before Walter shows up.*

Out we go, and the screen door slams behind us. Jimmie puts his hand under my elbow and helps me down the steps. Help I do not need. But I decide to let it go. Men like to hover and protect. I don't want to make him mad.

His car is a Ford, fairly new, maybe about a 1938 and black. He opens my door and I slide in, tucking in the hem of my skirt. He closes the door with a little slam and hops around to the driver's side. We are off.

1941 March 20
Kathleen
Walter Slover

That flaky Doris has done it again! Right after I get home from the Candy Kitchen, a guy shows up at our door. I was way back in the bedroom when he knocked, and it took me a while to get to the door. He is peering through the front door glass side panel, probably wondering if anyone is home.

I open the door. "Is Doris here? I came to take her to a movie."

Right off, I can tell he is a Yankee by the way he talks. But very handsome, tall, with dark hair that falls in a curl over his forehead. His smile of anticipation flattens when I tell him Doris is not here.

She left earlier with another boy, giving us no indication that she was expecting another date. I am getting pretty good at lying for her. Maybe I should just tell him that she has stood him up. But I lie once again. "No, sorry. Umm...she sent a message with a co-worker who lives down the street. She has to work until nine to get a big order ready. And she asked me to apologize to you for canceling."

He doesn't look like he believes me and says, "I'm Walter Slover. Didn't she mention my name?"

"Oh, yes, I think she did. I know she is real sorry she missed you."

"I already bought the tickets for the show. It is *Come Live with Me* at the Colony. Uh, uh... would you like to come live... I mean...go with me?" He lets a little ironic laugh slip out as he realizes he has used words that mimic the movie title. I giggle. He adds, "We can get a little supper afterwards?"

So here I stand, looking at one of Doris' leftovers. But he is handsome, so I think, *what the heck.* "Yes, thank you, I will but I need to be home fairly early because I have a theme to write for English class. By the way I am Kathleen."

"You are still in high school? You don't look it."

I don't know whether to take that as a compliment or not. "Let me get my coat." I take a long time since I want to freshen up my face and put on my new Revlon Super Red lipstick. I tell Mama I won't be home for supper, and off we go. He has no car, so we walk down Roberson Street and up Hay Street to the Colony.

"Where are you from, Walter? New York?"

"No, I grew up in southern Indiana in a small town called Shelburn."

I feel a bit shy. We really don't talk a whole lot on the way, but I get a good look at him and notice he is wearing sergeant stripes on his uniform. I wonder how old he is. My guess is somewhat older than me since he has risen to this rank.

Come Live with Me is a just ok movie, but it does have Jimmy Stewart, my favorite, as the leading man. His character is a writer and marries Heddy Lamar's character who is from Vienna and wants to stay in the USA but is in danger of being deported. The outcome is predictable as they arrange a marriage of convenience but fall in love later. It is a bit strange being with Walter who I don't know at all and watching such a romantic story.

At supper in the New York Café, talking is a little easier. We chat about the movie and then about my school and the rest of my family. When I get to Daddy and say that he had passed away a few years ago from leukemia, Walter gets a strange look on his face.

"My Dad is gone too. He died in a coal mine accident. About the only job in Shelburn was working in that mine which I didn't want to. So, I joined the Army when I turned nineteen three years ago. I needed to make some good money to help support mother and my sisters."

So, he's twenty-two. Way too old for a sixteen-year-old. I suddenly feel like a child.

Walter continues, "I know you miss your father. I really miss mine. We used to fish and hunt together. He was a real outdoorsman. Guess when he was not working in the dark, close mine, he wanted to be in the wide-open spaces."

"My dad was fun," I offer. "He was always smiling and making up jokes. He drove a truck for Swift and Company and was on the road a lot. We missed him but got so excited when he was about to come home."

On the walk home, I chatter too much about school and the things that happen there which must be extremely boring to him since he is older and away from all that. But he makes a comment or asks a question now and then, so I know he is listening. Very polite.

I really enjoy talking to him and would have invited him in if I didn't have that infernal theme to write. I wish Doris would write it for me. She owes me for covering for her. On second thought, that is a bad idea as she isn't much of a writer. I wrote a lot of themes for her when she was in high school.

"Thank you, Kathleen, for going with me. I had a good time." And he reaches for my hand and brushes it with a little kiss. I have never had a fellow do anything like that before, and it makes my heart do a little flip!

Hmmm ... this one might be a keeper. But he will probably come back for Doris and that will be the end of that.

1941 March 20
Doris
Spellbound

I am wide awake in bed. Kathleen is sitting at the desk writing an English theme.

I loved Jimmie whirling me around the dance floor. He must have had lessons when he was growing up in Kentucky. Probably Cotillion dances. I can tell his family is well to do because of his description of their house. Separate bedrooms for him and each of his three brothers. Not like us where all the girls are in one bedroom and the boys in another and Mama in the lean to off the kitchen. That difference in our backgrounds made me a little nervous. But he was so open and obviously doesn't care about that.

He was full of energy; we danced every dance. I was grateful for a rest when they put on a slow record, Tommy Dorsey's "I'll Never Smile Again." When his arm went around my waist, I got that speedy heart rate again. I hope he couldn't feel it or hear it. He pulled me very close and bent down and gave me a little kiss. Oh, he is a very good kisser! When he left me at the door later, he kissed me again, just once but held it longer. Oh!

Kathleen got home before me, and she bawled me out for leaving Walter in the lurch. But her little snit was brief. Because when I asked her how her date with Walter went, she smiled and started to twirl a curl on the nape of her neck like she does when she is excited.

I wanted to talk more about our dates, but Kathleen fell sleep quickly after she finished her theme. I don't know how she does it. She just whips them out. Writing was so hard for me when I was in high school. I'm glad it's not part of my job now.

Jimmie is unlike any other boy I have dated. He is so self-confident and knows how to treat a woman. He is a bit forward. I need to be careful not to fall totally under his spell and lose my good sense! But I can't stop thinking about him.

1941 March 22
Kathleen
Ginkgo Tree

Walter does come for me again! When I get home from a bit of Saturday morning shopping with Betty Sue, he is sitting on our couch. He smiles big and stands up.

"Hello, Kathleen, so good to see you again. I was wondering if, since it is a nice warm day, you would like to go for a walk and look for signs of spring."

What a swell idea! Just up my alley as I love the beauty of the outdoors.

"Well, yes, Walter, I think I would. Let me go put my packages away."

I take a few minutes in the bedroom to powder my nose and put on some fresh lipstick. Doris comes in the bedroom and says that she just apologized to Walter for standing him up on Thursday night. He was kind but did not ask her out again. Anyway, she is no longer interested in him since she met Jimmie. So, all is well, and I am happy to be going out with Walter.

The early afternoon sun is so bright that it hurts my eyes. The air is warm and soft. Just a perfect day. We may have an early spring.

We walk down Roberson street and stop at Gibson's grocery for a chocolate ice cream bar and then continue up to the high school. I point to some windows of my classes and the cafeteria door, and then we walk around back to the football field. I recount a little about our Bulldogs' football games last fall, but I am not much interested in football. He talks about playing on the Shelburn team, but then switches topics and describes his hometown.

After we walk the length of the field, I am getting tired since I walked all morning in town, so we sit down on the first row of the bleachers. Walter says that Shelburn is a very small town, much smaller than Fayetteville, centered around the coal mine. I can't imagine how terrible working underground in a dark and dangerous place would be, and I tell him so.

"Yes, my Dad took me down a couple of times, and it was just awful. Men's faces covered with black coal dust, strong smell of the sulfur, explosives, and sweat. Piles of rock left from dynamiting the walls to reach the veins of coal.   Dark like a dungeon. I think that Dad thought I would just follow in his footsteps, and he wanted to prepare me."

I want to ask him if his father's body was recovered after the accident, but I dare not bring up such a thing. Mama always says to remember to load your brain before you shoot your mouth off. No need for shooting off that question which could be too sensitive since I hardly know him.

I tell him how much my Daddy's absence still hurts. "Dad was so much fun. He made jokes, sang, and made us all feel loved and special. We always had good meat for our meals as he brought home leftovers from his route. I sure miss the stews Mama made and the chopped steak she fried with onions. We can hardly afford meat now, so we mainly eat the chickens Mama raises in the back yard, and those meals are few and far between because we spare the hens for the eggs."

"My mother raised chickens too! Chicken, chicken, chicken. My sisters Maxine, Euleta, and I got so sick of it. I don't like to eat it now. And when I get out of the Army and get a good job, I'm going to eat steak every day!"

We continue up to Fountainhead Street, and I show him where our friends Bea, Earl, Becky and Edna Rogers live. One of Bea's Japanese cherry trees is showing a bit of pale, pink fuzz, just waiting to burst into brilliant mauve blooms.

"I love to go the Rogers' house at Christmas because Mrs. Rogers is the best cook and always has lady

26

finger cookies and fruitcake to share. Actually, I don't much like fruitcake, too heavy, more fruit than cake."

Walter laughs. "Well, I guess you could pick out the fruit and eat the cake crumbs."

"That would be pretty hard work for a precious few crumbs, and besides, I don't want to be rude to Mrs. Rogers. I bet that one of her cakes weighs five pounds!"

Walter chuckles, leans over, and gives me a little kiss on the cheek. We look into each other's eyes, and he plants a soft kiss on my mouth and then another a bit harder and longer.

We continue up the hill near the hospital and stop under a big ginkgo tree.

Walter pulls down a small, new leaf and examines it. "This is strange. It looks like a little fan. There is no center stalk."

"My science teacher said that the ginkgo is one of the oldest trees still in existence. In autumn, the leaves turn bright yellow, and all fall together in a single day. It's beautiful."

"Hey, Kathleen, let's come back here again in the fall when they are golden."

Oh! He must be planning on a long relationship. Hmm… Right now, standing next to his tall frame, dark hair, and kind manner, that sounds good to me.

1941 March 29
Evo
Jimmie vs Slover

Doris and Kathleen have gone out tonight with their beaus Jimmie and Slover. Slover's first name is Walter, but everyone calls him by his last name. I like that.

Maybe I could be Brantley. I don't like Evelyn because it sounds like something old Queen Victoria might have named one of her many children. Old, old. I tell everyone to call me Evo. But most people insist on Evelyn. My middle name is Lou which is worse even though it is my grandmother Coggins' name. I love her but not that name! What I hate the most is when Mama or Doris gets mad at me and calls me the whole blame thing: Evelyn Lou Brantley!

Slover brought me a bag of candy and asked me about school and my piano lessons. He wanted to hear me play something, so I played a little of "Amazing Grace." I wish I knew some popular songs, but Mrs. Loy thinks that new songs lead to the devil. Old, old, old. Times are changing. People should get with it.

Jimmie ignored me completely. He only is interested in Doris. Doris kept giving me these sharp looks and motioning with her head that I should skedaddle. Jimmie looks at Doris in a funny way and talks just about himself He corrects some of the things Doris says, and sometimes they get to arguing. I wish he would go away.

1941 April 1
Ethel
Kidney Stone

I was awake all night with a kidney stone. The pain was so bad that I threw up several times. Doris hovered around me and did everything she could think of to help from hot compresses to massaging my abdomen and back. Nothing helped, but Doris sure tried. She is so good when someone is sick, Kathleen isn't, and Evelyn just cries and looks scared. I made them stay away from my room.

The attacks are coming more often. The doctor told me the next time, I would have to have surgery. I don't want surgery as we can't afford it, and it scares me. Doris has insisted that I go to the doctor today, so I guess I'm going as she will not change her mind for love nor money.

Janie came early this morning to cook breakfast for everyone and start on my washing. She is such a blessing, helping us out when she has young children of her own and other jobs. She is the most hardworking woman I have ever known, and her husband Sam is a hard worker, too. He works at the Candy Kitchen where Kathleen works some and as a janitor at the bank.

There are people on Roberson Street who don't like Janie's family living here since they are colored. This is unfair because they are the kindest folks. The people who don't like them don't hesitate to hire them to help with housework, ironing, or yard work. Then, they complain that Janie charges too much … which she doesn't. When she works for me, she often does extra things for no charge. I don't care if she is colored. She is a good friend to me.

I am still in bed. The pain has eased off some. Maybe the doctor will say I am ok and don't need surgery.

1941 April 3
Evo
Hospital

I can't believe it is April, and it's snowing! Doris, Kathleen, Gene, and me are walking up the hill to the hospital to see Mama. She had her kidney removed yesterday!

I was scared when Mama and Doris came home from the doctor on Wednesday and said Mama had to have an operation. She was in so much pain, and an ambulance came and took her to the hospital that night. I could not stop crying because I was afraid that she would die like Daddy when he went to the hospital for a leukemia treatment. I never got to see him again or say goodbye and give him a hug or hear him tell me another joke.

Mama came through her surgery fine. When she gets home, I'm going to be extra good and try not to irritate anyone or talk too much. I'm going to stay right by Mama and get things for her.

Highsmith Hospital is close, just to the end of Roberson Street and up Hay Street hill a bit. Doris was afraid to drive her car because the roads are icy.

I stop to grab some snow and rake it into a snowball. Everyone else gets a little ahead of me, so I hang back and lob my snowball right at Doris's butt. It does not have much impact because the snow is soft. Doris turns around, and I try to pretend it wasn't me. "Golly, Doris. Where did that come from?"

Of course, she doesn't go for my lie. She would have blamed me even if I didn't do it. I had hoped she would throw a snowball back, and maybe we could have a little friendly fight with Kathleen and Gene. No. She grabs me by the arm and gives me a little swat on my butt. I don't care. It was worth it!

When we get to Highsmith Hospital, everyone is wore slap out from climbing the hill. We spill in the door, and the unsmiling lady at the desk takes one look at me and asks how old I am. I say nine.

She frowns. "You have to be at least twelve to visit a patient."

Drat! Doris told me about this stupid rule before we left home. But I really wanted to see my mama and cried and begged them! They gave in but said I would have to stay in the waiting room and sit on a hard bench while they saw Mama. I really thought I could charm my way in. My tears do nothing to make the mean lady let me go up to Mama's room.

Kathleen puts her arm around me. "Sorry, Evo, we will tell Mama you are here and that will make her feel better. Give me the picture you drew for her, and I will be sure she gets it."

I storm outside and run to the ginkgo tree, kick at the snow, and cry. After a while, Kathleen comes to get me and says Mama will be able to come home in two weeks.

1941 April 11
Doris
Mercurochrome

With Mama in the hospital, we girls are helping more. Since I work, and Kathleen and Evelyn are in school, supper is a challenge. Kathleen can't cook much without burning things, and she complains. Evelyn wants to help, but she makes such a mess. Tonight, she tried to make Mama's biscuits which are always delicious and perfectly round and golden brown. That child covered the table with flour and poured in too much buttermilk. When I got home, there was a soggy mess and lopsided biscuits with burned tops. Mama never uses a recipe. Evelyn had watched her, so she thought she could do it. When I get home about five-thirty, much of the cooking is left to me. Some neighbors have brought food for us and that has been a big help.

Kathleen and I still manage to go on dates or have friends over. Jimmie is always on my mind. He doesn't ask me out regularly, so I still date others. So does Kathleen. But I think her heart is with Slover. After she went out with him a few nights ago, she said it was nice to date "a real man" instead of silly boys.

As for Evelyn, she misses Mama and is sad that she cannot visit her. Today after school, she went right to Edna's, and she came home with skinned knees but would not tell me how she got them. Probably doing something foolhardy!

She howled like a cat when I put the mercurochrome on, and Kathleen blew on her knees to soothe the burn. That child did not wait to let it dry, so now she has big red stains on her skirt. Another job for me, getting that stain out. Good luck! Maybe I can get Janie to come do the wash. She might know how to get it out. She is smart for a Negro.

1941 April 12
Kathleen
Tomato Sandwich

It's Saturday, and I have a new job at F. W. Woolworth's Five Ten and Twenty-Five Cent Store. That name is a lie. Even though many things are within the advertised price range, they sell clothing and household items for up to six dollars.

My job is to roam the floor and help customers find things. I'm happily moving among the glass cases and racks and enjoying talking to the customers.

But, wouldn't you just know it, someone called in sick at the lunch counter, and the manager moves me to fill in! So many customers rushing in for lunch and wanting it fast. I just cannot keep up! At least I'm am not asked to cook anything because I would be in a real pickle. I take orders, set up silverware and napkins, bring the food to the counter, settle the bill, and clean the spot and start all over again. I can't work fast enough, and several customers get real snippy. I'm nervous and that makes it even worse!

A customer's elbow bumps me, and I drop a bacon and tomato sandwich on the floor! The plate breaks. Bits of tomato go everywhere and fly up on my dress! I forgot to put on an apron. The cook is mad that he has to make another sandwich, and the customer doesn't even give me a tip after I brought the new one. The manager squints his eyes at me. "Thanks for losing us fifty cents!"

I wish I could disappear and take a twenty-five-cent banana split with me. I hate F. W. Woolworth's and will probably lose my job!

After three o'clock, the lunch traffic trickles off, and I only have to serve an occasional king size Coca-Cola or milkshake. I'm told to go back to the floor. I'm sure those lunch counter folks are happy so see me go.

Not much to do, so I'm thinking about my upcoming date with Walter tonight.

Oh, foot! I have to help with supper when I get home. Doris and I always argue because I do something wrong. I wish she would just do it and leave me out of it! Evo tries hard to help us, but she's just not up to the task. I think we have some leftover roast and some sweet potatoes. Doris, of course, will want Mama's biscuits and expect me and Evo to have them in the oven when she gets home. Oh, yes, and she wants gravy which will stick to the pan and make a mess.

I hate cooking, and sometimes I even hate Doris!

It's almost five o'clock and time to close. FINALLY! I will hurry home, help cook, and get ready for my date. Drat! My dress is stained from the tomato attack, and I will have to change.

1941 April 12
Kathleen
Gasoline

Walter whirls me around, and my skirt flares out behind me. It feels so good to have his strong arms around me. We laugh as we spin, and it is wonderful! He is a great dancer, and I am having so much fun!

He invited me to his Thirty-Ninth Infantry Division dance on base. He borrowed a car and came for me at seven, bringing me a little white carnation corsage. I'm wearing the pale blue dress that Mama made me before her surgery, heels, and nice hose that I got at Woolworth's with my employee discount. Hope I don't run them.

When the music stops, a private comes up to us. He looks at me with kind eyes. "So, Sergeant Slover, this must be your Gasoline!" He has a foreign accent and his attempt to say Kathleen comes out as Gasoline! I think he may be Japanese or Chinese. He is charming and smiles broadly at me. "Well, Sergeant, Gasoline is certainly lovely and what a good dancer."

"Thank you, Private," I say. Walter introduces him as Private Wong, one of his best men in Company K. I imagine he would say that about all of his men as he is always telling me how proud he is of his platoon.

We jitterbug and lindy hop to the live band. I am exhausted after "The Boogie Woogie Bugle Boy," and we sit out a while and drink some punch. I love the slow ones, in particular "Stardust" and "You Made Me Love You" as Walter holds me very close.

On the way home, we talk about our families. My sisters and brothers and his two sisters Euleta and Maxine. And our parents. Walter loved his daddy so much, and it was so hard when he died. He taught Walter so many things. They hunted and fished and fixed things in the house.

"I know how you feel. When my Dad died of leukemia, a big hole was made in my heart which can never be filled. How did the accident happen that killed your father in the mine?"

We are just coming up to my house on Roberson Street. Walter stops the borrowed car and puts on the break. "No, Kathleen, I am not sure you really know how I feel."

He pauses for a while. Did I say something wrong?

"I am going to tell you something that I haven't told anyone since I left Shelburn. I haven't felt that I could share this until I met you. My dad did not actually die in the mine. There was a terrible explosion, and he was burned so badly on his face, arms, and chest. He suffered bad with pain all the time and was ashamed of his appearance. He had been a very handsome man."

"So eventually he died from his injuries?"

"Yes, in a way but not actually. He shot himself a few days before Christmas and was buried on Christmas Eve."

Silence grows into a great gulf between us. I don't know what to say.

"Oh, Walter, I am so sorry. How hard that must have been for you and your family."

"Yes, yes," his voice is so low I can barely hear him. "Times were tough. We had no income, and mother had to go to work as the janitress at the school. Now that I am in the Army, I send them half of my pay."

His voice trails off, and the silence grows again. I slide over and put my arms around him.

1941 April 27
Doris
"Be Kind to Your Web-footed Friend"

It's Sunday afternoon, and we have just gotten home from church and finished lunch when some boys from Fort Bragg arrive. Today, Jimmie is one of them. I think I am in love with him, despite the fact that he can be nervy and a little too proud of himself. He brings two pals who are not at all interesting to me, but they are fun and add to the good time.

They want me to play the piano so we can sing. We crowd around the old upright in the dining room. The piano is out of tune. We can't afford to hire a tuner. No one seems to mind because we just sing loud and laugh a lot along the way.

Kathleen sings "Evelina," and everyone just falls out laughing and joins in singing it over and over. This is a song Daddy sang to us.

> *Evelina and I went fishing one day*
> *Down on the banks of the Chesapeake Bay.*
> *I fished for mackerel, Evelina for bass*
> *Evelina fell in up to her...*
> *Don't get excited, don't be misled.*
> *Evelina fell in up to her head.*

Mama comes in from the kitchen. She is recovered from her surgery, although sometimes she looks a little weak. But that would not stop her from staying home from church to cook a big meal. Janie came yesterday and helped her get everything ready. She would not hear of us staying home from church to help.

She wipes her hands on her big plaid apron and starts removing the lunch plates. She is blushing and says, "Phsaw, you youngins are bad." But she laughs along with us for another verse of "Evelina." Mama, like her mother Grandma Coggins, does not think much of fun on Sunday, particularly card playing. But she tolerates singing as long as a few hymns are thrown in. So, we follow up with "Kneel at the Cross" and "I'll Fly Away."

The dining room is full now as Roger, Gene, and Evelyn join in. I wish Evelyn would butt out because she says silly things. I have to correct her and she huffs off to the bedroom. Mama later chides me for being harsh. Well, that child deserves it!

Kathleen suggests "Be Kind to Your Web-footed Friend" which she hums all the time. Her constant humming habit is an irritation. She must think I don't hear her. She can be a loon sometimes.

Jimmie starts off a tune set to "The Stars and Stripes Forever." I can't play it, so we just sing. I stand up by the piano and feel Jimmie's arm go around my waist. Hmm.... he likes me.

> *Oh, be kind to your webbed footed friend,*
> *For that duck may be somebody's mother*
> *She lives in a hole in the swamp*
> *Where the weather is always damp*
> *You may think this is the end:*
> *Well it is… but to prove we're all liars*
> *We're going to sing it again,*
> *But this time we will sing a little higher.*

Then we start again and again until Jimmie sings louder and ends the song with:

> *You may think this is the end:*
> *Well it is well it is, well it IS!*

I could keep singing forever if Jimmie would keep his strong arm around my waist.

1941 May 14
Ethel
War News

It's hard to ignore the news about the war in Europe. Germans bombing England and occupying France, and marching forces all raising their hands to "Heil Hitler." What a scary man, bent on taking over everything. I hear all this on the radio, and the children tell me about the *Fox Movietone News* at the movies. I never go to the movies even though they ask me. I have too much to do.

Everyone talks about the war, and most want just one thing: keep the USA out of it. But should we just let Europe fall to this devil man? Then, what will happen if they come for us?

I'm so torn when I see the suffering in Europe, but I'm afraid for my boys, Buck and Roger. Gene is only fifteen, so he should be safe with the draft age at twenty-one. I can't imagine a war that would last long enough for him to get involved. I'm glad Evelyn is so young because with her nature, she would probably be hankering to get involved in some way if the government decided to let women join up. Surely not! What a horrible idea! Women are too weak and have too much to do at home.

Doris and Kathleen have sweethearts. Well, Kathleen definitely does, but I'm not sure about Doris and Jimmie. Their relationship is somewhat wild. What if the girls marry, and their boys go to war? I don't want them to go through being a widow as I have. Lord, I miss Wesley. He was my rock. I could be much braver if he were still here. He would cheer me up with his humor.

A speech from Congress today proposed that our country provide more war relief. England is so short of food, and their food is rationed I pray that helping out with relief will be the only way war will touch us. That ought to be enough.

1941 May 18
Kathleen
White Lake

After we get back from church, Walter and Jimmie come to take me and Doris to White Lake. Woohoo! One of my favorite places to go, only about an hour from Fayetteville and just outside of Elizabethtown in Bladen County. The water is clear, and the bottom and shore are white sand. Tall pines on the shore and cypress trees in the water's edge and an amusement park. The story is that the lake was formed centuries ago when a meteor hit and made a crater of crystal white sand.

Doris and I pack a lunch in Mama's big wooden basket. Peanut butter sandwiches, apples, Mama's sweet iced tea, and a few slices of coconut cake.

When the boys arrive, Jimmie says to me, "Hello, Gasoline." I guess I am stuck with a nickname thanks to Private Wong's accent. Everyone laughs, especially Doris who can't seem to stop.

On the trip, we roll all the car windows down and sing and tell jokes. My hair gets blown to smithereens, but not Doris' because she has brought a scarf.

Walter and I are in the backseat, holding hands, and he learns over and gives me a kiss now and then. No other boy I have been out with can measure up to him. He is everything on the positive side of my list of qualities for a potential boyfriend: tall, handsome, kind, funny, honest, and loyal. The only thing on the negative side is that he might have to go to war if we get in this thing. I couldn't marry him if he asked because being a war widow is not one of my goals! I don't think he is going out with anyone else, even though I have an occasional date with others.

It is sunny and warm, and the lake surface glitters and rolls in tiny gentle waves to the shore. We spread out Mama's old quilt and lay out our food. Walter and Jimmie gobble it down like they are starving. Mama will like hearing about that since having people appreciate her food is her favorite thing.

Jimmie suggests we go to the amusement park before swimming. Doris says this is a good idea because everyone knows you need to stay out of the water for at least thirty minutes after eating so you won't get a cramp in your leg and drown. I don't believe this, but Mama and Doris certainly do.

At the amusement park, we go to the arcade first. Jimmie and Walter head right to the shooting area, so they can point guns at little sitting ducks and win prizes.

Walter hits every duck right off because he has earned expert marksman certification. He wins me a big teddy bear, and then asks if I would like to try it. I hate guns and am afraid of them, but I try anyway and hit the first duck right off the bat.

Slover claps and says I have a real talent for this. "No, Walter, it was truly blind luck because I closed my eyes." I never hit another duck in my remaining nine tries!

Doris and I are anxious to get out to the rides and pull the boys out of the arcade. We ride the roller coaster even though neither of us really likes it because of the height. But it is worth it to sit with our protective dates who put their arms around us. Then to the Tilt-a-Whirl which is my favorite. Doris gets sick after getting off and leaves her lunch in the bushes. Jimmie gets her a Coca-Cola to settle her stomach.

Lakeside, back to our quilt spot, we strip off our outer clothes, and Doris and I struggle to pull on our bathing caps. We have our bathing suits underneath our street clothes which makes getting ready easier. Both boys have hard, athletic bodies with muscles from all their training. Oh, the sight of them renders my knees a little weak! I feel Slover's eyes on me, so I must look ok despite my poor old bathing suit.

Jimmie grabs Doris' hand and pulls her to the water. They splash in about knee deep, and Doris orders, "That's far enough! And the water is cold!"

"What!?" barks Jimmie.

Doris, who can't swim, is truly afraid of water. "Yes, we can sit down here in the edge and enjoy it."

Jimmie ignores this and puts his arms around her waist and takes her out deeper. "I can't touch the bottom. Stop, Jimmie!" Jimmie lets her go but holds her hands and she sort of floats. "Take me back where I can touch. Now!" He maneuvers her back to the shallows, lets her hands go, and pushes off to the deeper water.

This is silly because the lake is only about ten feet at its deepest, and you can walk a long way out and still touch. What did she expect at a lake?

Walter and I go in and pass her in the shallow water and join Jimmie. We are splashing each other and laughing. Walter blows a stream of water out of his mouth that goes high in the air. Then he puts his hands together and produces a little spout like it might have come from a baby whale. I try this and fail miserably.

Doris is still a shore flower. She looks mad. I don't feel sorry for her. She should be more adventurous.

Walter pulls me out away from Jimmie, encircles me in his arms, and bends down for a kiss. "Kathleen, my Gasoline. Will you be my girl? I don't want to see any other girls except for you. You are such a swell girl, and I want to spend as much time as possible with you."

I feel all tingly and safe and before I think, I say, "Yes, Walter, yes."

1941 May 24
Ethel
Grace's Chapel

One of my favorite days of the year. We are at Grace's Chapel in Sanford for the annual Coggins family reunion.

This year all my children are able to attend. We are in two cars, Doris' and Buck's. This does not happen every year as they are all busy with their lives and don't care so much for seeing relatives. None of them seems to enjoy it much except for Doris who loves to talk to everyone and enjoys herself.

First, the service in the chapel. I am so happy to see my Daddy Robert Bruce Coggins lead the singing. He taught Doris to play "I'll Fly Away." Roger, Buck and Gene play a little guitar. I guess they got some musical genes from Daddy.

It is stifling hot, and we all have our handheld funeral home fans. Flies buzz. Farm smells float in the windows. Freshly cut hay. Cows and faintly, their excrement.

Ladies dab their faces with hankies, and men take off jackets. Evelyn fans herself real fast to let everyone know how uncomfortable she is. I keep giving her looks and raising my eyebrows which is my signal that she is on her way to getting a whipping when we get home.

Yes, physical discomfort is real in this sweltering room. But there is the heart comfort to be in the presence of my family. Mother sits on my left, and I feel wonderful. On the rows behind us are my seven surviving siblings: Raleigh, Flossie, Ira, Robert, Mattie, Bill, and Mamie along with their families. The room is overflowing over with Coggins kin.

The preacher sure has a lot to say today, and the service goes on and on. I think Evelyn might explode.

When we stand for the last hymn, she breathes a little sigh that comes out too loud. She will definitely have a meeting with a hickory stick when we get home!

The congregation spills out into the churchyard, families meandering to their family plots. I point out the graves of my mother's firstborn twins. The words are fading. Julia - August 23, 1891 - August 24, 1891and Maggie - August 23, 1891 - September 6, 1891. They were both too small to live long. My sisters who knew nothing of life. I try to hold back the tears that are rising in the corners of my eyes. Mother had only a few precious days with Julia and Maggie.

Then, the grave of my older brother Marshall David Coggins, who died in 1914 at just twenty-two. I was twenty when he passed from scarlet fever. We were so close and had fun together. He was very protective of me; he would scare off my boyfriends if he thought they weren't good enough for me. But he did like Wesley. Marshall was a lot like Daddy, strong and sweet and sang with Daddy in church.

I move off from the big group and my children follow, knowing that we are going to their Daddy's grave. Buck had gone there when we first arrived and put the flowers on the grave, a few roses from the florist and a big bunch of forsythia from our back yard. Wesley always loved that bush and said it looked like an eruption of a yellow sunshine on sticks. Thomas Wesley Brantley, September 28, 1897 - August 25, 1939.

Buck speaks. "Daddy, we loved you so much. You gave us sustenance, wisdom, and laughter. You soothed us when we got into scrapes as small children. You worked hard to provide for us. You were a good husband to Mama and the best of fathers. May your soul rest in peace until we see you again."

By this time most of us are holding back tears except for Evelyn, who wails loudly. She was so young and took her daddy's death the hardest of all. Doris and Kathleen stoop down by her and put arms around her as she cries more softly into Doris' blouse.

Next to Daddy is Adele Louise Brantley, May 27, 1919 - October 26, 1937, with some of Buck's flowers by her headstone. She was my firstborn whose behavior was strange and unruly. The doctor called her a moron and said she would never be normal.

When she was a teenager, we had to send her to Dix Hill Insane Asylum in Raleigh when we could not control her anymore. It broke my heart. She was only there a short time when she passed in an instant on a brilliant fall Tuesday from what doctors thought was a brain aneurism.

A child lives on forever in a mother's heart. I hope to meet her again in heaven with Wesley. I imagine her vibrant and standing next to her smiling father.

After a few more minutes of remembrance by the graves, we dry our tears and turn toward the tables of food spread on the other side of the chapel. I pause to think of Wesley's family, none of whom are in attendance. Since he died, we never see much of them.

The lunch is, as always, a celebration of food. Every woman has brought her special dishes and plenty of them. There is crispy and perfectly brown fried chicken, pot roast, ham, pork chops, peas, corn, fried fat back that Wesley called Tennessee ham, butterbeans, string beans, fried and stewed okra, tomatoes, mashed potatoes, macaroni and cheese, scalloped potatoes, pickles, chow chow relish, numerous Jell-O salads that are melting in the sun, deviled eggs, fried cornbread, biscuits, several kinds of cakes, brownies, cookies, and sweet, sweet tea to drink. A feast to soothe the sadness of the grave visitations.

So many relatives to talk to and catch up with that the task is overwhelming!

"How is your tobacco coming this year?"

"My, my how your boy has grown. You must be feeding him fertilizer!"

"What a lovely dress! Did you make it?"

"How is your Uncle Bill? Is his bad back better?"

And on and on, until the afternoon sunlight begins to soften. Everyone starts to pack up their leftover food and give goodbye hugs and move toward their cars. Mother hands me the rest of her caramel pound cake and gives me a big hug that lasts and lasts.

I feel happy and full. In the car, several are drowsy, and Evelyn falls asleep. Her head rests on my shoulder.

The Burma Shave advertising signs pass by:

DON'T STICK YOUR ELBOW...

OUT SO FAR...

IT MAY GO HOME...

IN ANOTHER CAR...

BURMA SHAVE.

"Eugene Fields Brantley! Get that elbow in this car, right now!"

1941 May 25
Evo
The Great Dictator

What a great Sunday for me! Not at first. I have to endure the usual afternoon of sitting around in the front room and listening to boring talk and boring Rev. Fosdick on the radio. About two o'clock Slover shows up to take Kathleen to the movies. Lo and behold, they ask me to go with them! To see *Gone with the Wind*.

We have all seen it lots of times since it came out last year, but we love it every time. Even Mama went with us once. Doris and Kathleen swoon over Clark Gable. Scarlett O'Hara's strength and bossy ways remind me a little of Doris, and Kathleen reminds me of sweet Melanie. Actually, Melanie is pretty weak; Kathleen only a little. Come to think of it, Janie Ringo reminds me of Mammy. Janie even wears a head scarf like Mammy's. And Jimmie Rice looks a bit like Ashley Wilkes. And Slover is as handsome as Rhett Butler!

Mama did not like the end where Rhett says, "Frankly, my dear, I don't give a damn." Damn, damn, damn. I like to say it but never in front of Mama. Mama hates swearing of any kind. She said that normally Rhett would not have said such a thing unless he was very mad. Roger said that Scarlett deserved it.

I want to run down Hay Street to the Carolina theatre, but Slover and Kathleen just stroll, hand in hand. Love birds! I have to keep slowing down for them to catch up. *Slover and Kathleen, sitting in a tree, k-i-s-s-i-n-g. First comes love, then comes marriage, then comes Kathleen with a baby carriage. How many babies will they have?* We sing that when we jump rope at school recess, and then count our jumps to see how many babies the couple will have! One time I got up to forty-five babies before I tripped over the rope. Egads!

When we get to the Carolina, *Gone with the Wind* isn't playing. Instead a Charlie Chaplin movie called *The Great Dictator* is on the marquee. Kathleen looks at Slover and says she is not sure this is a good movie for a nine year old.

I thought all Charlie's movies were silent, so what problem could there be since I cannot hear any bad words? I tell them that, but Slover says he had read that this is Charlie's first talking movie. So strange since most all movies are talkies now. Of course, Charlie is so funny in the way he movies that words don't matter. They finally give in and say I can go after several choruses of "pretty, pretty please and pretty please with sugar on it" from me.

Slover buys me popcorn and a Coca-Cola, and he and Kathleen get Almond Joys which they say are "indescribably delicious" just like the ad says in *Life Magazine*. We get settled in the theatre below the balcony where all the Negroes sit. I don't understand why they sit there. It's dark in the movie, and you can't tell a black face from a white one. Why don't they sit with everyone else?

In *The Great Dictator,* Charlie Chaplin looks funny as always. But the movie is serious which really confuses me. There is a plane crash, and the pilot can't remember anything afterward. Then some people are put in a big fenced in place to live, and the dictator is mean to them. The pilot, who can remember again, and his girlfriend try to get the people out, but the dictator tells them to stop. I start to get sleepy, so I miss most of the rest of the movie.

When I wake up, someone is talking to the pilot's girlfriend. "Look up, Hannah. The soul of man has been given wings, and at last he is beginning to fly. He is flying into the rainbow — into the light of hope, into the future, the glorious future that belongs to you, to me, and to all of us." Everything must have turned out alright since that sounds pretty happy with rainbows and all.

48

I hope Slover and Kathleen didn't notice that I was asleep because they might not want to take me to a movie again. They don't say anything. They were probably too busy holding hands and looking at each other to notice.

Slover asks when we get out on the street, "How did you like that, Evo?"

"I did. (*I lie.*) That Dictator guy reminded me of that bad Hitler with the funny moustache who I saw making a big, loud speech and holding his arm out to the crowd in the newsreel we saw before the movie. The one that marched into Paris and took it over."

Kathleen is the one to answer. "Yes, Evo the movie is making fun of Hitler."

"That Hitler is not funny. He scares me."

Slover says, "Wow, Evo. You are so smart. Yes, Hitler is scary. We Americans may have to help Europe fight him."

Kathleen gets a funny look on her face, lifts her hand to the back of her hair, and begins to twirl a curl around her index finger. "But, Walter, surely you would not have to help do that."

"Let's hope not. But if called upon to help, I am ready and trained. Now, let's go in the Caroline Soda Shoppe and get malted milk."

That is the end of movie and war talk. As I sit and sip my chocolate malted, I wonder why people have to be mean to each other like that Dictator was.

1941 June 3
Ethel
Postcards

It's early afternoon and oppressively humid. I force myself to get up from the porch swing and *Better Homes and Gardens*. Robert Jennings, the mail carrier, who just lives over on Franklin Street, is walking up to the porch and straining under the weight of his big leather pouch. I step into the yard, so he won't have to drag his bag up the steps.

"Hello, Robert. So hot today! Wouldn't you like to come in a while and have a glass of tea?"

"No, thanks, Mrs. Brantley. Got to finish this route and get home. My boy Danny has a baseball game this evening. He is getting pretty good on third base. The coach reckons he has a chance to play pro someday."

"Hope you can get home soon. Wouldn't want to you miss Danny's game. He is such a fine boy, well spoken, kind, and ever so handsome." He hands me the mail which includes the light bill, a letter, and two postal cards.

I sink back into the swing to look at the post cards. Since the messages are written on the back behind the picture, it is understood that anyone is free to read them. I would never open any sealed letters. Kathleen and Doris get scads of cards from the boys they meet. They send them even after they leave Fort Bragg and go to other assignments. I read the two:

To Kathleen from Fort Bragg:

Dear Cat, how is the weather in Fayetteville? It is hot enough to pop corn out here and the orders are so strict you can't even smile what they don't call you down. Boy, it is tough and gets tougher. I had rather sell Dr. Pepper, three to one. Tell everybody

50

hello and don't court too much. Write soon. Pvt.
John Mansfield.
To Doris from Uniontown, Pennsylvania:

Miss D, wish you well. Having a swell time. Tell all
the girls I said hello. Joey L.

Ok, Ethel, that is enough procrastinating. Get to the kitchen! I go in the house and leave the mail on the end table in the front room and head to the kitchen. It is steamy even with the window and back door open. Lifting my apron skirt, I wipe the sweat from my face.

The radio distracts me from the heat. Oh, no! Lou Gehrig died last night. The New York Yankee, the "Iron Horse." Only thirty-seven-years old from a strange muscle disease. Gene and Roger will be upset as they are mad about baseball and idolize Lou.

I feel so sorry for his wife as I am very familiar with how it is to lose a husband. Like my Wesley, Lou suffered a long time and got worse and worse. I wish death could always be quick.

What am I thinking? Those English boys overseas die immediately from some bullet or bomb. Or perish at sea. A thousand men lost when the German Bismarck sunk the Hood in the Atlantic just a few days ago. No chance to say good bye to friends or family. Just alive one moment and gone the next. Maybe the long, sad goodbye is better.

I pray and pray that we won't get in this horrible war. Surely, Hitler can be defeated without our help. No. I am deluding myself. In the last war when I was a child, we had to join in to help make the victory happen.

Now yet another war is waging, and we are probably going to be in it. When will we ever learn?

1941 June 6
Kathleen
Class of 1941

It's my graduation day! I've been trying on my cap and struggling to decide how to wear it. No matter how I arrange it, I look ugly under that tight cap and my nose looks big, which it is, without hair to frame my face. Hair just pokes out everywhere. Mama will say, when someone's hair looks bad, that they look like the "Wild Woman of Borneo" from the circus. Well, that's me today! Doris said not to bother as every girl will look awful in that thing.

Something else very important happened today. We got a telephone! Oh, how swell it will be to call friends and talk about the latest without having to wait until I see them. I can even call Walter at Fort Bragg. Joy, oh, joy!

Since it is a week day, Walter can't come. He came by last weekend and gave me presents. A card, a cute pocket book, and a pretty gold compact with powder. He said that I really don't even need makeup because I am so pretty. Ha, ha! I doubt he would have said that if he ever saw me before I fixed my face! Or with that dad-blamed graduation cap on.

I went by the school at ten o'clock to pick up my report card. I got all A's in English, Citizenship, Shorthand, French and Bible. But in typing I squeaked by with a D-!

I could never type the required number of words per minute without numerous mistakes. Miss Ray said I had no focus and must be daydreaming. Not true because I couldn't think of anything else during the timed drills. She walked the room with a yard stick and would bang knuckles if she saw mistakes. Had she seen all my errors, my hands would have been black and blue. I was just too nervous to do it well. I'm going to have to work harder when I go to Worth's Business College in the fall. Thank the good Lord that shorthand is easy for me.

I got my yearbook *The Lafamac,* which Buck paid for as my present. This is what the yearbook staff printed under my picture: "Kathleen Marguerite Brantley. She's quiet, ambitious and also sincere. Nothing at all does she ever fear." Ha, ha! They don't really know me with that "nothing does she ever fear" part because I get so nervous sometimes that I feel like I am going to throw up. I guess they had to stretch a bit to create a rhyme!

There was a lunch party in the cafeteria after we picked up our yearbooks, and we sat all afternoon and signed each other's books. The procedure went like this: we passed our books around, we signed our pictures, and then wrote something on the blank pages at the end. Nothing very significant, just wishes for a good life, how great a person you were, or how much they enjoyed a certain class with you.

My favorite was what Betty Sue wrote: "Gasoline, always remember me and how you used to have to get me out of bed every morning." Sometimes when I stopped by her house to walk with her, she was still in bed. Her mother and father had already left for work. All her brothers and sisters were out on their own, so she was left alone to get up.

I don't think the Arthurs ever knew how Betty Sue was almost late for school many days. I guess I did save her from tardiness and punishment at home.

Even when she got up late, she could put herself together in a flash! Her hair is naturally curly in a way that she never has to roll it the night before on bobby pins or twist it with paper bag strips like I do. She can do the fastest teeth brushing, dressing, combing her hair, and throwing on a bit of powder and lipstick I have ever seen. She doesn't worry so much about perfection in her appearance as most girls do. This does not keep her from having lots of dates as she is so much fun and very outgoing and a natural beauty to boot.

For supper, Mama had cooked my favorite Italian spaghetti. I got more presents from Mama (a new homemade dress in pink), Doris (a pretty blouse), Roger (a picture of some of Mama's zinnias that he painted and framed), Gene (some candy), and Evo (a book of coupons she created with her crayons: "this coupon is good for one brushing of your hair, one washing the dishes when it is your turn.") That kind of thing. So sweet.

Now it is eight p.m., and I am sitting in my gown and lopsided cap with hair hanging out in the ugliest manner possible in the auditorium of Fayetteville High School. We are the first class to graduate in the new school building just finished before the term began in September. We, the class of 1941 with one hundred thirty-nine graduates, are the largest class in the history of the school. Most of us have finished grade eleven which is the requirement for graduation. There are a few who chose to study an additional year. Eventually twelve grades will be required of all.

I'm feeling somewhat nostalgic when I look around at my classmates and realize I probably won't see some of them ever again. For some, I am truly happy about that! My irritating critic Tommy Bruce, for one.

I wonder what the future will bring for us with our country possibly on the brink of war. Some of the girls may marry soon, and their husbands will go off to war and die.

No, no, no! We will stay out of the war, and none of that will happen. The boys will be businessmen, doctors, lawyers with wives at home making beautiful and delicious meals for them when they come home after a hard work day. There will be children to cherish. And the couples will go out in the evening to dance and laugh with friends. Happy endings.

There is a band prelude, a prayer, a bunch of speeches by the Salutatorian, Valedictorian and others about preparedness, the theme for the evening. I don't hear much of this. It just washes over me as background droning. It's hot in here, and I am sleepy during this important moment in my life.

I am thinking of Walter and wondering what a life with him might be like. Would we live in Indiana, a place foreign to me? I have never been out of North Carolina.

Images of Paris swirl around in my head, and I see again my daydream. Not going to happen. Ever. Even if I could, by a miracle, go there, the picture is ruined with the Germans tromping around.

Finally, a benediction. We turn our tassels and throw our caps in the air. Then hugging of friends and family and picture taking. I am now a high school graduate.

Tomorrow, I will take my diploma to Quinn-Miller Furniture on Hay Street to pick up my miniature cedar chest. The company gives these to all the female graduates. Of course, they are expecting to get some business by selling full-size hope chests that girls can buy to fill with linens, dishes, and flatware to be used when they marry. I could never afford one of those or buy anything to put in it. I have no intention of marrying any time soon, anyway. I love the little chest, however, and I will put my letters in it.

1941 June 10
Evo
The Wayward Grape

Kathleen asked me to be her guest at her senior banquet at our church. I'm tickled pink! She's allowed to bring only one guest, and she picked me! I would have thought she would take Mama, but Mama had already promised to go over and spend the night with Mrs. Rogers who just had her gall bladder yanked out. I was her second choice, but I don't care because I am getting to go to an event for grownups!

We dressed up real nice. I put on a blouse and the new plaid skirt Mama made me. Kathleen, as always, looked beautiful in her pale pink dress. When we got there, several people said how pretty I looked. Last night Doris twisted my hair on paper bag strips, and I had some nice curls. I wanted to wear some lipstick, but Mama said no.

The tables in the ladies' parlor had place cards. Kathleen Marguerite Brantley and Evelyn Lou Brantley. Dagnabbitt! They just had to use that long, awful name. Kathleen whispered in my ear, "It is customary to use formal names for an event like this." We sat with Mr. and Mrs. Downing because he was Kathleen's escort. Mr. Downing was Kathleen's Sunday School teacher all through high school. There was a fancy introduction of each graduate and escort.

Some of the teenagers in the church served us plates of chicken salad, fruit, and little cheese biscuits. I tried to be neat and not drop anything, but wouldn't you know it, a grape rolled off my fork and onto the floor. I don't think anyone saw it. After that, I speared them with my fork. Dessert was little chocolate eclairs, two on each plate. I could have eaten a dozen of them. Kathleen gave me one of hers.

After the meal, we sang "Onward Christian Soldiers" and "God Bless America." The choir director stood up and waved his arms, but we didn't need that as everyone knew the songs.

Then, Dottie Jones pretended to be a fortune teller and gave each graduate a little piece of rolled up paper tied with a bright blue ribbon. The grads had to stand and read them aloud. Kathleen is shy about standing up and talking in front of a crowd. But she did it nicely even though her voice sounded a little shakey. Her fortune was:

Well, there's no doubt about it. You are sensitive, extremely sensitive, and extremely capable. You have a good deal of pride in your own ability and a sort of determination to live up to the best that is in you.

I thought that was a nice thing to say. But on the way home, Kathleen said she didn't like being called sensitive because it sounds weak. I told her I thought it means that she cares about people and tries to help. Which she certainly does with me.

1941 June 18
Ethel
Sunshine Cake

Summer, my favorite season. My zinnias are blooming, and my garden is giving us cucumbers, green beans, and onions. Tomatoes are coming on, and I can't wait for a tomato and mayonnaise sandwich. We go to Sanford more often now to help Mother and Daddy and my brothers' families with their huge crops that need to be picked and frozen for the winter. I get to spend more time with my family and also bring home some of the vegetables.

We always go on the weekend when no one is working at their weekday jobs. Kathleen rarely goes with us because she has Saturday work sometimes. I suspect that the extra Saturdays are often by choice. Walking the floor at Woolworth's is clean work, and she does not like to get her hands dirty.

Evelyn is another matter entirely. She is helpful with the picking and works fast so she can be dismissed to go fish at the pond or just run around with the cousins.

She is bored in the summer except when she is outside playing with Edna. They stay out all day and just come home as the street lights are coming on. Sometimes after dark, she asks for a jar with holes punched in the lid to catch lightning bugs. Then as it gets totally dark, she will sit in the swing on the front porch and watch them flash on and off. She always releases them before she comes inside. She would not think of leaving them in the jar to die. Such a tender heart and a lover of creatures.

Doris still goes out with various boys from Fort Bragg and often with Jimmie Rice. He is a strange one. Very handsome and very attentive to Doris, but I over hear them having little spats. Doris is very quiet for the days following. Kathleen now has Slover as her one and only.

No other boys. If they come to the door, she turns them away.

Slover got leave to go visit his family in Indiana. Kathleen is sad. A letter comes almost every day, and once he called on the telephone. I am wondering where this relationship is going. They certainly appear to be in love, but you never know. If it goes more serious, I hope she won't marry him until she finishes her courses at Worth's. She won't be seventeen until October, and she needs to learn a few domestic skills before she becomes a wife with household duties.

I try to teach my girls cooking. They worked hard to keep meals going when I had my kidney surgery, but now they are too busy to develop much domestic skill. Doris usually gets home from work too late to help, and on weekends she is either combing the downtown stores for the perfect dress or going on a date.

Kathleen is hopeless as a cook. She just can't seem to get everything going at once and has a tendency to burn things. She is so smart in other ways: almost all A's in school and can write such beautiful letters. I cherish the ones she wrote me when I was in the hospital with my kidney.

Evelyn is too young to do much although she wants to help. She has big ideas that she can't carry through. Today she wants to make a Sunshine cake with oranges that she saw in *Better Homes and Gardens*. She kept "pretty pleasing" me and looking sad until I finally relented.

I have all the ingredients except the oranges. I let her go to Winslow Street Grocery for the oranges because the smaller Gibson's up the street wouldn't have them. I told her to be particular crossing the streets and not to talk to strangers. She replied with her usual comment when she wants to do something risky by herself. "Mama, really? I will be ten years old in October!"

1941 June 18
Evo
Mr. Wolfe

Mama is letting me go by myself to Winslow Street Grocery to buy oranges for my cake. I walk down Roberson toward town but take a shortcut across Franklin Street to Winslow. Not very far. Why does Mama have to make such a fuss and give so many warnings? "Look both ways before you cross. Don't talk to strangers. Be particular about not stumbling on those crumbly bricks outside the store." Does she think I am five years old?

I hope that old Mr. Wolfe isn't working today. My palms are getting sweaty, and my stomach feels funny as I get near the store. I go in and right to the produce section and spot the oranges. They smell so good! I take them to the check out where the big display of candy bars beside the register catches my eye. I can almost taste a Snickers! But no, Mama did not give me any extra money. Only the ten cents for two oranges.

Yikes! Creepy Mr. Wolfe is here. He looks creepy and even his name is scary. Drat! He gets up off his stool which is a chore because he probably weighs three-hundred pounds. His big belly touches the counter. He leans over, grins, and bares his crooked, brown-stained-teeth. "Hey little girl! I saw you looking at that candy. Come around here and sit on my lap, and I will give you one for free."

He has asked me this before when I came in with Betty Sue. He wanted both me and Betty Sue to sit on his lap. We didn't, and he kept calling out to us until we got out the door. He never asks if Mama or Doris or Kathleen is with me.

I will not tell Mama about this. She would never let me go anywhere alone again.

"No, thank you, Mr. Wolfe. I just need the oranges, and I am in a pretty big hurry."

"In such a hurry that you can't be nice to an old man and enjoy some delicious candy?" He smiles even bigger, and I can see chewing tobacco juice in the corners of his mouth.

"No, got to go. Bye." And I am out.

I walk a lot faster on the way back trying to get the picture of Mr. Wolfe out of my head.

It's hot, hot. I want to stop by my school friend Tomoko's house on the corner of Franklin and Winslow to get a drink of water. But we would get to talking or try to get doodle bugs out of the ground with a piece on straw, and I would stay too long. Mama would worry if I didn't come right back.

I like to play with Tomoko, even though she is only six, because she loves to laugh and gets so excited about doodle bugs. You just find a little hole with a little dirt pile around it, stick in the straw, and wait till it starts to wiggle. Then you pull it out slowly and hope the doodle bug holds on. We don't keep them. We put them near the holes, so they can go back in. Her back yard has dirt and some grass and is a good doodle bug hunting place. But I go straight home.

My cake turns out tasty even though it is a little cockeyed, and I spilled flour and butter smudges on the counter. Mama and Kathleen say it is the most delicious cake they have ever eaten.

1941 July 11
Kathleen
I Love You

Walter is on furlough in Indiana visiting his family. He'll be back soon, and I can't wait. I'm filling my time working extra hours at Woolworth's. I made ten dollars last month which I am saving for Worth's Business College tuition. I wish I could find an office job and use my shorthand skills and improve my typing.

I am bored out of my head at home. Since I am accepting no dates, I spend my free time with my girlfriends window shopping or going to movies. I do enjoy it when some Fort Bragg boys, including Jimmie Rice, come to the house to chat, play games or sing.

Not sure what will happen with Doris and Jimmie. She moons over him, but she still goes out with others. He wants her not to date anyone else, but she says no. I hear them arguing when they are sitting in the swing.

The phone rings, and it is Walter! Oh, joy, joy, joy! So good to hear his Yankee accent that I've come to love. His voice envelops me in a soft warmth. And he says, right off the bat, "Kathleen, I miss you so much and I love you." Oh, he has never said that before, and it takes my breath. I can't answer.

"Did you hear me, my Gasoline? I love you."

"Yes, Walter, and I do love you too." It just slips out of my mouth, but then I get a sinking feeling in my stomach and start twirling my hair.

"Well, that makes me the happiest and luckiest man in the world!"

When we hang up, I am happy but a little dark cloud slides into my head. If he loves me, I fear the big question may be coming. My habit of thinking too far ahead brings my old resolve that I won't marry a soldier.

1941 July 16
Kathleen
Prince Charles Hotel

Walter is back! He called me from Fort Bragg and asked if he can take me to supper tonight. Of course, but strange that he can come on a weeknight. He said to wear something dressy.

He comes at seven sharp wearing civilian clothes, a beige shirt open at the collar and slim black pants. When I say how good he looks, he says that it is ok not to wear his uniform since he does not officially check in from his furlough until tomorrow. He looks so good that I can hardly restrain myself from grabbing him and kissing him right in front of Mama.

He has borrowed his friend Franklin's car, so we ride in style. I ask where we are going, and he replies that it is a surprise. Well, it is a surprise indeed when he pulls into a parking space right in front of the Prince Charles Hotel, which has the swankiest and most expensive restaurant in town.

"Walter, are we going here? Really? It is so expensive!"

"My girl is worth it, and this might be a special occasion." Oh, no! He might pop the question, and I am just not ready.

We are seated at a corner table in a secluded area of the room. Pristine white linen table cloth and napkins with a single red rose in a crystal vase in the center of the table. And candles.

The waiter asks if we would like to see the wine list. Walter says yes and starts to look it over.

"Kathleen, would you like red or white?"

"Neither, thank you. You know that I am a Baptist, and we don't touch alcohol."

"Not even wine?" He is a Methodist, and they just drink up a storm whenever they want.

"Not even wine."

"Ok. But do you mind if I have a glass?"

"No, go right ahead."

The waiter brings him a pale golden liquid in a crystal stemmed glass. It does look tempting, but I would not be a good Christian if I drank any.

Walter orders for us. Shrimp cocktails. Salad which is served on a cold dish. Steak, medium rare. Parsley potatoes. And rolls. Mama always cooks her meat well done; but the medium rare, once I get over the fact that is pink in the center, is delicious. For dessert chocolate fudge pie with vanilla ice cream.

My heart quickens as the waiter removes the dessert plates and brings us coffee. The sun is going down and casts a pale, smoky haze over the room. Walter shifts in his chair, and puts his clasped hands on the table. A big smile spreads across his face. He looks as if he is going to make a speech. And he does.

Reaching out for my hand (oh, no), he looks so deep into my eyes that I feel embarrassed. "Meeting you has been the best thing that has happened to me since…. well, since forever. You are beautiful, sweet, smart, and funny. I love every minute I get to spend with you. I cannot imagine living my life without you."

Oh, no! I need to do something to slow this down, but I can't speak. I feel as if I just was put on a speeding train. I need to jump off.

"Will you be my wife?"

There it is! I want to marry him. No, I don't. I don't know. Help! My free hand goes to the curl on the back of my neck, but I will myself to put it back in my lap.

When I don't reply, he continues to make his case. "I know this is fast. We have only known each other for a few months. But I am sure. I will be a good husband and take care of you." (Not if he is off in Europe rescuing the French and English.)

I know I must speak. "Walter, I do love you. This is just all so quick. I am only sixteen and just graduated from high school. I plan to go to school at Worth Business College."

"You seem older than sixteen. You are wise beyond your years. You can still go to school after we are married, and I will help pay for it. When I get out of the service, we can settle down here or in Indiana and have a nice life. Maybe children."

Ok, here they come, my words, once spoken, that may drive him away forever and break his heart. And mine.

"Yes, Walter, I love you, and I can imagine how wonderful it would be to spend my life with you. I would even move with you to Indiana, a place I have never laid eyes on and is so different from the life I have known here."

"So.... are you saying yes?"

"I am just not ready. I need some time to find out who I am before I join my life with yours. I also need to know where this war thing is going because if we marry, I don't want to be without you for God-knows-how long if you go to fight. And maybe lose you."

"But if you really love me, does any of that matter? The most important thing is that we can be together through whatever happens. No war will make us stop loving each other."

"I just have to have more time, Walter."

His smile melts away. "Well, I guess that answer will have to do, for now." With that, he pays the bill, and we walk to the car in silence.

1941 August 3
Doris
The Waterworks

Kathleen and I are going on a double date tonight with Slover and Jimmie. I'm glad Jimmie and I won't be alone because it's increasingly difficult to stop him from getting too intimate. He argues with me over this, saying that if I care for him, I'll go right along with whatever he wants. He knows I still date others and that makes him mad. The only phrase I remember from that boring Latin class in high school is *"carpe diem,"* which means seize the day. Why can't we just do that and enjoy our time together and let that be enough? I just want to be free to enjoy myself. No commitments.

While we are getting ready, Kathleen talks about Slover's marriage proposal and how she put him off and how miserable she is because she doesn't know what she wants. After she said she needed time, he didn't show up for about two weeks. She was so sad and nervous in his absence, driving me crazy with her whining and pining.

He finally came Sunday with Jimmie for afternoon games and music along with a full house of other boys. Tonight will be their first real date since the refusal. Kathleen is also happy not to be alone with Slover.

We go to the Broadway to see *The Wolfman* which is terrifying. Jimmie puts his arm around me and holds my hand. The boys love the movie and find it funny. I don't follow the plot very well as I keep covering my eyes during the wolf attacks, stabbings, and people turning into werewolves. And blood. Lon Chaney, Jr., stars in the title role, and creepy Bela Lugosi co-stars.

The *Fox Movietone* newsreel is almost as terrifying as the movie with scenes of German bombs being dropped on London and the burning houses. Real horror followed by made up horror.

Jimmie drives us out to the waterworks, and we sit on the grass to watch water spill over the dam, pure silver in the moonlight. Lots of couples come here to be alone, but we are the only ones tonight.

There are no clouds. The nearly full moon and stars seem so close. We can easily see the man in the moon. Kathleen wonders if people will ever be able to go to the moon and walk on it. She would like to go there and see how the earth looks from the moon. Jimmie replies that if anyone were sent to the moon, it would not be a woman because she would have to fix her makeup and hair every five minutes. Everyone laughs even Kathleen.

There is lots of smooching between both couples and quiet conversations. No serious talk from Slover or Jimmie, and we all have a beautiful time.

Later in bed, Kathleen and I whisper (because Evelyn has big ears and is always happy to leak our secrets). Kathleen is relieved that Slover was back to his old self without any mention of marriage. I am glad that I didn't have another wrestling match with the charming but confounding Jimmie Rice.

1941 September 11
Ethel
War Department Jobs

Kathleen started at Worth Business College on September first. The tuition is fifteen dollars per month with twelve for books for the Stenographic Course. A lot of money, but she has saved enough from her job at Woolworth's to cover most of it. She is taking Business Arithmetic and Rapid Calculation and Gregg Shorthand. She likes the Shorthand but not so much the Arithmetic. The campus is on Hay Street in the Huske building. She can walk with Roger, who works in the hardware store on the first floor. I make her a sandwich to take so she won't have the expense of lunch.

I know this direction is not the life she has dreamed of, but there is just no money for a regular college. She brought home a flyer today about a possible job. It read:

WANTED: WAR-OFFICE WORKERS
Thousands of stenographers are needed in the War Department, in the Navy Department, and in many other war agencies in the country.
Stenographers working a forty-eight- hour week begin at $1752 a year, typists at $1533. Qualified stenographers may be advanced to secretarial positions at $1971 a year or higher. Enrollees in Worth Business College graduate well-qualified for these positions.

A job like this would require her to move. She needs to finish Worth's first and, by then, she may be married to Slover and won't work because she would need to stay home and take care of him. I hope they don't move to Indiana. I want all my children to stay close.

1941 October 6
Kathleen
A Very Displeasing Letter

I'm extremely tired all the time. I go to bed when I finish studying and sleep like a log. Between working at Woolworth's part time and going to Worth's, my days and nights are full. Good thing I'm just dating Walter and not going out all the time with every Tom, Dick, and Harry that Doris drags home. No time for that life anymore.

I don't see Walter either since he is on maneuvers near Rock Hill, South Carolina. Not sure what this is all about, but Walter did say that the troops would be practicing for a possible invasion. Invasion of what? Where? Walter would not say more. But knowing that they are preparing scares the devil out of me! Are we going to join the war and invade Germany? Or France to rescue them from the Germans?

In Walter's last letter, he wished me a happy October first birthday and put a pretty lace handkerchief that had "I love you" embroidered in the center with flowers. He said this was to remind me of his offer of marriage because he loves me forever, and now that I am seventeen maybe I am ready to marry. When I wrote back, I thanked him for the hankie and said I loved him too but did not mention the marriage invitation.

Today's mail brought a very displeasing letter. I could feel my face getting redder with every word. I've never heard him angry, but this letter is mean, just plain ol' mean! He's mad that I didn't mention his proposal.

I feel like you are just stringing me along, and I think you are probably dating other men while I am away. Perhaps I've misjudged you, and you are just a fickle flirt playing with my emotions. Maybe it's best for both of us if we don't see each other anymore.

I drop the letter, and tears erupt and escalate into sobs. Mama comes running and asks whatever the matter is. I get up and run to the bedroom.

Oh, I am furious! The accusation of my dating others! A flirt! Playing with his emotions! The nerve of him!

Then my tears stop, and I think he must be dating South Carolina girls and has found someone he likes better than me. This may be his way of breaking off in favor of some Rock Hill floozy. He is so handsome, girls probably are flocking to him and he likes it!

My anger sinks into fear that I will lose him. What have I done?

1941 October 10
Evo
Wonder Woman

Right after school, I ask Mama if I can go to Edna's. I don't like to be here when Kathleen gets home around four from Worth's. She's driving us crazy with her crying, sitting on the sofa and staring into space, constant fiddling with her hair, and biting our heads off.

Slover. He's doesn't want to go steady anymore. He's in South Carolina, so there's no chance of making up. I think she should say she's sorry or just go on with her life. There are plenty of boys everywhere. But I like Slover. Other than Kathleen, he is the only grownup who doesn't treat me like a baby.

I run as fast as I can up to Fountainhead Street where Edna is in her back yard gathering pine cones and acorns from their trees. She's loading them into a Gibson's grocery bag. "Pretty good haul, Edna. Let's take these to the woods."

Edna and I have a secret place in the woods behind her house. It's hard to climb the hill, and we grab onto the pine limbs and wild dogwoods to pull ourselves up. We don't have to worry about any grownups finding our place because they would never climb up there. Edna's mother sees us climbing, but she is too old to follow us. We just tell her we are going up and will be back soon.

We struggle to the flat place with no trees. This is where we are building our fort. We collect sticks, rocks, and sea shells when we go to the beach and are now adding the pine cones. We've collected seed pods from a wisteria vine. They look like little green knives. We call them our daggers.

Our fort is just large enough for the two of us. We've used sticks for the sides and woven them together with pine boughs and daggers. We have a door opening and a roof decorated with shells and nuts. Rocks for the floor, and a piece of one of Mama's old quilts to cushion our butts when we sit. We found an old tarp to cover the whole thing in case of rain.

This is where we go to tell our secrets. We need a door that will open and close, so we can really have privacy. We call this a "work in progress" like Miss Jones said about the story I am writing for her class.

Our fort needs a name. We've considered B and R ranch (for our last names), Buckingham Palace, Edvo (combining our two names), or Eleanor Estate in honor of the First Lady that both of us love.

Edna has a surprise. A new comic book from *All Star Comics*. I'm flabbergasted when she pulls it out of her Gibson Grocery bag! On the cover is a woman! *Wonder Woman*! We sit side by side and can't read it fast enough.

A US pilot crashes near the island of Paradise where Amazon women live. Diana, who is later called Wonder Woman, rescues the pilot. After winning a contest to see who is the strongest, Diana gets picked to go to the United States to help the pilot search for Nazis spying on the US. She has a red, white and blue costume. We can't wait to read the next issue!

It's starting to get dark as we scramble down the hill. I tell Edna bye and skip back down to Roberson Street before Mama sends Gene after me. If she has to do that, I'm likely to get a whipping.

1941 October 12
Doris
Rock Hill

Kathleen is hopelessly depressed, and I have to do something. I told her to write Slover and ask if we could come to visit him on Sunday at the post in Rock Hill. She was very nervous about writing for fear that he wouldn't write back or would send another devastatingly mean letter.

"Look, Kathleen, you can sit here and cry, or you can do something. But you cannot stay like this. You'll get carted off to Dix Hill Insane Asylum in Raleigh." That was a terrible thing to say because of what happened to our sister Adele. I immediately wished I could stuff those words back into my mouth. But it seemed to snap Kathleen back to reality, and she said she would write.

Lo and behold, he called her on the phone and said yes, he would like to see the both of us in Rock Hill on Sunday. He would be waiting at noon at the base gate. It is over a hundred miles from Fayetteville, so we leave around seven.

So, off we go, me looking at the map to get the turns right, and Kathleen biting her nails and squirming in her seat. She keeps taking out her compact to check her makeup.

When we get to the gate precisely at noon, Slover is there, as promised, looking wonderful in his uniform. He is truly an attractive man. Maybe I should have not broken that date with him!

He walks up to my side, leans in the window, and says, "I would like to take you two ladies to St. John's Court in town. The food is delicious, especially their fresh seafood from the coast. I have to be back here by three."

He slides in the back seat, and says, "Hey, Kathleen, you look very pretty."

"Thank you, Walter, we would enjoy some good seafood."

I am wondering if he has taken Rock Hill girls that Kathleen has worried about to that restaurant.

When we get to St. John's, Slover gets out and opens my door and races around to the other side and opens Kathleen's and takes her hand. But he doesn't look her in the eye.

The lunch is delicious, and we make small talk about Slover's base and what kind of physical training he's been doing. He asks about every member of our family. Kathleen opens up to talk about her part time work at Woolworth's. She tells a funny story about a lady customer who kept trying to fit into a cheap dress that was too small for her and ended up ripping the seam and tried to say the dress was not well made. The manager was called to settle it and agreed with the customer and did not make her pay for the dress. The customer is always right.

Kathleen and Slover need time alone, so I say, "Let's go for a little walk," thinking I could hang way back behind them. Walter points out a little park, just beyond the main street.

"You two go on. I'll just stay in town and window shop even though the stores are all closed on Sunday. I love to look."

After about an hour, they come walking back up the street, hand in hand. Kathleen is beaming. Slover, grinning. "Doris, we want you to be the first to know because you bringing Kathleen here is responsible for our news. We are getting married!"

"Well, isn't that just the bee's knees! Congratulations and best wishes. I am very happy for you two."

On the way back to base, Slover sits in the back with his arm around Kathleen. When we arrive at the gate, he doesn't get out immediately. From the rear-view mirror,

I am witness to the most passionate kiss I have ever seen. I could have been on the other end of that kiss.

Kathleen is quiet until we get a few miles out of town. Then the words flow like an open faucet.

"Oh, Doris, he was so sweet at the park. He apologized and said he should never have been so mean and must have been out of his head to write that letter. He was going nuts missing me and wanting me so badly to be his wife that he went to extremes in that letter. He only has eyes for me. Some of the guys went out with girls here, even if they had girls back in Fayetteville. But not him. No girl even got a passing glance from him because my face just filled his head day and night.

"I told him to stop talking and let me speak. While he was away, he was all I could think of and after our letter spat, I felt like my heart had died. Whatever our future holds, I want to be his even if we are parted by war. And then I said, 'Yes, Walter, I will marry you.'"

1941 November 1
Kathleen
Ginkgo Shower

It is a spectacular autumn day. The sky is clear and cloudless, and the trees are russet, golden, and brilliant red. Walter and I are crunching through the school yard where descending leaves cover the sidewalk.

I want to make a big pile and jump in it, like a silly child. I am still childish in certain ways. But those ways need to end as I am soon to be a wife. I content myself with kicking up the brittle, crackling foliage.

Walter joins in the kicking, and the swirling colors surround our legs.

He puts his arms around me and comes in for a kiss. I am enveloped in warmth and happiness. He pulls away and looks into my eyes. "You know, Kathleen. We should pick a wedding date."

I get that familiar twinge in my stomach as I do every time he brings it up. Yes, I want to marry him. But I'm not in a hurry because of the nagging fear that we will go to war and Walter will have to go. If that happens, I want to wait until he returns. My hope is that, even if there is a war, he will stay at Fort Bragg or serve in the US.

He continues to push. "How about Christmas?"

"Too soon. I need to finish at Worth's and find a job first."

"Ok. Sounds sensible. How about Valentine's Day?"

"Everyone gets married on that day. I want our day to be just remembered as our anniversary."

"How about the spring? We could be married outdoors since we both love nature so much."

I can't resist that pleading look in his eyes, so I give in. "Ok, Walter, I will marry you in the spring."

He gives out a whoop and jumps up sending a burst of leaves into the air. Then, grabs me for a long series of deep kisses. I feel dizzy and don't want the kisses to end.

"Hey, Gasoline! Let's go visit the ginkgo tree to celebrate!"

We continue up the hill to the tree. Right on the corner of McGilvary and Bradford, there she is, rapidly unloading her treasure. We are here on what might be the last day of the ginkgo's leaf fall!

Walter grabs my hand, and we run under the limbs, giddy with delight as leaves sprinkle around us. We laugh and scoop them up and throw handfuls at each other. Walter drops to the ground and stretches out on the growing pile. I join him and put my head on his shoulder.

The afternoon sunlight catches the cascading leaves, and we become one with the shower.

1941 November 10
Evo
Halloween

Halloween has come and gone. It just doesn't last long enough!

Edna and I talked for weeks about our costumes. She wanted to be a witch, and I wanted to be Frankenstein. We drew pictures of how we wanted to look, but we could never find parts for a witch hat or Frankenstein's neck bolts. So, we went through Mama's material scraps and found plenty of strips that we could wrap around our bodies like mummies, and we smeared our faces with coal dust.

Roger said we looked like mummy clowns because the material pieces were all different colors. Not dingy and dull like the mummy we saw in a Boris Karloff movie. Boris was an Egyptian mummy that some scientists made come back to life. After living a while and trying to find his true love, he crumbled into dust. It wasn't really scary.

Even though our costumes were not what we wanted, we could still trick or treat and get candy. When it got dark, we toted the old pillow cases Mama gave us and started out. We were allowed only to go on Roberson or Fountainhead.

Our mamas warned that they would tan our hides if they heard of us doing any tricks. We wanted to do a few mild ones like toilet papering some trees or throwing a little hard corn against windows. But we didn't because neighbors would be sure to tell our mamas. The adults on our streets are such tattle tellers!

Real tricks are soaping windows, smashing pumpkins in gardens, throwing tomatoes, or hiding front porch plants and furniture. We itched to do those things, too. I bet Mrs. Kelly would never miss that ugly, dead geranium left over from the summer.

There was no moon, so it was real dark. Lots of kids on Roberson Street. But walking up to Fountainhead, we were alone.

Fountainhead has some pretty old trees that hang over the sidewalk. When we got about to Edna's house, we thought we heard a rustling sound in one of the trees. There was no wind, and it was too loud to be a bird. Edna said it might be the ghost of old Mrs. Glenn who just died in her dark, falling down house. She dared me to run up to a window and look in. I didn't want to be a scaredy cat, so I almost did it. But I got off by reminding Edna that we had to be home by eight, so we best finish our route.

I left Edna at her house and walked back home by myself. By that time there were many other trick or treaters out and the streets were crowded, so I wasn't scared.

When I was about to our house, a sheeted ghost flapped out from behind a tree. My heart just about stopped, and I started running when I heard laughing. Turning around, I saw Gene's wild hair emerging from the sheet. "Got 'cha," he yelled.

"No, you didn't, Eugene Fields Brantley, I knew it was you all the time."

"Really? Then why did you run?"

Fuming, I skipped up the steps and slammed the door a little harder than necessary. When I dumped my bag out on the dining room table, I had a nice haul. Five apples, two pears, several homemade popcorn balls (my favorite), lots of penny candy, a few homemade cookies wrapped in waxed paper, and ten pennies. Gene came to snoop through my stuff. He grabbed a piece of candy. I yelled at him, but too late, as he had already popped it into his mouth and gone to pick up a comic book. I am rationing out my stuff, one treat per day and keeping them hidden from Gene. I am saving the pennies.

Kathleen got a letter today from her Canadian pen pal Marj. She let me read it because Marj told her about Halloween there. This was the best part:

> *You spoke about Halloween in your last letter. Well...the boys practically took the town apart here. The next morning, you'd hardly know the place. They climbed up a telephone pole and turned out practically every street light in the whole place, took all the park benches and piled them at the high school door, took gates and put them on top of telephone poles. Don't ask me how. I haven't figured it out yet.*

Gads! Those Canadians are pretty wild! I wonder what their costumes were like. Maybe some dressed up like that mean, terrifying Adolph Hitler since they are at war with him. I wonder how you could make that silly moustache. Maybe I can try that next year if the war isn't over by then.

1941 November 20
Ethel
Thankful

I look around the table at each of my children. Everyone is here, including Kathleen's fiancé Slover.

I count my blessings. Buck continues to work at Horne's drug store and has been promoted to assistant manager. Roger works at Huske Hardware and now paints signs. Gene does well in school and is part time at the photo shop. Doris still works at Verne's, and Kathleen is at Worth's and working at Woolworth's on the weekends. With my alteration work, we are doing well with our money.

I'm thankful that I'm over my kidney surgery and have no more of those awful attacks. I am pleased that Evelyn is growing up as a happy child, and I see signs of maturity. She made the biscuits today, and they looked and tasted wonderful. She continues to keep us all laughing with her sometimes wild ideas.

We decided to buy a ready-to-cook turkey this year, so I didn't have to kill one and pluck all those feathers. It's big, so we will have leftovers. Rice and gravy, cranberry sauce, butter peas, corn, deviled eggs, Evelyn's biscuits, and coconut cake.

After we get the dishes cleared, there is a knock at the door. Lenna Kelly and Margie and Frankie bring us some of their homemade jelly. It will sure be good with leftover biscuits in the morning. They stay a while, and we all listen to the radio. There is some good gospel singing that plays in the background while Lenna Kelly and I talk. Margie, Frankie and Evelyn play Chinese checkers.

There is love, friendship, and peace in our house today. I say a little prayer in my head. "Lord, keep us always close and safe. Protect those in war abroad. And please help us stay out of it."

1941 December 4
Kathleen
Window Shopping

It's Walter's birthday, and he comes for supper. Mama surprises him with a chocolate pie, his favorite. I give him a new wallet, and sweet Evo drew him a picture of the two of us sitting in the swing. It looks a lot like us with Walter in his uniform and me in my blue dress. Roger shakes Walter's hand firmly and says, "Happy birthday. This time next year I will be your brother-in-law, and how lucky you will be." Everyone laughs.

Walter and I go to the Broadway to see *An Appointment for Love*. It's about a couple who decide, immediately after they meet, to get married, and then have all sorts of problems adjusting to each other. But they work everything out. I hope Walter and I will get along after we marry.

When the movie lets out, the stores are closed, but we walk Hay Street talking about our future and window shopping for things we might like in our home. Walter likes a big easy chair in Market Furniture. I spy a washing machine in the appliance store, a wringer type. That would surely make washing easier than doing it in a pot in the back yard like Mama used to do before we got ours.

Walter pulls me into the little foyer outside the door of Henebry and Son Jewelers and comes for a long kiss. I feel a little faint and want kissing and more. "Let's look at the engagement rings, Kathleen."

"Hmm. They are so expensive, Walter. Just a nice wedding band will do."

"No, I want you to wear a diamond, so the world will know you are mine and are as rare as a diamond."

Some of the rings are so big and flashy, as are their price tags. I spot one that has a small diamond and beautiful little filigree etchings in the gold band around it. "I like that one, Walter. It is so delicate. I don't like flashy."

"Well then," says Walter leaning in to see the price tag, "it shall be yours … after a few more pay checks."

Arm in arm, we start home. Everything is perfect, and I have pushed war worries far into the back of my mind.

1941 December 7
Doris
Radio

It is Sunday afternoon, just the way I like it. Mama is finally out of the kitchen to sit with the rest of us in the front room. Jimmie Rice is here too, next to me on the sofa. Jimmie and I touch hands between us but don't hold them.

Gene, his long legs stretching out in front of the sofa, is sprawled out reading the latest Marvel Comic *The Human Torch*. Buck is in the front bedroom picking out some notes on his guitar. Roger, in the rocker, is doodling on his sketch pad. Kathleen is playing Maj Jong in the dining room with Betty Sue Arthur, Mrs. Kelly from next door, and Polly. They are lining up their walls of tiles. I know that Kathleen would rather be out with Slover, but he is on training maneuvers at Fort Bragg.

The only Brantley missing is Evelyn, who started begging Mama, the minute dinner was over, for permission to go up the hill and play with Edna Rogers. Just as well that she is not here. She would squirm and talk and irritate all of us until Mama relented and let the girl go. Sometimes that child won't give us a moment's peace.

The radio plays in the background with the Rev. Harry Emerson Fosdick preaching away about sin. Gene, Roger, and Buck would rather listen to Dodgers football, but on Sunday afternoons, Mama's program choices rule.

"Y'all need another slice of cake?" Mama interrupts just as a commercial for Martha White flour begins.

"No, thank you, ma'am," is the collective response that accompanies a satiated groan from Roger and Buck. Mama's primary mission is life is to cook a mountain of food and watch us, in addition to anyone who might be visiting, eat away at that mountain. Today's mountain consisted of fried chicken, butter beans, peas, chow chow relish, rice and gravy, mashed potatoes, biscuits, fried cornbread and chocolate cake. She cooks just like her mother Grandma Coggins does on the family farm in Sanford.

Just as Betty Sue throws a tile on the table and says, "One bam," the commercial ends. Not Reverend Fosdick but an announcer,

All heads turn to the radio as if expecting to see something. Roger tosses his sketch pad down, reaches over from the rocker, and turns the volume up.

Hello, NBC. Hello, NBC. This is KGU in Honolulu, Hawaii. I am speaking from the roof of the Advertiser Publishing Company Building. We have witnessed this morning the distant view of a brief full battle of Pearl Harbor and the severe bombing by enemy planes, undoubtedly Japanese. The city of Honolulu has also been attacked and considerable damage done. This battle has been going on for nearly three hours. One of the bombs dropped within fifty feet of KGU tower. It is no joke. It is a real war. The public of Honolulu has been advised to keep in their homes and away from the Army and Navy. There has been serious fighting going on in the air and in the sea. The heavy shooting seems to be . . .

There was some static and a little interruption.

We cannot estimate just how much damage has been done, but it has been a very severe attack.

Kathleen bursts into tears. I look at Jimmie and think *he won't have to go. He isn't even finished with his flight training.* I grab his hand and squeeze it tight.

Everyone looks around blankly and no one speaks until Mama turns to Gene. "Run up to Fountainhead Street and fetch Evelyn home."

1941 December 7
Evo
Keep an Eye on the Sky

I take aim with Edna Rogers' Daisy Red Rider BB gun right at the middle can.

Me and Edna have set up three cans on a log in the back yard for our target practice. The big hill makes a safe place to shoot since the BBs will not go anywhere except into the dirt. Even so, my mama would be mad as fire if she knew that her daughter was using a gun, no matter how harmless it is. I'm willing to risk Mama's scolding and a possible trashing with a switch because shooting is ever so much more fun than sitting in the Brantley front room for Sunday afternoon visiting with assorted dull relatives and friends. I am ten years old now, and I deserve to do what I want on Sunday afternoons.

Just as my shot whizzes and kerplunks off the side of the can, Edna's mama Bea Rogers explodes out the back door and shouts, "Y'all get in this house right now. The Japs might drop bombs on us like they did on Pearl Harbor."

Me and Edna look at her wondering where Pearl Harbor is and look up into the sky for signs of airplanes. I aim the gun upward, thinking I might shoot at a plane.

Bea Rogers yells louder. "Throw that toy down and get in here, or I will tan your hides!

I pitch the gun aside, and we scramble up the steps as Mrs. Rogers shoos us in. In the kitchen the radio is playing, not its usual Sunday afternoon preaching and gospel music, but a man talking in a booming and hurried voice: "… distant view of a brief full battle of Pearl Harbor and the severe bombing of Pearl Harbor by enemy planes, undoubtedly Japanese."

"Where is Pearl Harbor, Mama? How big were the planes that dropped bombs? What kind of noise do bombs make? Why did they drop bombs? Did they kill anyone?"

"Shhhhh! Close that door and you and Evelyn Lou go pull down all the window shades. We don't want the Japs to see us and drop a bomb on us." Still wondering where Pearl Harbor is, I am beginning to feel a little scared and want my mama.

"Come on, Evo. Help me," Edna orders.

We have just pulled down the last shade in the living room when Mrs. Rogers flutters in, knocking over some of her salt and pepper shaker collection that sits on a three-tiered table. A little elephant salt shaker bounces on the floor but does not break. She picks it up, replaces it, and rushes over to her antique dining table, which she uses as a display area for her porcelain figurines. It has two sides that fold up to make it bigger. But now the sides are down. The table looks like a little cave with an open mouth.

"Quick, girls. Get under this table with me. We'll be safe from the bombs here!"

Just as we get set under the table and Mrs. Rogers wedges herself between us, there is an urgent rap at the front door. She squeezes out.

It is Gene. "Mama said you have to come home, Evelyn."

"Oh, Eugene," Mrs. Rogers answers. "Did you know the Japs are dropping bombs on us? You and Evelyn better just stay here until it's night when they can't see us."

"Uh, Mrs. Rogers, I don't think we have anything to worry about. The bombings were over five thousand miles away in Hawaii. Don't think the Japanese have any planes that could fly that far."

"OK. But be particular as you walk home and keep an eye on the sky and listen for airplane motors."

"We will. Thanks for letting Evelyn play here this afternoon. Bye, Edna." We are out the door and down the long line of concrete steps to the street.

I feel better after Gene's words set my mind at ease. Still, I hold Gene's hand real tight, and it is hard to keep up as he walks fast.

1941 December 7
Ethel
Mrs. Roosevelt

Since the announcement this afternoon, we haven't moved away from the radio. Some of the regular programs have been on with interruptions for bulletin updates. The last one told of more bombings on other Pacific islands. The president will address the nation tomorrow.

We had a supper of leftovers, but no one ate much except Gene, who can always eat to fill that growing body no matter what's going on.

Mrs. Roosevelt presented her regular broadcast. She summarized the news and gave a little speech which made me feel a little better:

> *I should like to say just a word to the women in the country tonight. I have a boy at sea on a destroyer. For all I know he may be on his way to the Pacific. Two of my children are in coast cities on the Pacific.*
>
> *Many of you all over this country have boys in the services who will now be called upon to go into action. You have friends and families in what has suddenly become a danger zone. You cannot escape anxiety. You cannot escape a clutch of fear at your heart. And yet I hope that the certainty of what we have to meet will make you rise above these fears.*
>
> *We must go about our daily business more determined than ever to do the ordinary things as well as we can. And when we find a way to do anything more in our communities to help others, to build morale, to give a feeling of security, we must do it. Whatever is asked of us, I am sure we can*

accomplish it. We are the free and unconquerable
people of the United States of America.

Evelyn fell asleep during the broadcast, and Roger carried her to bed. I think it best to send her to school tomorrow and keep things as normal as possible, and everyone should go to work and Kathleen to Worth's.

As Mrs. Roosevelt said, we should go about our daily business determined to do our tasks as well as we can.

1941 December 8
Evo
Day of Infamy

It doesn't feel right to be in school after what happened yesterday, but Mama said we should go about our business as a sign of strength. That is what Mrs. Roosevelt said last night. No point in sitting around moping. When I grow up, I want to be strong and brave like the First Lady.

I can hardly keep my eyes open in class. Yesterday was so exhausting. And to top it off, the phone rang at four a.m. and woke everybody up. It was Slover telling Kathleen that he was leaving Fort Bragg on sealed orders. I guess that means he is going somewhere but can't tell anyone where. Is he going to Japan to fight?

Kathleen was crying and saying she didn't even get to say good-bye and she may never see him again. Roger tried to console her by saying he thought the Army is just trying to get organized and decide how to react to the attack and that Slover is probably going somewhere in this country.

After all that, I never went back to sleep, wondering if the Japanese might drop bombs on us here like Mrs. Rogers said. Fort Bragg is a base like Pearl Harbor, so maybe the Japs will bomb it too.

Of course, everyone at school is talking about yesterday and what they were doing when they heard the news. The boys say they would sign up if they were older and fight the dadblamed Japs. Girls are mostly scared, and some are crying.

The teachers try to keep to the lesson, but there is too much talking among students. Mr. Blaylock just let us talk in history class, and he listened. That was good. The only thing he said was, "You will each remember all your lives what you were doing on December 7, 1941. Life as we know it is going to change in many ways in the coming days. But you are all smart and strong, and you will be able to handle whatever comes."

The president addressed the nation, and we got to listen over the classroom loudspeaker. He said yesterday was "a day that will live in infamy."

Stupid Albert Jonas said, "What the heck does infamy mean?" and made us miss a couple of sentences of the speech. I wanted to say that it means it will always be remembered as a day that something really bad happened, but I didn't.

There have been more Japanese attacks on some more islands in the Pacific Ocean. In history class, we got out maps and the globe and located all those places. None anywhere near us, but that does not stop the fear that we could be attacked.

Myrtle Martin said we should kill any Japanese living in our country. Several people agreed. Or at least round them up and put them in jail, added Billy Smith.

That sounded pretty mean to me. What about Japanese people who are US citizens and were born here? I thought that, but was afraid to say it, since everyone was so stirred up.

I thought of my friend Tomoko Sugano. She is a first grader. Her daddy is a gardener and does work at the homes of some rich people and for the city. Her mama Kazuko cleans houses. Some kids make fun of Tomoko's mom and call her "kudzu" like that big vine we see along the roads outside of town. Tomoko must be scared if she hears ugly things kids are saying.

I am scared too, but I won't tell anyone.

1941 December 9
Ethel
Stanley Applegate

The shock of Sunday's news of Pearl Harbor has kept me awake most of the last two nights. I am up at five-thirty as usual making breakfast. Evelyn will want to eat some of the Cheerios that Slover brought her from the base PX. I am not sure about that being very nourishing food, but all the young people are mad for it since it just came on the market. I put out a bowl and milk for her and then start on the real food. Eggs, sausage, grits, and toast. I feel shaky all over as I crack the eggs, and one slides out of the shell and plops on my shoe.

I can't keep my mind from going to scary places as I think about my boys. Buck and Roger: will they join up on their own or be drafted?

Buck called his friend Stanley Applegate in New Jersey last night. Buck and Polly met Stan last summer when his family was vacationing at Carolina Beach. The two talked about what they would do if we go war. Stan said he would join up.

Yesterday afternoon, Stan had been horseback riding with some friends and had not heard the news. They stopped in a restaurant for a bite to eat and were laughing and making jokes. The waitress rushed to their table and asked them what in the world was wrong with them having such a jolly time when our country had been attacked.

The next morning Stan, without telling his family, took the train from his home in Montclair, New Jersey, to New York City to enlist. He was turned away from the enlistment center when his physical revealed a bunch of wax in his ears and poor hearing.

The induction officer told him to go see a nearby doctor the military had contracted to help with such matters. He went down the street, the doctor flushed the wax out, and Stan went right back to the center, passed the hearing test, and was accepted. Just like that.

He and the others who had passed physicals were transported in a big open truck to another facility to take the oath. Some of the men in the truck yelled insults to men just walking along the street, calling them stragglers, sluggards, and cowards for not enlisting. The chief petty officer told them to knock it off.

Emotions are high and young men are mad to get into the war and resentful of those who won't join up.

When Stan returned home that evening, his father just looked at him and asked him which service branch he joined. The Navy. He reports for duty on January sixth in Newport, Rhode Island. I wonder how Stan's mother feels about this. I would be glad if physicals prevented my boys from being inducted.

I hear the children stirring in their rooms, so I hurry up with the sausage and toast.

1941 December 10
Doris
Welcome Neighbor Day

The city of Fayetteville is having a "Welcome Neighbor Day." Mayor McFadyen planned this several months ago to show the city's support for our military. We thought this event would be cancelled after bombings and our declaring war on Japan. But the mayor decided that the boys from Fort Bragg and the city people alike needed a little cheering up.

Our whole family is on Hay Street in the huge crowd of city folks and others who came from surrounding counties. It is cold, but we are all wrapped up, and the closeness of the crowd keeps us pretty warm. Grills are set up cooking barbecue, and there's music and dancing in the street. The USO building is open on Ray Avenue and is packed with people wanting to escape the cold.

The sky is a murky grey with that trace of brown which sometimes means snow is coming.

Mama is ready to go home before the rest of us, so Roger walks her back to Roberson Street. Kathleen and I dance with any soldier who asks us. I am glad that Jimmie could not leave base to come because he would be furious if I danced with someone other than him. I am having fun with a new partner for every dance. I feel like Scarlett O'Hara being surrounded by a host of suitors at a ball at Tara.

It gets dark and street lights and store lamps are off, as ordered by the government to keep us less visible to possible planes looking to drop bombs. I think this is a bit premature since Jimmie says that the Japanese don't have the capability to fly so far.

We stumble back to the intersection of Hay and Roberson. Several cars have bashed into each other in the darkness. Nothing serious as far as we can see.

As we pass the music store, the door is open and Bing Crosby's "Winter Wonderland" is playing at full volume.

Sleigh bells ring
Are you listening?
In the lane
Snow is glistening
A beautiful sight,
We're happy tonight
Walking in a winter wonderland

We sing along as the sky decides to let go of a few snowflakes and the weight of the darkness lightens a bit.

I wonder if next Christmas will be beautiful and happy if the war isn't over.

1941 December 15
Kathleen
Fayetteville Industrial Bank

I have finished my courses at Worth's Business College, so it's time to look for a job. I've sent applications to Fayetteville Industrial Bank, Sears Roebuck, and a few lawyers on Hay Street, all within walking distance of Roberson Street since I don't have a car.

I need a better job than Woolworth's. I hate that job, and it doesn't pay much, and I want to be able to use my secretarial skills. I did well at Worth's and feel prepared. Even my typing is pretty good now.

I meet the mailman and receive an envelope with a Fayetteville Industrial Bank return address. Most likely a "thanks-but-no thanks." I open it anyway, and to my astonishment, I am requested to come for an interview with Mr. W. C. Downing, the president, tomorrow at nine am!

My initial excitement quickly turns to fear! What will I wear? Will I say the right thing?

Mama stops her sewing. She notices that I am agitated and shaking a bit. She knows me well and senses my every mood.

My eyes well up with tears as Mama says, "Kathleen, what is the world is wrong?"

"I have an interview tomorrow at Fayetteville Industrial Bank."

"Isn't that good news?"

"Yes, but they probably won't like me. What will I wear? It is probably a waste of time."

"You can wear your white sweater with your nice jacket and borrow my pearls. You can use Doris' hat with the little net on the front. You will look professional and lovely. As you excelled at Worth's, you are well qualified. How could they not want to hire you? Just try to remember not to twist your hair."

Calmed down thanks to Mama's pep talk, I get ready. I wash the sweater since it has a little stain in the front and stretch it out across the oil heater in the front room to dry and go to bed.

1941 December 16
Kathleen
Interview

I am sitting on a little bench in the lobby of Fayetteville Industrial Bank, staring at the glass window which repeats my reflection in every block. A hundred Kathleens look down on me. I resist the urge to twirl a curl of my hair. The receptionist tells me that Mr. Downing will see me shortly.

The day did not begin well. I was shocked to discover that the heater imprinted two indelible parallel brown lines on the front of my sweater. If only I had put the back of it down on the surface, I could have worn it anyway under my jacket.

Doris, seeing my tears, let me borrow her white silk blouse, an act of generosity she would never have done under any other circumstances. Doris is not one to share her pretty clothes.

The door marked "Mr. W. C. Downing, President" on a shiny brass plate opens with a flourish and out steps a tall man, graying at the temples behind his glasses. He is regal in his movements. When he calls "Miss Brantley," I think my heart will stop. Stupidly, I raise my hand like I am still in school answering roll call.

He smiles and offers, "Please do come in, Miss Brantley."

I stand on wobbly knees which I pray he can't see and walk through the big polished wood door.

"Please have a seat." He extends his hand toward a plush Victorian chair in front of his big desk.

I sit. I want to say something like, "Thank you for seeing me," but my mouth won't work.

Mr. Downing rescues me. He gets right down to business. "Miss Brantley, do you see this stack of application letters?" He points to a pile about an inch thick.

"Yes, sir." My mouth does still function.

"Well, Miss Brantley, out of all of these, your letter was the best one, grammatically perfect, all words spelled correctly, neat, and logical. You have high praise from Worth's, and you are proficient in both typing and shorthand. This is all I need to know. You are hired. My secretary will discuss salary and other matters with you. We look forward to having you as part of the Fayetteville Industrial Bank team. Welcome aboard."

I stand as he does, we shake hands, and he sees me to the door.

I talk with the secretary, walk out the front door, and float down Hay Street. I have a real job. Happy! Happy! I pass Woolworth's on the corner and hold my head high and laugh.

Christmas Eve. Mama, Doris, Jimmie, Evo, Walter, and I walk to church. In enthusiasm for the holidays, some have violated the order to keep lighting to a minimum. We pass lit trees in windows along Roberson. Fayetteville is beautiful tonight, and I feel more cheerful than I have in the last few weeks.

We're supposed to hang black out curtains like they do in London. Mama is working on some for our house. So maybe next year, if the war isn't over, we won't see any Christmas lights twinkling in homes.

Back home, everyone goes inside to warm up except Walter (who returned to Fort Bragg a few days ago but couldn't tell me where he had been on those sealed orders.) He reaches for my hand and leads me to the swing.

"It's cold, Walter. Let's go in."

"Not yet, please. I need to talk to you." We sit for just a minute, then he gets up, turns around and goes down on a knee. "Kathleen, I love you more than life itself, and I can't wait for you to be my wife." He reaches in his pocket and pulls out a little box covered in velvet.

Oh! This can't be the ring we picked out. How did he save enough money? But it is! I open it to see the sparkling diamond surrounded by the perfect filigreed gold band. He takes it out and slips in on my finger, a perfect fit even though I never tried it on.

I throw my arms around him, and we stand for the most thrilling kiss of my life. I'm too excited to let my fears about the war and possible separation ruin this moment. I am his, and he is mine.

"Let's go and show everyone, Walter!"

"Yes, my Gasoline, let's do.

1941 December 29
Ethel
Blackout Curtains

I wake with a start as the pale blue of dawn slips through the space where the heavy black out curtains don't quite meet.

Lenna Kelly laughed at me when I ran my treadle machine day and night to get those curtains done. "Those Japanese can't fly all the way over here, and the Germans are too busy bombing London," she said.

I don't want to leave the warmth of my bed. My arm lies across the opposite side of the bed where Wesley should be. I'll never stop missing him. He was my rock, and I desperately need him to help me through this war.

How pleasant it would be to close my eyes again. I can always sleep in the early hours even though I sleep little in the deep of night. Yet, I sit up and slip on my fraying bedroom slippers and pull on my housecoat.

Even without the light on, I can see in the mirror the wrinkles that creep across my face in increasing numbers. Forty-seven years old, but I feel and look older. I brush my long, salt and pepper hair, gather it into a pony tail, wind it round and round into a loose bun at my neck, and fasten it with bobby pins. I will myself into the kitchen to start breakfast.

A new year is upon us. 1942. Will there be the usual New Year's excitement? Or will fear steal our celebration as we brace for the uncertainly of war?

Kathleen, January 1941 Evo, Ethel, and Kathleen Doris

Eugene Roger Polly and Buck Kathleen, Betty Sue
jitterbugging

Kathleen, Evo, Walter, Ethel, Roger, Gene   Wesley, 1936

Ethel on the new phone   White Lake

104

Kathleen's graduation

Walter Slover

Kathleen Brantley

Walter and Kathleen
on high school steps

Jimmie Rice

Stanley Applegate

Kathleen's engagement ring

Kathleen and Walter

1942 January 1
Kathleen
You Made Me Love You

New Year's Day. How my life has changed since this day a year ago when all I worried about was whether to wear a plaid skirt or plain one to school after the Christmas holidays.

Now I'm out of high school, engaged, and working at the bank. I like it my job but vanished are my foolish dreams of living in France and speaking the language and being in love with a Frenchman.

I have found my love right here.

Walter wants to marry in the spring. It scares me to think about being separated and wondering if he will return from war alive and in one piece. All of this happened so quickly, and I was swept into an engagement that I was not completely sure of. A song we danced to at his company party is stuck in my head:

> *You made me love you*
> *I didn't want to do it*
> *I didn't want to do it.*
> *You made me want you*
> *You know you've got the brand of kisses*
> *That I'd die for*
> *You know you made me love you.*

Yes, Walter, you made me love you. I didn't want to do it. But I did.

1942 January 5
Evo
Everything Will Be Alright

I'm back at school today after the holidays. Happy to be busy again. It was pretty glum around our house now that we are at war with Japan and Germany. We all wonder if my brothers and Slover and Jimmie will have to go.

I hear Doris and Jimmie arguing about who knows what, and Kathleen and Slover sitting on the front porch swing and talking. Kathleen looks very confused when Slover leaves. I don't know what they were talking about even though I try to listen through the front bedroom window. Yes, I am curious, but I just can't help it. Secrets are so delicious!

Not so much war talk among students as before Christmas. Maybe we are all getting a little used to being in war.

Except Billie Wilson in my math class. She lives on a farm way out of town and says she is afraid the Germans will come marching up the road to her house. Teacher tries to reassure her. She says that the Germans would have to come way across the ocean and that our soldiers would fight them off before they got very far.

I wonder if they would try to land at Carolina Beach where we go in the summer sometimes. No, on second thought, it would have to be at a port, like Wilmington, because the waves at the beach would just wash them out to sea and they would drown. I tap Billie on the shoulder and tell her so.

After school, I decide to stop by Janie Ringo's house to see how they are doing. Abby comes to the door when I knock and lets me in. I notice that the screen door is loose. Janie's husband Sam is probably too tired to fix it after he gets home after his two jobs, at the Candy Kitchen and as the janitor at Fayetteville Industrial Bank. I know it's real late when he gets home. I might ask Gene if he will fix it for them. He is so good at fixing.

"Hi, Janie. How are you doing?" She looks tired and hot, even though it is cold outside. She is standing by the ironing board with a big pile of clothes to be streamed and ironed. She takes in washing and ironing.

"Hey, Miss Evelyn. How is your Mama? Is she still feeling good these days?"

"Yes, she is, but she is pretty worried about what might happen to my brothers with this war on. Me too."

"Don't you worry, child. Everything will be alright. No matter what happens, the Lord will protect us because we are fighting to stop a devil from hell, and the Lord just can't abide such evil. Now, would you like a cookie, girl?"

"Oh yes, thank you, I don't mind if I do."

The cookie is sweet and comforting. Especially with milk to wash it down. I feel happy and safe. For now.

1942 January 9
Doris
Banjo

Friday afternoon and Verne let me go early from the tailor shop since business was slow. It is not cold for January, so I am sitting in the porch swing while my nails dry. Jimmie is coming to take me to supper.

At four o'clock, Horace Purvis pulls up in front of the house. I have never dated Horace, but he comes to the house with other soldiers occasionally. He brings his banjo and plays along on our songs.

He opens his door and waves me an invitation to join him in the car. I open the passenger's side door and stick my head in. "Hey, Horace. How are you? Why don't you come in and sit a spell?"

"No, thanks, Doris. I'm in a bit of a hurry. Could you get in for a minute?"

I slide in, and he gets to the point immediately. "I am being shipped out tomorrow to New York. That means I am going overseas."

"Oh! I didn't expect anyone would be leaving for war so soon! Surely, you will be stationed somewhere in the US. Not everyone needs to go over; there are plenty of jobs soldiers need to do here. Protect our coastline, for one."

"I wish that was true, but I don't think this war can be won unless we get over there and help. Well, anyway," he reaches in the back seat and pulls his banjo forward, "I was hoping you would keep this for me until I get back. I don't have time to mail it home. And if I don't make it back, it's yours forever. Hey, you or maybe one of your musical brothers can learn to play it."

"Horace, don't talk like that! You don't know for sure you will be in any dangerous places and even if you are, you'll stay safe and come back just like you are now."

"All the same, Doris, I would be grateful if you would keep the banjo."

"I will be happy to keep it and when you come back, you better come right here for a piano and banjo duet with…"

Crash!

The window on Horace's side shatters as a fist forces its way into the car. The fist withdraws, and Horace is bleeding, and some shards of glass are stuck on and in his face.

What in the world! I push open my door and jump out and look across the top of the car to see Jimmie Rice with his bloody right fist cradled against his chest with his left hand covering it.

"Jimmie Rice, have you snapped your cap?"

His mouth begins to spew loud venom, and his face is red with rage. "Doris, you little khaki wacky cheat! Here you are making time with another man right before you were going out with me! How many men are you stringing along? I bet your string reaches all the way to Fort Bragg!"

He pulls open Horace's door and jerks him out by his shirt collars and is about to punch him when Mama yells from the porch, "Stop! Stop it right now! You two boys get your sorry selves right up to this porch. Now!"

They stop. Mama is a gentle soul who never raises her voice, and in the surprise of this unexpected show of power, the two bloody boys freeze. After a little pause, they glare at each other, and we all head to the porch, me a little behind the boys.

I wonder what I should do, but I do nothing as Mama takes charge. "Jimmie, you sit in the swing, and Horace, you sit in the chair on the other side of the porch. Don't move or speak until I get back with some things to clean you up."

I sink down on the steps, and no one says a word. I study my shoes. Mama comes out with a pan of water,

110

towels, alcohol, cotton, and some band aides. She turns to Horace first who looks worse than Jimmie, picks out what glass she can, washes the wounds, dabs them with alcohol-soaked cotton, and sticks a band aid here and there. She turns and goes back in the house, the screen door banging hard behind her.

"Let me see your hand," she orders Jimmie as she returns with clean water and towels. She picks out some glass and cleans off the blood and wipes his wounds a little roughly. Jimmie winces at the sting and sucks in air with each dab. She wraps the offending hand with some band aids. "Now, Jimmie Rice, you get in your car and high tail it back to base. I wouldn't want to be in your place to explain a bummed-up hand to your CO."

"But Mrs. Brantley ..."

"No, buts. Just go." At that, he passes me, still on the steps, and looks back but doesn't speak.

Jimmie drives off slowly. The car jerks as he tries to shift gears with his banged-up hand.

When the car is out of sight, Horace says, "Mrs. Brantley, I apologize for causing such an altercation outside your home. I was here just to ask Doris to keep my banjo while I am away at war."

"From where I stood, son, you were not the cause of the problem but rather the recipient. Doris, walk Horace to his car and get the banjo. Then, Horace, you best be going back to Bragg too as you will have to deal with your CO."

When we get to his car, Horace opens the door and collects the banjo from the floor mat where I had dropped it in the fray. "Sorry, Doris, I caused a tiff between you and your boyfriend. Will you still keep my banjo?"

"Yes, of course. And I am not sure if that maniac is my boyfriend any more. Be safe, Horace. I will pray for your safety. Please drop me a line now and then. And when you get back, we will be happy to see you."

As Horace pulls away, I lift the banjo up across my midsection and strum across. The resulting chord is mournful and discordant, not happy and bright like the tunes its owner played around our piano. A little chill runs up my backbone. *Come home safe, Horace.*

1942 January 10
Kathleen
Dillon

After yesterday afternoon's explosion by Jimmie Rice, Doris is in a snit. She is mad as fire, but when he came this afternoon and apologized, she agreed to go with him to supper.

I'd like to hear that supper conversation! His hand was all bandaged. We did not expect to see him anytime soon because we figured he would get in trouble for fighting and be confined to base. He must have made up quite a story to explain the injury!

None of us kids were home at the time of the fight, and we had to drag the details out of Mama as Doris would not tell us. We were sorry we missed the show. What is it about a fight that draws people with such a perverse interest?

Walter comes a few minutes after Doris and Jimmie left, and we go for a little walk, since it is not too cold. We walk up to the high school and sit on the steps. We snuggle close since the air is cooler as the sun drops lower in the sky.

"Kathleen, when do you want to get married?"

"In the spring, like we said. Perhaps in early May outdoors or at the church. I want blooming flowers, Doris and Evo as bridesmaids, and Roger or Buck can give me away. Mama said she would make me a white dress with lots of tulle and lace…"

"I want to get married right away."

"Why? It takes time to properly plan a wedding. Invitations, getting the church…"

"I am not sure I will be here in the spring."

"What? Why?"

"There is talk that the Ninth Division will ship out soon. Something big is coming."

"Oh, then maybe we will have to wait till you get back."

"That could be a long time. We might go to North Africa or England, and there is sure to be an invasion of France eventually. I might not get home until all that happens."

I could not speak.

"I want to get married as soon as we can. We can go to Dillon, South Carolina, to the marriage chapel with no blood tests beforehand and say our vows the same day."

"But I am not eighteen, and Mama would have to give permission."

"I think she would. Kathleen, I want to spend as much time with you as I can before I go overseas. With a little luck, we won't ship out until September. If we marry in early February when I have a few days leave, we might have seven months together. Please, I want to have you as my wife before I leave."

He leans in close and delivers a long, deep kiss that leaves me breathless and feeling all over that I want more, to be touched by him, and to feel him against me and then everything else. His arms move around me and pull me in closer.

"Yes, Walter, I will marry you in February."

I am about to do what I said I would never do: marry a man going to war. But he kisses me again, and my yearning for him grows into an intense, all-consuming ache which is all I can think of.

1942 January 17
Ethel
Things Happen Fast

Well. I knew Kathleen and Slover would marry. But was surprised that they will do it in early February in Dillon, South Carolina, which is just over the border. They want to have time together as a married couple before he has to leave for war. Dillon is the place for secret elopements and quick ceremonies. They can be married by the Justice of the Peace in his home.

Since Kathleen is not yet eighteen, I will have to give my permission which I will do because nothing I can say will stop them. I wanted to make her a pretty white dress and have my Sanford family present, but I don't expect them all to trek down to Dillon. Just our immediate family will be there. Kathleen has asked Buck to give her away. She wants to wear a suit to be practical, something she can use for work or church later. And a hat, a big one.

She and Doris have gone shopping for the outfit and accessories. Gloves, of course, and a little suitcase to take on her honeymoon. Slover wants to take her to Carolina Beach. Bea Rogers said that the winter is a strange time to be going to the beach. I answered that the newlyweds probably won't spend any time on the beach anyway. We both blushed and giggled. Well, it's true!

Of course, they have no place to live. They have priced small apartments, but all of them require a lease and who knows when Slover will have to leave? I told them that they could stay with us. What was I thinking? We are crowded as it is. I would give them the front bedroom, but we still have roomers and can't throw them out because we need the rent money.

The plan is to have me take Kathleen's place in the middle bedroom with Doris and Evo, so Kathleen and

Slover can have the small back room. Not ideal and not very private, but that is the best we can do.

Slover is so sweet about it, and he insists on paying me rent. I guess I will let him because I don't want to hurt his pride. He really is a good man, and I know he will take care of Kathleen. And they obviously are deeply in love.

My one worry is that Kathleen is so young and inexperienced. I was twenty-two when I married, and I could manage a house since I was well trained by my mother. Kathleen can't cook a lick on her own, but maybe she will improve if I have her do more of the cooking while they are living with us. And in many ways, she is still childlike and not very self-confident. I had hoped she would get to experience more of life on her own before marriage. But this is just the way it is, and she will have to grow up. Things happen fast in wartime.

1942 February 1
Kathleen
Letter from Marj

Walter and I will become husband and wife one week from today. I have my new blue and tan suit and big matching hat, gloves, new hose, and little brown going away suitcase. I'll wear some heels that I already have since I spent so much on the other items, and I will use my Sunday purse. I am excited.

I am also scared. Am I doing the right thing? I do love Walter and when I am with him, I tingle all over in anticipation of being his. But after he leaves, I have doubts. I am seventeen and he is twenty-two. I can see my life stretching before me where I am a wife keeping house and cooking, neither of which I enjoy. What if I get pregnant immediately, and he goes off to war and leaves me with a child? I know nothing about taking care of a baby.

A letter came yesterday from Marj, my pen pal from Canada. I had told her I was getting married in my last letter which was a big surprise to her as I had never even told her that I had a serious boyfriend. Why did I not tell her that? Was I secretly hoping it wouldn't work out? Is marriage not really what I want? Was I ashamed to tell her that I was planning to be married so young?

I moved the rocker near the heater to read the letter since it is freezing even in the house, and I am bundled in Grandma Coggins' wedding ring quilt. She has already given it to me as an early wedding gift.

Dear Kathleen,

I was very glad to hear from you and enjoyed your letter very much. But I haven't recovered from the shock you gave me. Phew! You could have knocked me down "avec" (she throws in a little French) a feather. You are getting married in

*the spring. I feel like an old maid (or do I)? I'm
very happy to hear it though, and I wish you and
your sergeant (you didn't mention the name) a very
happy and prosperous life.*

Why did I not tell her Walter's name? Is this
another sign that I don't want to accept the reality of my
situation?

*I guess what shocked me so much was you
getting married at your age. Why, over here, we
never think of getting married until we're
twenty...and then the marriage age is considered
twenty-five, so I suppose I have eight more years to
wait. But maybe you're different over there?*

The more I read of her reaction, the more doubts
crowded my mind. What was I thinking to agree to marry
so young?

*A government man was at the school the
other day and took down all our ages, boys and
girls, and whether or not we were experienced in
farm work. Of course, I said, "No." Can you
imagine me pitching hay, feeding the pigs and
chickens and milking the cows! Not for me. I am
going to dig out appendixes, help cut off arms and
legs. In short, I am going to be a nurse. You can't
go into training here until you are eighteen but
maybe I can get in sooner because of the war and
the need for nurses.*

Marj has career dreams that she is free to chase
after. Not me. I will be a wife. The rest of the letter spoke
of all the dances and other activities in her school. Her
carefree life makes me jealous.

I am so conflicted. I have so many worries about being a wife. But when Walter arrives tonight, looking so handsome and smiling at me with love, all my fears will go out the door.

1942 February 8
Kathleen
Wedding Day

Mrs. T. W. Brantley of Fayetteville, N. C., announces the marriage of her daughter, Kathleen Marguerite, to First Sgt. Walter Slover of Fort Bragg, N. C. and Shelburn, Indiana.

The wedding took place Sunday, February 8, 1942, at the home of V. L. McLean in Dillion, S. C. The double ring ceremony was used. Several friends and relatives of the bride were present. Burgess Brantley, brother of the bride, gave her away. Roger Brantley, brother of the bride, was best man.

The bride was attired in a blue and tan plaid suit with luggage accessories. Her corsage was of pink roses.

Mrs. Slover is the daughter of Mrs. T. W. Brantley and the late Mr. Brantley of Fayetteville. She is a graduate of Fayetteville Senior High School, attended Worth Business College, and is now employed by Fayetteville Industrial Bank.

Sgt. Slover is the son of Verna Slover and the late Mr. Slover of Shelburn, Indiana. He is a graduate of Shelburn High School. In 1938, he enlisted in the U.S. Army at Fort Benjamin Harrison and is now serving with the Ninth Division at Fort Bragg, N. C. The couple is making their home at 229 Roberson Street in Fayetteville.

I am sitting close to Walter in Franklin's car on our way to our honeymoon at Carolina Beach. It's getting dark, but I look at his handsome profile. He has a great nose. He turns his head and smiles at me with a slightly wicked grin. "Finally, my Gasoline, we will spend this night together and all other nights forever."

This thrills me but also scares me as I don't know what to expect in bed. I have saved myself for marriage.

At two o'clock, we were married. My immediate family was present and a few friends including Betty Sue, of course, and some of Walter's men from base. The ceremony was brief with the Justice of the Peace's wife playing a few tunes on the piano. Buck escorted me to the little altar area while she played "Here Comes the Bride." Then she sang "I Love You Truly." It was hard standing there in front of everyone for what seemed like an age waiting for her to finish.

Doris held Walter's wedding band and gave it to me at the right time. Roger held my ring, my engagement ring. We didn't buy a band to save money.

While we were signing the license, everyone went out to the lawn and were waiting to shower us with rice. By the time we got to the car, rice was pooled in the brim of my hat and in Walter's hair. We were laughing and brushing off rice furiously. Away we went, trailing tin cans and ribbons attached to the back bumper most certainly by my brothers.

A little way out of town, Walter got out and ripped the stuff off the bumper. Without the jangling cans behind us, we are riding in relative quiet. Until Walter starts jabbering on about the wedding and who was there and how he wishes his mother and sisters could have been there. We'll visit them when he gets leave. I'm nervous about that since I have never traveled so far, and I worry if they will like me. I say this to Walter and he answers, "Of course, they will love you because I do, and you are such a wonderful girl!"

We stop at a little roadside restaurant for supper. I order lemon meringue pie and coffee. I am not hungry and leave a big part of my pie. Walter orders a big plate of roast beef, mashed potatoes, greens beans, and rolls. Then, pie to boot. He finishes my pie, too. No worries for him, evidently.

When we arrive at the Ocean View Hotel in Carolina Beach, a bellhop takes our luggage to our room while Walter checks in. He wants to walk out on the boardwalk before we go up. So, we do. We are standing on the wood planks looking down the deserted beach, when Walter says, "Let's go down to the beach." I answer that I will get sand in my good shoes. "No, we can take our shoes off."

"But what about my hose?"

"There is no one out here to see us, so just take them off." I reach under my skirt and detach my new hose from the snaps of my garter belt and stuff them into my purse.

The sand feels good under my feet. So free, cool and thick around my toes. The night is beautiful. Crescent moon and many stars clearly visible since we are away from lights. The sea is calm, and the slowly lapping waves make soft splashes as they fall on the shore.

I am cold, but Walter stands behind me and puts his arms tight around me, and I feel warmer. It is a perfect moment, and Walter turns me to him and kisses me gently and then harder. I tingle at his touch and think of nothing else.

I wish I could freeze the moment forever.

1942 February 11
Kathleen
Mrs. Walter Slover

I open my eyes, and Walter is propped on his arm and looking at me. "Good morning, Mrs. Slover. You look beautiful! Hey, it's not quite dawn. Let's go out on the beach and catch the sunrise!"

I don't want to get out of the warm bed, but I do. Soon we are standing on the boardwalk. Even in my coat and with Walter's arms around me, my teeth are chattering uncontrollably. The eastern sky is putting on a show of purple and pink. Bit by bit, the sun peeks over the horizon showing more and more of itself until it lets go of the sea and rises higher in the sky. A golden reflection spreads toward us in a perfect contrast to the deep navy of the sea. I wish Roger could paint this for me.

"Hey, wife, let's go get breakfast before we drive home." Reality strikes. This is the last day of our honeymoon. Walter will have to go back to the base in the morning and me to work.

And then, what? Will he get orders to ship out soon? I don't think I can bear that. Worries start to creep in like night falling. Where will he go? Japan? Europe? How long will he be gone?

I turn and grab him around the waist and reach up for a kiss and plant one on his lips and don't stop.

When I let go, Walter blinks and says, "Whew, girl! That was quite a kiss."

"Oh, Walter, I don't want you to go to war. Can't you break a leg or something to get out of it?"

He laughs. "No, can't do that, Kathleen. I love our country, and I must help protect us and stop the march of that bastard Hitler. I am prepared to fight. Don't worry. I know how to protect myself and the men in my platoon. And, hey, this war could be over before you know it. I figure it might last another year or two, tops. When the Nazis and the Japs see that we mean business, they'll surrender."

He makes it sound so easy, but I know what a mess the last war was. I give him a look of doubt and reach up and twirl the hair on the back of my neck.

Walter pulls my hand away and kisses it. "Mrs. Slover, will you please accompany me to breakfast in the Ocean View Café? I am starved. I could eat a dozen eggs and a pound of bacon!"

He grabs my hand and pulls me toward the restaurant.

1942 February 18
Evo
Mattress Springs

Kathleen and Slover got back from their honeymoon last week. They are sleeping in the little room behind the kitchen next to the girls' room.

I am sleeping with Doris, Kathleen's old place, so Mama can have my small bed to herself. It's strange to have someone else in my bed. Doris is a restless sleeper and sometimes pokes me when she turns over.

It is about ten p.m., and I just can't get comfortable and go to sleep. I keep thinking about the newsreel at the movie last week and the scenes of Japanese planes bombing little islands in the Pacific Ocean. Will they bomb us? Gene says Japan is too far away and they would need an airbase close to us to bomb us.

Still, I am scared. At school, we have practiced what to do in an air raid. We put our heads down under our desks until the teacher says all clear. I don't like this. I imagine planes bearing down on the school and dropping bombs. I wonder if being under my desk would protect me.

I forget about the air raid because I hear sounds coming from Slover and Kathleen's room. A squeaky rhythm of bouncing mattress springs. I know what that sound is because I can make any bed squeak when I jump up and down on it. I am not supposed to do that, but I do when there is no one near to stop me. Like a trampoline. I would like to be an acrobat like the ones I saw in the Ringling Brothers and Barnum and Bailey Circus in Raleigh. They could bounce high and grab arms and do flips. Edna and I tried to do that one time on her bed, but we could never get high enough. Mrs. Rogers heard us and stopped us and made us promise never to jump on the bed again. But we do it anyway whenever we think we won't get caught.

Are Kathleen and Slover jumping up and down on the bed? I think the squeaky spring noise has to do with whatever married couples do to make babies. I know all about the "birds and the bees." The male and the female mate, but I don't really know how it works.

I would just love it if Kathleen had a baby. Jump higher, Kathleen! It might be a girl, and I could have fun playing with her.

She could be called Eleanor for the First Lady. Eleanor Elizabeth. Elizabeth for the brave Queen of England who goes out in London with her husband King George to check on families who have lost their houses to the bombs. And their daughter Princess Elizabeth who joined the women's military and fixes trucks for soldiers. I saw them on the newsreel at the Colony Theater.

Yikes! I am back to thinking about getting bombed, and now I really can't go to sleep.

1942 February 21
Doris
New York Cafe

Can't sleep. Evelyn is punching me. She says I keep moving over on her side. She is the one who hogs the bed and pulls all the covers off me. I pull them back, and she punches me again and pulls on the covers.

And I'm thinking of Kathleen and Slover on the other side of the wall enjoying their time as a married couple. This gets me thinking of Jimmie and how I feel when he kisses me and runs his hands in places that I tell him not to go but I want him to go.

Since the broken window incident with Horace, he has been a different person. He never pressures me. He doesn't know this, but I have refused all other dates since Kathleen and Slover got married. I'm in love with Jimmie and want him to ask me to marry him.

I never hear from him during the week as his air training has become more intense. But he called me this afternoon and asked if I would go to supper at the New York Café. We had a wonderful time at supper laughing about some dumb jokes:

He: Why didn't you answer my letter.
She: I didn't get it.
He: You didn't get it?
She: No, I didn't get it; and besides I didn't like some of the things you said in it.

And another:

Teacher: If you take a potato and divide it into two parts, then into four parts, and each of the four parts into two parts, what would you have?
Little Emily: Potato Salad

I liked the last one especially because I was not quick with math problems when I was in school. But working at Verne's has taught me a lot about practical math. Tallying up bills, making change quickly, creating charts to show profits versus expenses, and keeping an inventory of hangers, thread, cloth and paper bags that cover the clothes we alter.

After supper, we found ourselves at the waterworks but didn't get out of the car because it was bitterly cold. When Jimmie stopped the car, we were drawn together immediately as our arms went round each other and Jimmie pulled me close. He kissed me more gently than his usual urgent and hard manner.

Then, he pulled back, looked into my eyes. "Doris, I love you. Oh, your eyes and your deep brunette mass of curls! I want you so much."

I was dizzy with desire. "Oh, Jimmie, I do love you too!" Then, no more words. Just more passionate kissing from lips to cheek to neck. I felt his hands find new places to caress.

With Jimmie in my head, I drift off into dreams of sweet bliss.

1942 March 11
Kathleen
Answers in the Little Window

Walter and I have been married a little over a month, and it has been wonderful. He has been able to come home from base every night. I am doing more of the cooking, with Mama's help of course, and I am liking it more since I am doing it to please my new husband. He is so complimentary and eats like a horse. Tonight, I made Mock Apple Pie which is not apple pie at all because you use Ritz crackers in the place of the apples!

I love crawling into bed with Walter and being all warm next to him. Even though we have to sleep in the lean to, I am happy. But I will be happier when the roomers move out at the end of the month and we can have the front room. We are saving to buy us a bedroom suit, a maple colored one like I see in the magazines.

Today a got a letter from Marj. I had written her that we had married and put Mrs. Walter Slover over the return address. It felt strange to write that but also nice.

Dear Kathleen,

I was very glad to hear from you and when I saw the return address ...even before I opened the letter I knew you'd "gone and done it!" All through supper all I could say was "gosh," "imagine" and mother said, "Marjorie, will you quit sighing and repeating those words? It's getting monotonous."

Congratulations! Say, that was a marvelous picture of Walter. I am going to put it beside you in my photograph album.

Kathleen, thank you for the lovely St. Patrick's card. I was very delighted to receive it.

Last nite I went to a St. Patrick's supper at our church with my girlfriend and we had a swell time. The only trouble was, I had to come home early and write up my news for the Orangeville Banner and then go back again. We met about six other girls and finished the evening out with a bang. Write soon. Love, Marj

I have to admit the part about all the fun she had with her girlfriends made me a little jealous that I don't have time for anything like that now. A little dark voice whispered in a corner of my brain. *You're too young to be married! You are still a girl who needs to be carefree. Walter is so much older than you. You are just playing house.*

But reading over the wedding congratulations cards turns my mind in another direction. The verses are sweet:

To congratulate you and wish you all the luck and happiness in the world.
Just an old-fashioned wish on your Wedding,
That your mutual love will abide,
And that joy will be yours ever after,
Through the years that you spend side by side.

My favorite, from one of Walter's cousins, asks questions about what the future holds for us and has a little wheel that you turn to answer them. Will we ever be wealthy? Will the bride make good biscuits? (Ha Ha) Will the groom eat them? (He does, even though they aren't pretty.) Will we ever live abroad? (My dream. Paris, please.) How many times will we wish we were single? (Hmm. My imaginings go off in that direction with Marj's letters.) The answers come up in the little windows when you turn the wheel which I try to manipulate to get a good result.

If only life were that simple.

1942 March 23
Evo
Tomoko Sugano

I am worried. About Tomoko Sugano. I haven't seen her on the playground for two weeks. I asked her teacher where Tomoko was, and she said, "Yes, she has been absent a lot." I wonder why no one from the school has checked on her. I decide to find out.

So yesterday, Edna and I made a little detour on our way home by the Sugano house. The family lives upstairs in a little apartment over an old, empty store building. The store was dark as always. We went up the outside stairs that lead to the second story and knocked, but no one came. As we turned to leave, a truck pulled up, and some men got out. Edna and I watched.

The men must have had a key because they went right in. We waited. Finally, two men came out carrying a dresser, and two others had a chest. Another carried a beautiful blue and white vase kind of thing with mountains and trees on it. The family must be moving to a different house. Edna said we should go ask the movers where the Suganos are. We did, and one of the men answered, "Filthy Japs are going away. Good riddance!" Then, he went back into the building.

When I got home, Mama was in the swing reading the paper. I sat down next to her, and words tumbled out of my mouth as I told her what Edna and I had seen.

"Mama, where are the Suganos? Why did the man call them filthy? Tomoko always looks neat and clean in her pretty starched dresses."

"Evelyn. This will be hard for you to understand, but I just read in the paper that an internment camp is open in Manzanar, California, for Japanese living in America. They may have gone there. Japanese on the west coast are being moved to camps. I know that the Suganos have relatives out there, so maybe they went to be with them."

"You know, they were living in Fayetteville by accident. I first met Mrs. Sugano at Gibson's grocery. When they came to the United States before Tomoko was born, they wanted to see the whole country. So, they drove from California and did just that!

But when they got to North Carolina, they were in a car accident here in Fayetteville that destroyed their car, and they ended up in the hospital. They healed but had no money left after paying all the hospital bills. Mr. Sugano began to look for odd jobs like his gardening work. And they just stayed."

"What is an internment camp, Mama?"

"It is a place where people are sent who are considered dangerous."

"A prison? Tomoko and her family have not done anything wrong."

"Well, sort of like that but the news article said the interned families will have their own room or maybe a small house. Here, look at this picture."

The picture showed a long building sort of like the barracks I saw when we visited Slover at Fort Bragg. And a few smaller buildings that looked like houses. There were no trees or sidewalks or flowers or gardens. All around the camp, the land was flat and looked dry. It was awful and empty.

"Mama, if the Suganos are there, when will they get to come back home?"

"Hmm. I don't know, honey. Maybe not until the war is over."

"What about school for Tomoko? She will get so far behind everyone else by the time she gets home!"

"I don't know, sweetie. Maybe there will be school there."

"But, Mama, this isn't right! The Suganos are not like the mean Japanese who bombed Pearl Harbor and started the war."

"Some people think that Japanese living here will do things to hurt us since we are at war with the country they were born in."

"But Tomoko was born here. In Fayetteville. At Highsmith Hospital. Just like me. She is an American!"

I just don't understand. My friend and her family would never hurt anyone. They are so kind, and Mr. Sugano always bows and smiles when I see him on the street.

I tried to stop my tears, but I couldn't. Mama put her arm around my shoulders and pulled me close and smoothed my hair and just let me cry till I was done.

1942 March 24
Evo
Doodle Bugs

I can't stop wondering about Tomoko.

I thought about her all through school today. I got yelled at by teachers for not paying attention. Edna and I were talking about Tomoko at recess. Some boys overheard us. I had to fight hard not to cry when they said there were happy that the dirty Jap family was gone. I wanted to punch them, but instead I just said, "Tomoko is not dirty. She is an American citizen and a nice person."

"So what? She is still Japanese, and we need to kill every Jap after what they did to us at Pearl Harbor before they do something else," spouted Johnny Smithers.

After school, I just had to go by the Suganos' house in case they might be there. I did and saw Mr. Sugano coming doing the stairs with two suitcases. When he reached the ground, he put down the suitcases and bowed as usual.

"Oh, Mr. Sugano! I am so sorry y'all are moving away! I will miss Tomoko so much. I hope you will move back."

"Thank you, Miss Evelyn, but we will most likely stay in California with my brother's family. Thank you for being Tomoko's friend. She is in the back yard if you would like to see her."

Yes! I dash around to the back and see Tomoko's little body bent over a doodle bug hole. Just as I get to her, she pulls out a big one and stands up.

"Oh, Tomoko." I grab her in a big hug and her straw and big doodle bug go flying. "I don't want you to leave. I'll miss you so much."

"I'll miss you too and our doodle bug hunts."

"I hope there will be doodle bugs in California." I am thinking of that picture from the paper with dry land and thinking *probably not.*

"Yes. Me too." She kicks at the dirt with her foot. "I will try to write to you and maybe you can write me back."

Then her mother calls, "Come Tomoko, we need to get on the road." She turns and skips to the front yard. I don't follow.

I just stand feeling lonely and sad.

1942 March 28
Ethel
Hope Chest

Kathleen and Slover are settled into married life. The roomers moved out of the front room, and the newlyweds have moved in. They bought a bedroom suit. It is blonde with a big dresser and mirror and a chest of drawers. Kathleen has been saving up since the first of the year, and with Slover's contribution and a little money they got as wedding presents, they were able to pay cash. Market Furniture delivered it this morning.

Slover is on maneuvers at base. Kathleen is fussing around making their room look nice. Over the bed she hung the picture of my zinnias that Roger painted for her graduation. I'm making them some new drapes. All the children pitched in with a little cash, and they were able to buy a hope chest too.

Kathleen's hopes have already arrived in the form of Walter with no time to prepare. She has very little to put in the chest, but she is humming and smiling as she arranges what she does have. I made her pick out a sterling flat wear pattern, even though she protested that they could not afford this. I told her that people will give her wedding gifts and some of them will be silver, so she should not miss the opportunity to start her set and go to Henebry's and register.

She and Slover chose a pattern called Rambler Rose by Towle. It has a line of tiny roses in the center of each handle. They received two knives, a fork, and two spoons from Walter's family. The children and I pitched in and got them another fork ten dollars. (Mr. Henebry gave us a little discount.) Now they have two place settings.

She is carefully folding and placing some linens and towels in the chest along with a wedding ring pattern quilt my mama gave her. I remember watching Mama and her sisters work on it when I was still at home. In the intertwined rings, I recognize pieces of dresses we girls wore. Mama made them from flour sacks and then when we had outgrown the dresses, they became part of the quilt.

Watching my daughter so happy and just beginning to accumulate her household goods takes me to what I saw on the news reel when Doris invited me and Evelyn to see Walt Disney's *Bambi* last Saturday at the Colony. I needed to work on an order of alterations for Penny's, but Doris insisted that I should take a little break. The animated movie was beautiful and sweet, and I did enjoy it.

But I can't get the awful sight out of my head from the news reel of a poor old woman with a yellow star sewn on her coat being dragged out of her house and leaving behind all her belongings.

I wondered what things she might have left behind. Silver? Lovely handstitched tablecloths? Pictures of her children and grandchildren? Her mouth was set in a hopeless frown. She looked so defeated and sad that I just couldn't stand to look.

My Kathleen just beginning her life, and this wretched woman being forced from hers.

Evelyn was bothered by the scene too. On the walk home, she pulled my sleeve. "Mama. Why did the soldiers make that lady leave her house? Where is she going? Did she do something wrong?" I didn't have an answer, but I know where the wrong is and who is doing it.

Doris filled in the space opened by the child's questions. "They are just mean men, Evelyn. That is why we are having a war."

Yes, this is why our boys have to go. And stop this.

137

1942 April 1
Kathleen
The Train

Walter and I are on the train going to Indiana to see his family. Farther away from Fayetteville than I have ever been, and I am excited. But nervous about meeting his family. Will they like me? Will I know what to say? Will I feel like a stranger there?

As I watch the Blue Ridge mountains whizz by in the distance, Walter is telling me about the family. His mom Verna is a good cook and never takes her apron off because she is always either cooking food, washing the dishes, or laying things out for the next meal. She is forty-five, a little younger than my mama. His sister Euleta is nineteen and just beginning a job at the local newspaper. The youngest sister Maxine is fifteen and still in high school. I wonder what they think of having seventeen-year-old sister in law?

Walter tells me about his childhood. I already know the awful truth about his father's suicide which I have not even told my own family about. I certainly will not talk about it while I am in Shelburn. They probably don't know that I know. Walter says no one talks about it.

I ask him about his memories of his father Ernest, and the stories come rapid fire.

"After he and Mom were married in 1917, Dad was drafted into the Navy. He was on a freighter named the USS Fresno. He made one round trip across the ocean to the port city Le Havre, France, and was on a second trip when the Armistice was signed in November 11, 1918. I was born the next year.

"My family called me Daddy's boy. We went fishing and hunting together. Once when I was very small, Dad took me coon hunting, but I got tired and Dad carried me home sound asleep on his back. I don't remember that,

138

but Mom talks about it. As I grew older, Dad said that it was important to 'be a man' and try to do everything well. I idolized my Dad, and I tried hard to live up to his expectations."

I can see the effects of this teaching as Walter does strive for perfection. He is meticulous in his dress. He cleans up after my messiness in our room. Our first fight was over my leaving the bed unmade all day. His tone made me cry. But we kissed and made up, and now I try to be neater.

He expects excellence from the men in his platoon. He believes that going to war is doing his manly duty. As much as I fear his going to war, I am beginning to understand that it is important to him to do his part to set things right. Do I like it? No. But I have accepted that he must do what he believes he must.

He continues his family portrait. "Euleta is very smart. She can write well and got her job at the newspaper easily. She writes the obituaries and sometimes articles about happenings in and around Sullivan and Shelburn. Sullivan is a bigger town and the county seat.

"Euleta and I have always been very close, and she always followed me around and wanted to do whatever I was doing even if it was dangerous. Once some friends and I took a rowboat out on the Wabash River, and she wanted to go too. We boys were jumping off the boat and diving under it. The current was strong, but Euleta kept begging to try the diving. I gave in, and she dived off. We kept waiting for her to come up. But she didn't. I jumped in, saw she was tangled up in the undergirding of the boat, and got her out.

"She begged me not to tell Mama, and I didn't. Mama wanted Euleta to be more of a lady, but my sister had no interest in that. Dad, however, was proud of his 'try anything' daughter."

"What about Maxine?"

"Maxine is a more gentle and peaceful girl who sticks pretty close to Mom. She likes to cook and sew, two things Euleta has no interest in. Euleta and I were very protective of her. I was seven when she was born and Euleta, four. She was our baby. Euleta was sort of a second mama to her."

"Your family sounds wonderful. I can't wait to meet them."

But I have a big knot in my stomach and realize I am twisting the hair at the nape of my neck. *Bad habit, Kathleen. Stop. You are a grown up. Time to end your childish ways.*

1942 April 2
Kathleen
Shelburn

It's the final day of our railway trip. I am so tired. Night time in the little elevated berth was awful. I could hardly sleep with all the jolts and bumps. I kept waking up all night and hoping that day had come. And I missed sleeping with Walter. He, however, slept like a baby, saying the rhythm of the rails was soothing. Sleeping on barracks cots and on the ground during maneuvers has given him the ability to sleep anywhere.

We changed trains in Richmond from Atlantic Coastline to Chesapeake and Ohio line. Then, we passed through Washington, DC, a little of West Virginia, and Ohio. We are now in Indiana on the last lap to Shelburn.

I can't pull my eyes away from the window. All these places I have never seen before. I could see the top of the US Capitol in the distance in DC! Southern Indiana looks dry and flat except for a few hills when we crossed the Wabash River. I start singing "The Wabash Cannonball" that Roger and Buck play on their guitars. Walter laughs and hums along with me. I'm glad that he doesn't sing along because he has a terrible voice. He truly does. He sang a few times at home when we had folks around the piano. After he had left one time, Roger said, "Kathleen, I am sorry, but your sweetie can't carry a tune in a bucket. In fact, he can't even find the bucket!"

The singing helps me take my mind off my fears about meeting Walter's family.

From the great Atlantic Ocean to the wide Pacific shore
She climbs a flowery mountain o'er the hills and by the shore
She's mighty tall and handsome she's known quite

well by all
She's a regular combination on the Wabash
Cannonball
Listen to the jingle, the rumble and the roar
As she glides along the woodland o'er the hills and
by the shore
Hear the mighty rush of the engine hear those
lonesome hoboes call
Traveling through the jungle on the Wabash
Cannonball.

"Look, Kathleen! We are coming into Shelburn! There's my high school and the cemetery and Turner's store where I worked some."

The landscape of farms and fields slowly transforms into a row of sad looking stores. I see the rail depot as the train slows and slows. I grab my purse and pull out my compact and lipstick to freshen up. I am so nervous that I smear my lipstick up on my cheek and dig in my purse for a Kleenex. Walter pulls out his handkerchief and gently wipes away the smear. "You look fine, my love, beautiful as always." He plants a soft kiss on my cheek.

"There they are! Mom and my sisters!"

I see a tall woman in a black coat and two girls, blond Maxine and brunette Euleta. They are focused intently on the train windows but must not see us as we pass them even though Walter waves wildly. We come to a stop by the platform.

Walter gathers our suitcases, and off we go behind a group of soldiers and a woman with a baby. The second we step down off the train, Maxine and Euleta come running with their mother more slowly behind. Walter is hardly off the platform when Euleta throws her arms around him and does a little dance with him. Out of her grip, Walter pulls Maxine close and gives her a little pat on the head. He moves on to his mom who puts her hands on both sides of his face and gives him a long kiss on his cheek.

She turns immediately and envelops me in a big hug. "Oh, Kathleen. It is so very good to see you in person. You are even prettier than your picture. I am so happy that my Walter found you to share his life!" She hugs me again. My fears start to melt away in the warmth of her embrace.

Euleta and Maxine give me tentative hugs, and I find my voice to say, "So good to meet y'all at long last."

Maxine stares at me oddly. "Wow, Kathleen, you talk funny. How cute the way you stretched out 'goooooooood' and called us y'all."

I am embarrassed and blush and hate my accent. *They* sound funny to *me!*

Euleta champions me. "Maxine, people have different accents all over the world. I think she sounds charming."

Walter's mom takes my hand. "Let's get home. We have a big supper waiting for you two. Baked chicken and Walter's favorite chocolate pudding for dessert."

Chicken, hmm. I guess Walter never complained to her about all the chicken they had to eat. Of course, he would not say anything unkind to his mama.

1942 April 12
Kathleen
Church

It is Sunday morning, and I am sitting between Maxine and Euleta in the Shelburn Methodist Church. Walter is beside Euleta, and his mom is on his left. I can't much concentrate on what the minister is saying as my head is spinning from all the unexpected new experiences I have had since we got to town. We are leaving tomorrow.

I try harder to focus on the sermon, but my thoughts keep straying.

A big surprise when we first arrived was that the Slover home on South Buckley Street has no indoor plumbing. Just a well and pump outside the kitchen right next to Mom's bleedingheart bush, and an outhouse for a toilet! At night, you don't have to go outside to do your business. Instead there is a white enamel bucket with a lid that they call the chamber pot. The next morning someone takes it to the outhouse.

Much of Fayetteville has modern conveniences. I thought the North was supposed to be more advanced than the south. When I expressed my surprise to Walter in private, he said that some folks in Shelburn do have plumbing, but it is expensive. Nearby Terre Haute is a bigger city and is more modern.

Mom (that's what she asked me to call her) cooks all the time, and there are many bowls, plates, and dishes to wash after every meal. I help, of course, but it is hard and takes forever as we have to go out to the pump to get the wash water and then rinse water. Endless carrying out and dumping and pumping more water. And, just as Walter said, when the cleanup is done, Mom starts pulling out and preparing things for the next meal. She almost never sits. Which means I don't either because I feel I should stay in the kitchen with her. I also help her with the wash which is done in a big tub near the pump.

And then, last night just as they did last Saturday night, Mom and Walter dragged a big metal tub out of the pantry and started making trips with buckets to the pump to fill it. Community bath! Maxine went first and then me. I thought the water would be dumped and new put in for me. But no! I bathed in Maxine's water, then Euleta after me, Mom, and last Walter! It would take all night to change after each bather. But that water looked pretty nasty after Walter got out. The water was cold. In the winter, they warm it on the stove in batches.

I come back to the present as everyone stands to sing a hymn. Then, the congregation files to the altar for communion. At home we stay in our seats and just pass the bread on a plate, and then the grape juice in a tray of little cups. Here, you take a little piece of bread from a dish and dip it in a big cup of grape juice. At least, I think it is grape juice. Maybe it is wine since Methodist don't see anything wrong with drinking like Walter did at the Prince Charles. If it is wine, I don't see how that tiny dip could hurt.

Back in the pew, my thoughts meander again. There is a Holiness Church across from the house, and last night it was all lit up with cars pulling up and lots of noise. Loud voices praising God and singing and shouting halleluiah. Walter and I were sitting in the porch swing which faces the street. "What are they doing in there, Walter?"

"They are the holy rollers. People call them that because sometimes they get down and roll around on the floor if they get really filled with the Spirit. They meet on Wednesday and Saturday nights. It is always wild and goes on for hours."

I could see in the windows, and they were dancing! In church! Imagine that! Pastor Gaines at First Baptist would say they were going straight to hell.

Walter kept on about the holy rollers. "Me and my friends used to sneak up to the windows and watch. It was strange. The preacher would lay his hands on someone's head and pray and say, 'Be healed.' And the person would fall back, and people would catch him, and some folks would even pass out. Sometimes the person would say, 'I can see' or 'My pain is gone' or talk in gibberish. Dad caught us looking one time and whipped me good with his belt and told me never to spy on anyone ever again. He said that way of worshipping is different from ours, but that's ok. Leave them alone. It's none of your business."

I've heard lot of stories here about Walter's childhood. Mom said that she used to nurse him on her arm in the bed. When he had enough, he would always roll over on his Daddy's arm to go to sleep. He and his Dad were close from the start. I am realizing how very painful it must have been for Walter to lose his Dad in such an awful way.

When Mom and I were cooking breakfast yesterday, while Walter had gone for some early morning fishing, she started talking about Ernest's death. I guess she assumed that Walter had told me about the suicide. He received some disability from the Jackson Hill Coal Company after he was injured. But when he took his life, they did not want to pay anymore! The mine folks considered the suicide caused by his own free will, so they didn't feel they were obligated!

The family got a lawyer, who had doctors testify that he was out of his head because of his injuries. After an appeal, the family won and received a financial settlement. Mom decided to open a restaurant, so she could grow the money into more security. But this backfired because the restaurant failed. I knew about the restaurant because Walter told me about it, and that it failed because she was too generous to give free food to hungry people during the Depression.

Then she got a job as the janitress at the school, cleaning and getting coal to warm the classrooms. She still has that job. When Walter got older, he had odd jobs. Then, he joined the Army to help support the family. Life was hard for us after my daddy died, but not that hard.

Mom is a good woman who's had a tough life, but she has risen above it and is not in the least bitter. She's such a giver. Last week, in addition to cooking for the family, she made a meal for a neighbor who was recovering from surgery. She asked me to go with her to deliver it. Before we left, she went in her bedroom to select a pair of knitted slippers which she calls "house shoes" for the neighbor. She has boxes of them as she is always knitting if she has a free moment. She has given me three pairs for myself and one each for Mama, Doris, Evo, and Polly.

Communion is finished, and the choir sings a beautiful and slow version of "Nothing but the Blood of Jesus." I want to hum along but don't.

I look at Euleta's profile and see how much she looks like Walter. She has told me bunches about her growing up as his sidekick. He taught her how to wrestle and box, and she used these skills! When she was in first grade, there was a boy who was much larger than any of the other kids. He was always picking on the girls on the way home from school. He had a brother who was equally dumb and uncouth who would back him up. Mom had ordered Euleta to be a lady and never fight. One day she was telling Walter and Mom about the mean boys, and their father overheard it. Ernest told her to work the boy over the next time he picked on them and for Walter to take on his brother. That was what they did with the greatest of pleasure, and those two never bothered the little kids again!

My own Mama would probably have killed me if I did something like that. Mama always told us to use words to put off bullies. She called it "walking carefully and carrying a big stick" like President Teddy Roosevelt said.

Euleta, obviously so proud of her big brother, said he was always tops at playing marbles, shooting a slingshot, or BB gun and ice skating. Kettle Creek would freeze, and Walter would put her and Maxine on the sled and pull them as he skated along.

Walter was pretty mischievous as a child. Apparently, Halloween was pretty wild here, similar to the things Marj has told me about her town in Canada. Boys would do some serious "tricks" around town. Once Walter and his buddies decided to turn over an outhouse of a man who was always mean to the neighborhood children. They did, and when the structure hit the ground, there sat the man on the seat!

With that, my mind is jolts to the present as the minister announces the closing hymn.

1942 April 18
Evo
Hobos

I'm so happy that Slover and Kathleen are back from their trip to Indiana! They gave me a bracelet and candy and a pair of slippers made by Slover's mother.

Slover brought home the newspaper from Fort Bragg today. I like to read it because some of the articles are funny. I am lying on the sofa reading the latest about Slover's Company K:

> *Among the men in Co. K, I find the best dressed man to be Sgt. Bupp, the best athlete Sgt. Madison, the most handsome Sgt. Slover...*

"Walter, Kathleen! Come here quick!"

Kathleen jumps up from the piano where she was trying to play "The Chattanooga Choo Choo." "Whatever is the matter?"

Slover dashes in from the front porch.

I show them the paper. "Look, look! This says Slover is the most handsome man in Company K!"

Kathleen answers, "Well, of course, my husband is!" and gives him a kiss right on the mouth.

Slover laughs, "Wonder if I could get a pay raise for that? Come, Gasoline, and sit on the swing with me and enjoy this spring afternoon with the most handsome man!"

I read the rest of the article which is part jokes and part information about promotions:

> *Every time the first-class ratings are mentioned several men can be seen grabbing their razors or a shoe brush.*

Duty must be getting light again in the company for the last few days we have had several to return from the hospital.

Pvt. Mainous tried to knock down a fireplug with his knee Tuesday morning. Better luck next time!

Cpls. Bura and White have been appointed sergeants, and Pvts. Windham, Davidson, Barta, Darling and Jennings are now wearing two stripes.

Just as I finish the last sentence, Edna calls "Hey, Evo, Let's go to our fort. Meet me there in a few minutes"

I get Mama's permission and skip up the hill. Edna is waiting on the edge of the woods, and she has tears running down her face. "Our fort is gone!"

"What?"

And we stomp up through the woods to our spot. Yes, gone. No tarp, no door, no top, no quilt floor. Only the shells, nuts, wisteria seed pods and rocks scattered about.

"I know who did this, Evo. That Frankie Kelly and his pals. The nerve! Let's look around and see if we see our stuff!"

We climb higher and just before the crest of the hill, I see our tarp. A sort of a tent formed over some of the low growing bushes. Two feet in old broken-down shoes are sticking out from under the tarp. Big men's feet!

We high tail it down the hill, tripping a few times, as we glance back to see if the feet are following us. Safe on Edna's porch and out of breath. Mrs. Rogers sees us and asks why we were running. We tell her.

"You girls have no business in those woods. Hobos that get off the trains are always looking for places to live. Sometimes several of them will set up together, and they call that their 'jungle.' That is what you saw. The man would probably do you no harm, but you never know. Don't you dare go up there again!"

1942 May 9
Ethel
Rationing

So many things are changing as this war moves on. I'm trying to get used to the new "war time" that started in February. We had to set our clocks ahead one hour to save energy by not having to use lights as early. I keep getting mixed up as to what the time is. Yesterday, I cooked supper an hour early because it felt like supper time. The children had to eat a cold meal! *Ethel, remember to look at the clock!*

And now rationing! I walked to the high school this morning for our family's sugar rationing cards. Things will be harder to get. But providing food for our fighting men is more important, even if we citizens at home have to go without.

We are also asked to save and donate scrap metal to help build ships, planes, and war equipment. Evelyn has been roaming around the house asking for things for the drive they are having at school. I gave her some coat hangers and empty cans. She snooped around wanting some of my pots and pans, and she even asked Doris to give her the back bumper of her car because she read that some people have donated theirs! Doris replied, "Are you crazy, girl? Do you want me to get mashed if someone runs into me?"

I first heard of the sugar rationing on the radio. The Office of Price Administration said that this would be a fair system so that the very wealthy could not buy up all the sugar. Everyone, regardless of income, is limited as to what they can buy.

There was a long line waiting to get the ration cards. The lady in front of me was grumbling. "This is ridiculous! Those soldiers don't need sugar! They need more solid foods, like beans and meat! Not the luxury of sweet stuff." I wanted to bless her out for being so unpatriotic and tell her the fighting men need a little pampering with some good sweet things from time to time. But I just said, "Yes, this war will be hard on everyone."

Some of the teachers from the school were working with the distributions. I saw Miss Whitehead, Kathleen's French teacher from last year. She asked about Kathleen, and I told her she was married. "Oh, how, wonderful! I wish her all happiness. She was one of the best students I ever taught."

I had to give the number and ages of persons in our household. I had brought all of our birth certificates. But the girl at the desk just asked me to fill out a paper with the information. She didn't even look at the certificates. At the bottom, however, was a statement that said persons could be fined for giving untruthful information. It also said that having a ration card in no way guaranteed that the sugar would be available.

The OPA has already limited the buying of cars, tires, and gasoline. Also, prices have been frozen on almost everything, which to my way of thinking is a very good thing. Land of Goshen! I can imagine how those with plenty would just buy things up at any cost and create a shortage. As difficult as doing with less will be, it is a good plan. I am already used to doing that since Wesley died.

When I got home, I sat on the sofa to read all the particulars:

War Ration Book One - 1942
Your first ration book has been issued to you, originally containing 28 war ration stamps. Other books may be issued at later dates. The following instructions apply to your first book and will apply to any later books, unless otherwise ordered by the Office of Price administration. In order to obtain a later book, the first book must be turned in. You

should preserve War Rations Books with the greatest possible care.

When you buy any rationed product, the proper stamp must be detached in the presence of the storekeeper, his employee, or the person making the delivery on his behalf. If a stamp is torn out of the War Ration Book in any other way than above indicated, it becomes void. If a stamp is partly torn or mutilated and more than one half of it remains in the book, it is valid. Otherwise it becomes void.

If your ration book is lost, you report it to the local Ration Board. If you go into the hospital for more than ten days, you must turn in your ration book. I guess that is because the hospital will feed you. If a person dies, the book must be returned. Hmm...I wonder how they will control all of this. There will be some dishonest folks trying to abuse this. I am going to guard our books with my life!

I'll get Roger and Gene to help me plow up some space for a bigger garden this year. Mrs. Roosevelt is planting a Victory Garden like folks did in the Great War. For some cotton pickin' reason, the Department of Agriculture disapproved of her doing that! She did it anyway and encourages everyone who can to do the same. She is so intelligent and kind. I like her husband, but she could do the job of president.

I wonder if we will ever have a woman president? Probably not. Men would not like it. And how would a woman do the president's work and still do the cooking and cleaning?

1942 May 23
Doris
German Subs

Jimmie, Slover, Kathleen, and I went to the Colony tonight. The newsreel reported that some Royal Navy sailors patrolling our east coast were torpedoed by a German U Boat. Thirty-seven men died, and bodies washed up on Ocracoke Island. Just off North Carolina's coast! Scenes of the island's beach with men looking for bodies. How horrible! I leaned over to Jimmie and said, "Gosh! This is scary. German subs so close to us "

Jimmie whispered, "That's exactly why we are in this war, Doris. To stop that. Those British sailors died trying to protect us, and we need to get over to Europe and help them fight." I don't want Jimmie to go over there, but that is what he is training for. He has asked me to marry him, but I haven't given him an answer. I want to know what his future holds before I decide.

The second clip was about another camp for Japs in California, Tule Lake. A detention center and work camp. Good! Round up the Japs and put them to work far away from us. So we don't have to fear them doing anything to us. We should be looking for Germans in America and doing the same thing with them!

Other footage showed the German General Rommel, the "desert fox," riding high and looking smug on one of his tanks in North Africa. Those Germans are trying to take over the whole world. So many places to fight them.

Finally, the movie *My Gal Sal* started. It was a musical, a relief after that depressing newsreel. Gorgeous Rita Hayworth and handsome Victor Mature. A chance to escape the reality of life for a while. For two hours my mind filled up with the color and liveliness of the show. And with my handsome beau, his arm around me and his hand holding mine.

1942 June 10
Doris
Duck on a June Bug

So many things about life are changing at an alarming rate. Boys are being drafted or signing up every day. Danny Jennings from down the street received his draft notice and is going to be a marine. He has gone for training at Camp Lejeune on the North Carolina coast, not too far from Carolina Beach, our vacation spot.

From what I hear about boot camp, poor Danny won't be on any vacation as the training is just awful. He is such a kind and sweet young man. Jimmie and Slover told us about how the drill sergeant yells at new recruits in training to make them tough. Poor Danny. I hope he can take it.

Slover and Jimmie will be going overseas soon. I am worried about Buck and Roger being drafted. I cannot imagine those two gentle souls having to fight and kill Japs or Germans. I know Mama is also worried about this.

I still have not given Jimmy an answer. I keep stalling. I have stopped going out with any other men. Jimmie is very happy about this. He is becoming more intense with his romantic gestures. The minute we are alone, he is on me "like a duck on a June bug." Rhett Butler in *Gone with the Wind* used that expression when Scarlett was asking him for money to pay taxes on her plantation Tara. He said that all his funds were in Liverpool and if he tried to access them, that the Yankees would be on him "like a duck on a June bug." To Jimmie, I am a June bug for his duck!

The Japs constantly brag about themselves. That awful Tokyo Rose said on Japanese Radio that with the recent victories in the Pacific, the Japanese people can look forward to marching into London and New York City! I would like to jerk that woman baldheaded!

War on two fronts, Europe and the Pacific. More and more boys going. I got a card from Horace Purvis. He wanted to know if my brothers are playing his banjo and said he would be going to the Pacific soon.

And rationing. I know this is necessary, but things are tough because of it. We already have limited sugar which means very few of Mama's cakes on our table. Gasoline may be next, and I may have to find a job closer to home so I can walk if I can't get gas.

Now we have air raid drills which are pretty scary. There are civil defense volunteers and block wardens, who check on you to be sure you use the blackout curtains and comply during the drills. Evo is grabbing every bit of scrap metal she can find. I missed my bobby pins when I went to do my hair yesterday. There were only four left on the dresser. That child admitted that she had gathered them up and taken them to school, along with some coat hangers, and empty cans Mama had given her! She said I had too many bobby pins and I should be happy to sacrifice for the scrap metal drive to help build planes to protect us and our boys in uniform.

Patriotism is one thing but taking little bobby pins is going too far! That child!

1942 June 22
Ethel
Wesley

I'm a worrier. Especially about my children. I guess it got worse after we lost Adele, my sweet but flawed first child. Now, I worry mostly about my boys and when and if they will have to go to war. So far, no draft notices.

I wish my Wesley was still alive. He could always calm my worrying. He used to say to pray and let God do the worrying. He loved the verses from the book of Matthew about how worrying cannot add a single hour to your life. Even when he got leukemia, he was always hopeful.

This morning I got out my keepsake box and read some letters he wrote me. Once when he was on a long trip to deliver some meat for Swift Company up north, he sent this card:

> *Hello Sweet,*
> *Hope you are all feeling fine this morning. I am feeling pretty good. This sure is pretty country up here. Nothing but mountains. Seems like I get along mighty slow, but after I get out of this mountain country, I can make some time. I have already come about 500 miles of the way. I will get back just as soon as I can. Try not to worry about me. Be good till I see you and tell all hello. Wesley*

A letter from Sanford dated July 1939 when he was staying with his brother while he took treatment from Dr. Howard:

> *Dearest Ethel,*
> *How are all today? Fine, I hope. I am feeling pretty good. All but my old back. It is hurting some. They*

haven't put in Charlie's phone yet. I will call you
when they do. I don't have to take no shot today, so
I am just laying around and resting. Sister said to
tell you all hello.
I don't know yet when I will come home. Dr.
Howard said I could buy the medicine and get
someone down there to put it in my arm. So, I will
let you know when I will be home.
Don't forget to have the light bill paid.
Well, sweetheart, take care of yourself until I see
you. Tell all hello for me.
Love, Wesley

Wesley did come home in early August. Doris gave him the shots. She was the only one of us brave enough to do it.

It got hard for him to chew food, so I ground up liver to build his blood back up. He just got weaker and paler and finally could not get out of bed.

But he kept on being cheerful, telling jokes, and talking to the children about their days at school or work.

Every night when we went to bed, he said, "Tomorrow the sun will come up again, and it might be a better day." But there were no better days, only worse ones. Then on the night of August twenty-fifth, I awoke suddenly with a feeling that something was wrong. He was gone. And right next to me in our bed. Just like that. No more suffering, but our hearts were broken.

I will never get over the loss of him. He is always at the back of my mind. I see his smile in the girls' faces and his gentle ways in Buck, Roger, and Gene. But how I wish he was still with me to give me strength in these terrifying times.

1942 July 4
Doris
Fireworks

A bunch of us are going to White Lake to celebrate the holiday. Jimmie and me, Slover and Kathleen, Buck and Polly, Roger and his current girlfriend Irene, Gene, and Evelyn. Mama tried to beg off since it is a very hot day, and she had alterations to catch up on. But we badgered her until she relented. She's looked down lately, and we want her to have some fun. We all pile into Jimmie and Buck's cars and leave about four o'clock to swim, have a supper picnic, and watch fireworks.

Roger, tall and handsome and quick witted, is a magnet for girls. Kathleen says he is like I used to be before Jimmie, changing beaus often. Roger is a flirt which I certainly was not! Anyway, I hope this Irene doesn't last long. She has the most irritating habit of smacking her ever present mouthful of gum. She hangs all over Roger, and Mama is always cutting her eyes at this.

It's so hot that we practically jump out of the cars and head for the water, stripping off our outer clothes as we go. Mama, who doesn't go near the water, spreads our quilt and picks up our clothes and arranges them in neat piles.

Jimmie doesn't try to make me go far out in the water, thank goodness.

We are all splashing and jumping around, when Mama yells, "Where is Evelyn?" Everyone looks around. No Evelyn.

Polly shouts, "I saw her around the end of the pier." The men rush out and start diving to look under the pier. Slover goes under by one of the pilings, emerges with Evelyn in his arms.

"It's Ok. She's fine. She got tangled in the mooring ropes." He gently sets her up on the pier. When she stops sputtering water, she bursts into embarrassed tears. Mama comes running out on the pier and gathers Evelyn into her arms and escorts her to shore.

Mama has the food laid out, so we dig in. Evelyn doesn't eat anything. Slover puts his arm around her and tells her a story about how one of his sisters got pinned under a boat once. "Euleta is pretty adventurous like you. Both of you are brave girls. Don't worry about it. You will just be more careful in the future with your adventures." Evelyn smiles and grabs a sandwich.

When it begins to get dark, we go to the amusement park which is the best place to see the fireworks. When the show starts, Jimmie takes my hand and walks me away from the crowd to a fallen cypress tree on the water's edge.

The colors begin to shower the night sky, and booms and pops explode. Jimmie puts his arms around me and pulls me close. He whispers in my ear, "I love you, Doris. You are the woman of my dreams. I want you to be my wife. I am asking you to marry me. We will be more spectacular together than these fireworks."

I laugh. "I hope that doesn't mean we would be fighting all the time!"

"No, it means we will live a full and exciting life. I want to buy you nice things to compliment your good looks and take you to amazing places, like Europe. When the war is over, of course. And I want to settle down in a nice home and make beautiful babies with you."

Overcome by this offer, I answer, "Yes, yes, Jimmie Rice, I will marry you!" He jumps up and lets out a whoop that no one hears because of the crackling and booming.

As the fireworks end and we all head for the cars, Jimmie holds up his hand and says, "I have an announcement. Miss Doris Dean Brantley has just agreed to be my wife, and I am the happiest man in the universe." Hugs, slaps on backs, and tears ensue.

Only Mama, who has been cool to Jimmie since the car window fiasco with Horace Purvis, refrains from the congratulations. Then, she puts her hand on Jimmie's shoulder and says, "You be good to my girl." Jimmie replies that he will treat me like a queen and protect and love me always. Mama nods and lets a little smile slip out.

After we get home, Jimmie stays, and we sit in the swing. "I have something I need to tell you, Doris. In the fall, I will be going to Ft. Jackson near Columbia, South Carolina, to attend the Army Air Corps training school. We can get married before I go and find a nice apartment."

A bit taken aback, "Then I suppose you will be an instructor in the school and train new pilots."

"No, my love, I will be training to go overseas and be part of a flight crew, probably early next year, not sure where."

I suck in my fears and bravely offer, "We will have time together before that happens. And the war will probably be over by the end of 1943. You will come home, and we will begin the plans we have made for our spectacular life."

The future is so uncertain, but I am going to cling to what I just said to Jimmie, my husband to be, my man going off to war.

1942 July 30
Evo
Yankee Doodle Dandy

Today, the President said that women can be in the service! Women can be in the Navy and will be called WAVES. I guess that is because the ocean has waves. They will work in the US, so more men can go to sea. You have to be twenty years old. Dang! I told Kathleen about it and how much I wish I could join the WAVES.

"Evo, you're already doing things here to help. You have an eye for finding and collecting scrap metal. I was amazed at the huge wagon load you and Edna collected. And...you make us adults laugh with your happy ways so we don't focus on bad war news. We are all contributing, even if it's on the home front."

I just love Kathleen. She listens to me when some of the rest of my family don't. When Slover can't come home from Fort Bragg, she lets me sleep with her. She says it helps her not to miss him so much. I love sleeping in their new bed. It is so soft, and I just drift off to sleep easily.

I wish she would have a little baby. I know it takes nine months, and she and Slover have been married for only five. Maybe by November. But maybe not because Kathleen's stomach looks as skinny as ever.

Another nice thing that Kathleen did was to take me to the movies to see *Yankee Doodle Dandy* with James Cagney. I was mad for it. There was so much singing and dancing. She took me to the Carolina Soda Shoppe afterwards for a chocolate milkshake. Kathleen reminded me not to slurp loudly when I got to the bottom of the glass. She said, "Do you know what a straw is for?" I said to drink.

"No, Evo. It is to tell a fool that he is at the bottom! But you, of course, are no fool because you know not to do that."

162

1942 August 8
Doris
German Spies

The radio plays all day at Verne's since the war started. The morning news drones on while I am putting tickets on a large order of alterations dropped off earlier by a colonel's wife. She has painted on eyebrows that look like commas. I hate it when she comes in as she treats me like a fool, repeating every detail of how she wants the seams let out of a dress or skirt. She is always dissatisfied with the fit, and those commas squint in and get closer together when she storms in to tell me that that she wants something done over.

The problem is that she keeps getting fatter. I imagine her sitting on her large bottom around a bridge table while she and her girlfriends snack on fancy food prepared by her maid. She has the look of someone who has never done a lick of work in her life.

Verne's business is getting better and better. Since the war started, it is harder for folks to find new clothes. We are asked to make do with what we have so all manufacturing energy can go toward the war effort. Less buying new and more altering the old. Verne has hired several new seamstresses, but I am still the only front desk clerk and stay busy most of the time. Some days there is a line waiting outside when I arrive.

I listen closer to the radio when the newscaster raises his voice and gives a headline: *Dateline Washington DC. Six Nazi Saboteurs Executed in Electric Chair. Two who cooperated spared.*

Good riddance! I remember when they were captured. That news terrified me to think Germans could be everywhere spying on us and plotting to kill us. I have often wondered about Mr. Schmidt who works at Huske Hardware with Roger. Schmidt is a German name. Roger believes him to be a loyal American who was born here and has worked at the store for twenty years. But who knows whether he has turned Nazi to support the country of his heritage? I won't go in there anymore. I wish Roger didn't work with him. He might be finding out all kinds of information to use against us!

The problem is that Germans look just like regular Americans. Not like the Japanese who have squinty eyes and yellow skin. You can spot them immediately. I'm glad that the government is rounding up the Japs and moving them to internment camps.

Evelyn was upset when that Japanese girl stopped coming to school, and she learned that her whole family might be living in one of those camps. I tried to explain to her that the camps are set up to protect us, but she kept blubbering that the girl's family is loyal to America.

That child is too young to understand that people may not be what they seem. With a war on, we can't be too careful. I don't want to see any Japs around me.

Jimmie told me not to worry about German spies being here, and that all countries station spies in their enemies' lands. The US and England certainly have their share in Germany and France. It is just a fact of war, he says. That made me feel a little less suspicious, but, still, I will keep my eyes and ears open.

1942 August 11
Kathleen
Octofoil

Walter came home today with a strange look on his face. No smile even when we sit down to supper of fried chicken (which I finally managed not to burn, thanks to Mama's overseeing the process.)

After we finish our dessert of chocolate pudding, my husband speaks to all of us as he reaches over and takes my hand. "The Ninth Infantry Division will be leaving Fort Bragg in mid-September."

A gasp escapes my mouth. "We are definitely going to war, but we don't know where. Most likely to England, Scotland, or Ireland for further training." I relax a little as those are places where there is no fighting, except for the continued bombing of England.

Roger offers, "Maybe to North Africa where the Germans are pretty well entrenched or Italy?"

"I don't know, Roger, but that's a good guess. You know the Ninth Division was started during the last war but never saw combat." He points to the patch on the shoulder of his uniform. "I don't think I ever told you all the meaning of the octofoil insignia that we wear. It resembles the design given to the ninth son of a family in medieval times."

Evo, pointing to Walter's shoulder and counting, "Then why are there only eight leaves on it?"

"Good question. The circle in the middle for the first son, and the eight leaves around it represents more brothers. And the red, white, and blue colors for the USA, of course. The division men are like brothers as we will stick together whatever comes."

"Aren't you scared, Slover? I am scared for you." The child says aloud what I am thinking.

"Not so much, Evo. We have to help Europe. If the Germans lick them, they may turn to the United States as their next conquest. We can't let that happen. My men are well trained, and I trust that we will be protected by our skill and brotherhood. And, I will have my beautiful wife and this great family praying for me and waiting for my return. And I will come home."

Tears are pushing hard against my lids.

Reaching for the hands of Gene and Evo, on either side of her, Mama says, "I think a prayer is in order." We all join hands.

"Dear Heavenly Father, we ask that you protect Walter and all the men going to fight. Give them courage and strength to do the task that has been given to them. Also, grant us here peace and patience. Bring our men safely home. In Jesus' name, Amen."

After supper, Walter and I sit on the porch in the swing. Now the tears have broken through and are running down my cheeks. Walter pulls out his handkerchief and wipes them.

"Don't cry, my Gasoline. I will go do what I have to and will be home before you know it. When us Americans get in the fight, those Krauts will turn tail and run."

Trying to divert my attention, Walter picks up the newspaper. "Look at this, Kathleen! That traitor rascal Pierre Lavel, prime minister of the German sympathizing Vichy government, has publicly declared that 'the hour of the liberation of France is the hour when Germany wins the war.' What an idiot to think that France would be free if Germany won! We have to stop them."

My mind understands, but my heart is broken into slivers of fear and dread.

Evo slips out the screen door and squeezes in between Walter and me. She rests her head on his arm and takes my hand.

Three hopeful but hurting souls swinging gently in the spring twilight.

1942 September 6
Evo
Children Should Be Seen and Not Heard

It's Sunday afternoon, and we're speeding down the highway in Doris' old Nash toward Sanford where my grandparents live. The car is hot, and the windows are rolled all the way down. My hair blows around my face and into my eyes. But I don't care because it feels free. Doris and Kathleen have scarves around their heads because they want their hair to look good. And Mama's hair does not blow because it is gathered into the tight bun on her neck, as always.

I'm still in my church clothes which I hate: fancy pink and white dress and lace-topped socks and black patent leather shoes with straps. The dress is itchy, and the shoes are too tight because I am outgrowing them. No matter how much I complain, Doris says just to put up with it until we can afford a new pair. I'm going to be eleven this Wednesday, and I am sick of being dressed like a baby.

The trip to Sanford lasts only an hour, but it seems endless. Kathleen distracts me with a game of "cow poker" which involves us each choosing a side of the road and counting the cows we see. The winner is the one who "herds" the most cows. It's a dumb game; another proof that my family thinks I am a baby.

We turn off the main road and follow the dirt path past now bare tobacco fields, the vegetable garden, and the plum trees that line the way on both sides. I am happy that we aren't going there to help with the tobacco harvesting, vegetable picking, and canning that we often do in the summer.

As we near the house, two flop-eared dogs, rising from their afternoon naps under the house, bark out greetings that scare me. But as we get out of the car, their tails beat a slow, welcoming rhythm. One wags over, sniffs my starched Sunday dress, and plants a big, sloppy lick on my leg. Grandma Coggins hurries off the porch and shoos the dogs away as she puts her arm around my waist and ushers me up to the porch.

"Lord, honey, you sure have grown." She says this every time we visit even though our visits are frequent.

My bearded and bespectacled Grandpa Coggins, sitting and rocking on the porch, waves.

" Y'all hungry? Wouldn't you like a bite to eat?" invites Grandma.

Leading us to the sunny kitchen, Grandma displays her "bite" of lunch. A feast is spread before us on a huge table covered with starched, white cloths to shelter the feast from flies. Grandma hands us plates and pulls back the cloths to display her country food. Golden fried chicken, pot roast swimming in brown gravy, thin slices of salty country ham, golden creamed corn, stringed beans with ham hock seasoning, field peas with snaps, butter beans (my favorite), mashed potatoes, fluffy rice, homemade sugary pickles, perfect round hand-patted-with-love-biscuits, hunks of cornbread, and hand-churned butter. And the desserts: the whitest of coconut cakes, buttery pound cake, and a perfect pecan pie.

We take our plates into the dining room where assorted relatives are eating and gabbing. Grandma brings huge glasses of sweet, sweet iced tea for Mama and my sisters. For me, a tall glass of milk. I don't like the taste since it is fresh from the cow, not pasteurized like my "city" milk.

We eat. And eat. And eat. When everyone has cleaned their plates, Grandma keeps pushing us to have more. Inevitably, she will say, "Y'all sure didn't eat much."

The group moves to the front room for talk. This part is boring, boring, boring because I have to sit and listen and try to behave myself because, as Momma and Doris, always say, "Children should be seen and not heard."

I itch to go outside and play where fun awaits: chickens running loose in the yard to be chased, trees to climb, purple flowers to gather from the chinaberry tree, good dirt to draw a hopscotch grid, a big supply of rocks to skip across the pond or sort into piles of similar colors. But Grandma, like Mama, says playing would be a sin on this Lord's Day which is for church and visiting. So I have to sit and try not to fidget.

The adult talk fades into a drone. The heat makes me drowsy, and my eyes begin to droop. Gradually, my head leans onto Mama's shoulder, and I drift off...

I awake, and afternoon shadows are slanting lower. Folks are gathering themselves into cars for the trip home.

Grandma Coggins follows us to the cars and blesses us with, "Come back real soon. Drive careful, now, you hear."

The dogs circle her, wagging tails but not barking for our departure.

Grandpa waves from his rocker on the porch where he has spent the entire afternoon dozing and snoring. His big gray mustache makes him look like he has no mouth.

1942 September 9
Doris
Bombers

More Japanese "infamy." During dinner, the radio reports a massive forest fire was started today in Oregon by two bombs dropped by a Japanese plane.

"What?" I exclaim louder than I should. "I thought that Japan was too far away to fly a plane here!"

Roger said I didn't listen carefully. A float plane was launched from a submarine and was apparently retaliation for the Doolittle Raiders bombing Tokyo. The nerve of those Japs! My mind goes to an image of the same thing happening on the our coast! Maybe to Fort Bragg and Fayetteville! Big fires burning. People dying. I am horrified!

Jimmie puts down his fork from his second piece of pie. "See, Sweetie, this is why we must get to Europe and Japan. To protect our own homeland. You, your family, and all others in our country. I can't wait to finish training and go!" I give Jimmie a hard look, but I know he is right. He is going to South Carolina in October to get more training, and he wants me to marry him right away.

I blurt out, "Ok, Jimmie. Let's go to Dillon this weekend and get married." His mouth falls open. Everyone else just looks at me in shock.

Mama is the first one to speak, "Well, I guess my second daughter will have a hurry up wedding. Evelyn, promise me when you marry, there will at least be time me to make you a dress!" Laughter breaks the silence. Jimmie stands, reaches for my hand, and gives me a long kiss in front of everyone.

Roger says, "I am acquiring brothers-in-law at an alarming rate. First Slover, and now you, Jimmie." More laughter. Jimmie gives Roger a big pat on the back and then a hug. "Yes, Roger. You are fortunate once again."

171

1942 September 12
Ethel
Wedding Dress

Doris and Jimmie did not marry today as they had planned. Jimmie is scheduled to leave on Monday for Columbia, South Carolina and must stay at Bragg to get packed and loaded for the transfer. He will look for a place for them to live, and then they will marry.

So, I am starting on a wedding dress TODAY! It will be a simple one with a bit of lace. Mid-calf frock without a train. Doris wanted it to be short, so she can wear it later for church. I am going to work day and night to finish. I don't want her marrying in a ready-made suit like Kathleen did.

Slover came home with the news last night that his unit will move out on the seventeenth. After Monday, he will not be able to leave base again before his departure on Thursday. Kathleen can go to base the day before to say her goodbyes. There were tears and some hair twisting.

We are having a goodbye party for Slover tonight. All the children will be here, plus Buck's Polly and Roger's awful girlfriend Irene. I will be glad when he finds someone else. What he sees in her, I don't know. Doris said that it is probably her very large breasts! Land o'Goshen!

Kathleen has bought Walter a little locket with her picture, and Gene prepared a little booklet of pictures of our family and his Indiana family. I am giving him a very small New Testament that he can fit in his pocket. Evo plans to give him her rabbit's foot.

Kathleen, Doris, Evelyn and I are cooking a big meal with meatloaf, mashed potatoes, fresh green beans from my last batch from the Victory garden, biscuits (Kathleen is about to master them), gravy, and finally a chocolate cake that depleted the last of our sugar ration for the month.

172

Roger has been talking about enlisting! He thinks he will surely be drafted. He went to the recruiting office and learned that he will have a better chance of not serving in combat if he enlists.

My Roger is such a gentle young man that it is hard to imagine him with a gun in his hand. Perhaps he will get an assignment as a support soldier like a medic or a supplier of ordnance. I don't want him to go but feel a little better if he has choices. Buck is hoping that his having to support a wife and mother will keep him out of service. He plans just to wait and see what happens.

All this uncertainly about my boys' lives is maddening. The Jennings' boy Danny was drafted this summer and is now somewhere in the Pacific. We hear how the Japs brutally murder and do cruel things to captured soldiers. The Jennings are sick with worry.

Our lives are spinning, surrounded by dread and insecurity. I pray this awful war will end quickly.

1942 September 16
Evo
What's Up, Doc?

Miss Jones is putting long division problems on the board. She turns, she sees me staring out the window, and yells, "Evelyn Lou Brantley! You need to be writing these down!" I pick up my pencil but don't finish with the others. I get reprimanded once again.

I'm thinking about Slover going to war. And Danny Jennings, who is already there. I gave Slover my rabbit's foot for good luck. Doris said I should have given him a cross because the rabbit's foot is a superstition, not a truth like the Bible. I didn't have a cross. A rabbit's foot can't hurt.

Billie Wilson told me about going to the train station to see her brother Harry off. She thinks she will never see him again. I wanted to make her feel better but couldn't think of a thing to say because she might be right. I wonder if Harry has a rabbit's foot or cross.

When I get home, Roger is in the backyard with that pest Frankie Kelly and painting his bike. It's old, and he won't be getting a new one due to all the metal being used for the war. Frankie is watching closely.

I lean in too and am surprised at the most amazing thing! It's Bugs Bunny saying, "What's up Doc?"

"Thanks so much, Rog. The other kids will be jealous of my swell bike. Isn't it just the cat's pajamas? Hey, Evo, what do you think?"

"Yes, Frankie, it's swell."

"Would you like to ride it, Evo?" What? He's being nice to me? I don't have a bike.

"Yes, thanks, I believe would."

What a kind thing for Roger to do, making Frankie's old bike look new and colorful. I love Roger so much. I hope he never has to go to war.

1942 September 18
Kathleen
Victory Rolls

Walter is gone. A huge piece of me has been ripped away, and my mind is so cloudy that I can hardly focus at work. Tears keep dripping down my face and splattering on the letter I am typing up. I have to start over three times. I hoped that I could throw myself into work and not think of Walter so much. But, the more I try not to think of him, the more I think of him.

I feel him getting farther and farther away from me. Ft. Dix, New Jersey, to Staten Island, New York, and to the port of embarkation. I have no idea where he will land after that because the routes overseas are kept secret to prevent the Germans blowing up the ships. But I imagine he might go to Nova Scotia and then Ireland. Friends who have had their men go over got letters when they safely arrived and that seemed to be the usual route. I try to picture Walter in beautiful, green Ireland.

I visited him on Wednesday at base. He took a picture of me standing outside his barracks and said he wanted it to remember how beautiful I am. I was wearing the suit jacket I got married in because he likes me in it. He had to stop about three times and tell me not to cry in the picture. "Hey, Gasoline. I don't want to show you off to my men with ruined mascara. Smile, one last time for me so I can see that smile every day. Get Gene to develop this and send it to me."

"I will, honey. I will write you every day and send you pictures."

"That's good. I will write you every day, too, when I can. But don't get worried as I hear that sometimes it takes a long time for letters to get back home."

Private Wong came out of the barracks. "Hey, Gasoline! You look so pretty. I love your new hair style with those roll things around your face. You could be a movie star. Sergeant, your wife might get discovered, become a star like Betty Grable, and be famous when you get back."

"Private Wong, this style is called 'victory rolls.' Another way to support our boys."

"Gasoline, if I had someone like you waiting for me at home, I would whip all those Germans fast and get back to her. Sergeant Slover is a lucky, lucky man!"

No one was present to see Private Wong off. I felt sorry for him. What a nice man! Walter introduced me to some of his other men. Corporal Vincent Ammirato who was so cute with dark hair and flashing dark eyes. He looked far too young to be going to war.

There were couples and parents and siblings and sons around the barracks saying their goodbyes. The afternoon sun started to dim, and everyone was suddenly aware that it was almost time for the partings.

Walter and I embraced and just stood that way for several minutes. I wanted to pull warmth out of his body and absorb it into mine to keep. Suddenly, it was five o'clock, and we had to leave.

And then yesterday. Doris took me to the train depot to see him off. Standing under the shelter, I looked up at Walter's handsome face.

He smiled. "It will be alright, honey. I am prepared for this and will have the best men supporting me and me supporting them back. I will come back to you, and we will have a wonderful future together, and all this war will become a distant memory. We will have babies like we talked about. Girls named Cheryl Dean and Sherry Susan and boys Junior, named for me, and Ernest Wesley named for our fathers. Just keep those thoughts."

"Walter, promise me you won't do anything stupid or dangerous. Keep yourself under cover. Get plenty of rest." I didn't know what else to say. My mouth went dry. I willed myself not to cry.

My husband bent down for a kiss, and we held it for a very long time, and he hugged me tight and rubbed my back. He shouldered his duffle bag and climbed on the train.

I could see him in a window seat, and he pushed up the window and threw me a ball of paper. The train began moving, and I waved. He raised his hand in a salute and blew me a kiss.

I managed a big smile, saluted back, and blew a kiss his way.

The view of him faded with the acceleration of the train until I could not see him at all.

I turned and started to walk to the car where Doris was waiting. I didn't look back. I knew if I did, I would make a scene.

This was the most difficult moment of my entire life, but I managed to keep walking and holding back tears.

Finally, when I reached to open the car door, I turned slightly for one last view of the departing train that was ruining my life.

Doris looked at me and said, "Good job, Kathleen. I am proud of you. You gave your man a beautiful image to take with him."

I opened the wadded paper.

My darling wife, Remember I love you more than anything else in the world. I will be back before you know it.

1942 September 28
Kathleen
War Bonds

Walter has been gone for ten days.

I've written him every day as promised but have gotten no letters in return. I tell myself all is well and that the letters may take a long time to get here like Walter said. Still, I am dying to hear from him. I'm just going through the motions of my life. Work, home, sleeping and doing it all over again. This routine is broken on the weekends, and those are my worst times.

It's Monday, and we have a new bookkeeper at the bank. Barbara Emerson from Atlanta who decided to stay in Fayetteville after her husband left for service last month. She has thick blond curls and long eyelashes which she bats as she talks, particularly when she is talking to one of the male tellers. A bit flirty considering she is married and has a husband overseas. She lives in a little apartment above a home on McGilvary Street.

She asked me to go to the Carolina Soda Shoppe for lunch. She talked nonstop while we were eating, waving her long perfectly manicured nails. I like her because she is fun. And do I ever need a bit of fun in my life! Since we both walk to work, we decided we would come together. She will stop by my house on her way.

"Hey, you, Frenchwoman!"

I turn from the filing cabinet to see Tommy Bruce standing at the last teller's desk. "Look at you, all professional as a secretary! I figured you had gone off to France by now!" He laughs.

"No, Tommy, of course not. There is a war going on over there, in case you don't know it." He is probably as stupid as he was in high school and doesn't even know that France is occupied by the Germans.

178

"Just trying to make a joke, Kathleen. How would you like to go to a movie with me tonight?"

"No, thanks, Tommy. I am married now, and my husband just left for the war."

"Oh, sorry to hear that. I was lucky. I got my induction notice in May but was turned down because the doctors discovered I am deaf in my right ear! Not something that had ever been diagnosed before. I just thought people weren't talking loud enough." Maybe that is why he was so stupid in school and his French phrases came out sounding like gobbledygook.

"Too bad you can't serve your country, Tommy." Why couldn't my Walter have gotten a break like that?

"I am serving the country in a way right here. I am selling war bonds for the War Advertising Council. I stand outside of the theaters on the weekend and try to get people to sign up to purchase them. A nice benefit is that I meet a lot of pretty girls."

"That doesn't sound like much of job."

"There is more to it than that. I have to keep records, collect money, and make sure it gets to the government. That is what I am doing in here: depositing funds to forward to Washington, money that will provide uniforms, planes, ammunition, soldiers' provisions and whatever else is needed."

Insipid Tommy Bruce and his cushy job makes me angry, and I don't want to talk to him anymore. "Got to go, Tommy. Lots of work to finish before the end of the day."

"Nice to see you, Frenchwoman. Maybe we can get together sometime and reminisce about our high school days."

As the free man walks out the door, I hope this is the last time I will ever see him.

1942 October 1
Doris
Dillon Again

Jimmie called on Thursday to tell me he has found an apartment for us in Columbia. It was hard to find a place with so many couples and families living there while the men are training.

He is coming back to Fayetteville tomorrow. We'll go ahead and get married on Saturday and go back to Columbia because we have to take occupancy of the apartment on Monday or we will lose it! Whew! Mama is mad and doesn't understand why he can't just move into the place, and we can get married in a few weeks in a regular wedding.

She didn't hear his pathetic pleading on the phone about how he cannot bear to live without me. I am fine with this because I miss him something terrible.

So off we will go to Dillon on Saturday, tie the knot, and drive on to Columbia. Mr. and Mrs. James Cantrell Rice. I will wear the white dress Mama made, but she is not going to the wedding. Only Kathleen, Roger, Buck, Gene, and Evo.

When I told Verne that I would have to quit my job, he was not too happy as I am practically running the place. He made me promise that when I come back, I will work for him again. Actually, I am getting pretty bored with that job. I might apply to Sears Roebuck after Jimmie goes overseas.

I can't imagine how lost and fearful I will be when he leaves. Poor Kathleen is so sad and can't seem to brighten up. She practically runs home from the bank to check the mailbox, even though Mama told her she will call her at work if a letter comes. She is excited about my wedding, so maybe that will give her a little break from her misery.

180

Our apartment is in downtown Columbia on Lincoln Street in the home of J.E. Byrd. Jimmie says it is small but nice and has furniture in a small front room, a kitchen, and one small bedroom. It overlooks a park. I hope I can find a job as I don't want to sit home all day.

Many changes in my life and fast! But I am excited about finally being able to love Jimmie in every way. Oh, this makes my heart beat fast like it did the day I first saw him.

1942 October 5
Ethel
Worry Vacation

Doris and Jimmie married on Saturday and are now living in Columbia in their little apartment. The house feels empty without her sashaying around, chatting about her day at work, and trying to drag Kathleen somewhere to improve her mood. I'm a little sorry that I didn't go to the wedding. I was miffed that they eloped instead of marrying in the church. I should not have reacted that way and hope I didn't spoil their joy. She called me this morning and said they would visit on the weekend. Good news!

Other good news is the card that Kathleen got today saying that Slover had landed safe at his destination, whatever that is. She found every possible way to fret after he left in September: Germans might sink his ship, he might be seasick, or he might have fallen overboard and drowned. She danced around the dining room when she saw the card. Betty Sue had come home with her, and they turned on the radio and began doing the jitterbug right there.

The joy of the day only lasted till suppertime. Roger announced that he went to the recruiting office and signed up. He will be inducted at Fort Bragg on November twenty-fifth. My prayer is that my gentle giant of a son will not go to combat.

I was good and did not say anything, but inside I was dying. Evelyn was not so restrained. She got out of her seat and threw her arms around his shoulders and tears came. "Oh, Roger. Slover gone and Jimmie soon to be and now you."

It's late and everyone is sleeping, and the house is at rest again. I'm rummaging through my material basket. I pull out some scraps of red, blue, and white muslin.

Tomorrow, I will start on a service flag to honor our soldier boys. There will be blue stars for Slover, Jimmy, and Roger and some extra blue ones for other of my loved ones who may be called upon to serve. Our men are leaving us, one by one. I will not make a gold one! I say out loud, "I won't need a gold one. No one will be lost."

"What cha' doing, Mama?" Evelyn pokes her head in the door.

"Just planning for a little sewing. Why are you still awake, sweet one?"

"I can't sleep Mama. I had a bad dream about the soldiers in helmets with guns like I saw on the newsreel. I saw Roger's face under a helmet. And he got shot."

"Evelyn Lou, I think you have been seeing too many newsreels at the movies."

"I'm scared, Mama. What if Roger goes to war, and we never see him again?"

"Come sit with me in my rocking chair. Shh, shh. Don't think about that. Do what your Daddy always told you. When you are scared, make your mind go somewhere else. Remember how he talked about taking a 'worry vacation' to change the picture in your mind?" I pull her into my lap and drape a quilt around her.

"Yes, I do. I am going to think about jumping in the waves at the beach."

We rock and rock and slowly her body relaxes, and she is sleeping. Warm and safe and vacationing from worry.

1942 October 16
Kathleen
Scotland

My first letter from Walter arrived today! I could not tear the envelope open fast enough!

Dear Honey,
I guess you have got some of my letters by now, I have written you plenty.
I am now in Scotland so I can write you a letter hoping you will get it.
How are you getting along, are you missing me half as much as I miss you?
How long has it been since you have heard from Mother? I have never gotten a letter from her since I have been on the move and have only got one from you.
Has Doris ever got married yet?
Honey, I dream of you every night and most of the day, so you see I am thinking of you most of the time.
Write me long letters and tell me all the news because I get plenty lonesome over here without you and that it the only way I can keep my morale up.
This is very pretty country over here, plenty of good green grass and plenty of mountains.
How would you like to take a ride over some of those mountains that we rode over in the Blue Ridge Mountains when we went to Indiana?
Well, honey, it won't be very long till Xmas, but don't send me any packages of any kind unless I tell because they would only get all messed up.
Have you been getting your check okay? If something happens that you don't get it, be sure and let me know. I don't think you will have any trouble

184

getting it. But in case you do, let me know as soon as possible.

Tell Evo and the boys to be good. Tell your mother that I sure don't get those good biscuits over here that you and her make. Boy, what I wouldn't give for some of them now.

Sometimes, they serve us something called scones, but they are hard, not soft and flakey like your buttermilk biscuits.

Well, honey I will have to close for the present. Remember I love you more than anything in this whole world. I love you with all my heart.

Love forever, Walter

Walter has a beautiful, flowing handwriting. I read every word over and over, and they sound more dear to me than anything even Shakespeare ever penned.

1942 October 18
Kathleen
Duds

Two more letters from Walter arrived yesterday!
The first one was heart breaking:

> *Another day has gone by and I am a very lonesome*
> *one without you. It seems like I have been gone*
> *from you for years.*
> *Well, honey I have never gotten a letter from you*
> *yet. I guess I will get them all in a bunch. You know*
> *what? I was thinking about the waterworks and all*
> *the good times we used to have there. Those were*
> *the days and we will have them all over again*
> *someday, just wait and see.*
> *Think of me when you make those biscuits. I would*
> *sure like to have some of them now.*
> *Honey, I can't send you money like I thought I*
> *could but I will save it and send you a good bit at a*
> *time as soon as I can. Your allotment will keep you.*
> *Honey, put every penny in the bank that you can*
> *because we will need it when I get back. Your*
> *husband, Walter*

He sounds so sad and lonely, and that makes me sad
and lonely. And biscuits! I will never look at them the same
way. I wish there was some magic way I could
instantaneously dispatch them warm and buttered to him.

The second letter causes me once again the pain of
knowing he has not received any of my letters. What is
wrong with that postal system? Buck says it takes a long
time because someone has to read them all and censor
anything that might give information to the enemy if the
letters are intercepted:

I miss you so damn much that it hurts so you see I love you an awful lot. The only thing to do is to grin and bear it because we are not the only ones that are going through this thing. But think of all the things that we can do when I get back. I will take about two months off and I will take you any place you want to go. There are a lot of places over there that you have told me you want to go, like Niagara Falls and Florida. We will go to as many of them as we possibly can. I will make up as many of our lost days as I can.

Have you bought you any new duds? Go ahead and buy as many as you want. Because as I told you when we got married that I wanted you to look nice, so you buy all you want.

Honey, I want you to send me a small picture of you than I can put in my billfold. You know the little locket that you gave me? I lost it somewhere and I can't find it nowhere.

I showed your picture to one of the other first sergeants and he said you have a very nice-looking wife. That made me feel very good, but I knew that all the time. It was the one we had taken by the schoolhouse when you had your new Easter outfit. You looked real nice. I have just been looking at that picture and it brings back lots of feelings to me.

Well, honey, I am going to have to close so I won't be charged extra for this letter. Yours forever, Slover

The prospect of traveling with him after the war makes me happy. How I wish we could go to Paris! It will probably be ruined by the Germans. I pray that crazy Hitler does not do anything to the beautiful art works.

Walter losing his locket makes me sad. I'll send another one. It makes me feel good to read all the nice

187

things he said about my looks. I am not planning to go crazy buying "duds" as he said, but I know shopping a bit always cheers up a girl. I'll ask Barbara Emerson if she wants to go shopping on Saturday.

1942 November 1
Kathleen
Peepers

I'm running. Fast. It's dark. The street is narrow, lined on both sides with apartment buildings. There are no street lamps. Almost tripping over cobblestones that catch on my shoes, I am sweating and tired. But I cannot stop. I'm being chased by German troops! The evil cadence of the boots thuds closer, and I turn my head quickly to confirm that. I make a desperate decision to knock on one of the doors. I bang furiously, and finally, the door opens. A sleepy Nazi soldier yawns in my face, just as the men following me catch up. I have nowhere to go. I scream and scream.

I jolt awake and realize I am screaming. Mama stands by my bed shaking my shoulders. "Kathleen, it's okay. Go back to sleep."

More lucid now, I know where I am. In the big bed in the front room that Walter and I shared. Mama leaves, and I roll over and face the window. I can't tell if it is yet daylight as the blackout curtains make the room perpetual night.

I hate being alone in this bed. I am cold and miss the warmth of Walter's body. I'll be moving back in with Doris and Evo soon because Mama has rented this room to another couple. I will be glad not to be alone at night.

Can't go back to sleep. I turn on the little metal reading light attached to the head of the bed and reach for my book. *Seventeenth Summer* by Maureen Daly. About a girl and her romantic adventures. Not good literature, but it distracts me from my situation. Just turned eighteen, married to an absent husband, and working. I miss school parties, being in class and learning new things, sharing mindless chatter with girlfriends, and going on dates. But, more, I miss Walter.

I can't focus on the book, so I just get up. I pick up my watch from the dresser and see that it is four-thirty. The dresser that Walter and I had so much fun buying and moving into our room. The bed. The chest. All those pieces will be enjoyed by the new roomers. I hate the idea of some other couple sleeping in and making love in our bed. But there is no room for all that furniture anywhere else in the house. So, it will just have to be.

The room is so cold. I wrap in my robe, slide on my slippers, and go to the front room near the heater. I stand close and rub my hands together over the warmth. Turning on the table lamp, I plop on the sofa with my book but still can't take in the words. I read the same sentence three times.

Movement catches my eye. The window by the door. What? I stand to get a closer look, and a blurry image disappears. The neighbor's cat, maybe. Then a sudden thud on the porch. I'm scared now but force myself to look through the side window by the door. A man is getting up and high tailing down the steps, and then, he disappears from view.

I am proud of myself that I don't start screaming for Mama. I have created enough drama tonight with my nightmare.

A "peeper." Someone just looking in windows to see what he can see. He must have seen my light. This spying has become common. Sometimes the spied upon call the police, but by the time they arrive, the peeper is long gone. Folks must be pretty bored to sneak around in the night. Happens in the daytime, too. I decide not to tell anyone about this, especially Evo because it would scare the heck out of her.

Somehow this little excitement shakes me out of the memory of my nightmare. I stretch out on the sofa and go back to forgetful sleep.

1942 November 12
Kathleen
Initiations

I got a letter from Marj today dated November eighth. Mail sure does get here faster from Canada than Scotland. I haven't heard from Walter since the middle of October. I hope he is safe in Scotland and not in the invasion of North Africa. I have seen the newsreel of the Allied invasion called Operation Torch to stop that awful Rommel and get him and his tanks out of there. The Ninth Division is there fighting. I pray Walter's unit was not sent there, but most likely they were.

I don't write Marj very often because when she writes about her carefree life, it leaves me jealous and feeling sorry for myself. I want to be doing fun things. Life is so boring. My only happy days are when I hear from Walter or do something with Betty Sue or Barbara Emerson.

Dear Kathleen,
It was swell to hear from you again, and I enjoyed your letter tres beaucoup!
I hope you won't mind waiting for your birthday necklace a little longer. I really can't find much here, but I am going to Toronto November 18.
A week ago, our school had their Initiation. Really, Kathleen, Tweed is the only high school I've ever heard of to have initiations like they have at college. Usually this process happens when students start ninth grade, but since I am new to town, I have it as a senior. I had to turn my clothes inside out and take off my stockings. Some fun! Then they painted me up with lipstick, paints, eyebrow pencils, etc. And did my hair in a beautiful (?) coiffure of

pigtails tied with string! What a mess I was! Well enough of that nonsense.

Kathleen, do you have "square" dances over there? They have an average of about two at every dance, and I really enjoy them, even if they do heat one up a bit.

Do you do have Basic Training and Defense Training there? They do here and...ouch! We have to march...left, right, left, about turn, attention, stand at ease. That is the Training, and for Defense we have to make an air raid shelter in the basement, learn how to detect enemy aircraft and how to put out incendiary bomb sites. Terrible stuff!

I can't imagine how hard it is for you to be away from your Walter, and I certainly hope you hear from him again soon. Love, Marj

Hmm. She took that initiation thing is good spirit. I would have hated it, being singled out like that and laughed at. And all that preparing for possible attack is scary. Although we have practice raids some and blackouts, Canada is a lot more serious about preparing than we are.

1942 November 18
Doris
The End of the Beginning

I am loving living in Columbia with Jimmie, being with him every night in our own place and making love. He does not get to come home every night as his training is becoming more intense. I miss having a job to go to every day, but I try to keep our place nice and to have a good meal ready when Jimmie comes home.

I worry about all the practice flying he does. He is not always the pilot but is training as well for the other positions on the plane: navigator, bombardier, gunner, radio operator. He has to know how to do everything in case one of the crew becomes "disabled" which really means wounded or killed. He talks about the training when he comes home. He is very proud of all the things he can do. Sometimes, I don't want to hear about any of this. I pretend my husband is not practicing for combat but just has a regular job.

Mama writes me many letters and postcards filling me in on every detail of Fayetteville life. Her card today told me that Kathleen and Eugene have been sick with colds but are still going to work. Martha Medlin in our church had a big baby boy. Her husband is overseas with the Ninth Division just like Slover. How hard it must be for her alone and for her husband not being there to meet his son! I hope to high heaven that I don't get pregnant before Jimmy leaves and end up in the same boat!

Mama said Kathleen finally heard from Slover and he is ok and is in Algeria, North Africa. So now we know he was in Operation Torch to get the Germans out of there.

Mama is worried to death about Gene since President Roosevelt has signed a bill to lower the draft age from twenty-one to eighteen. Gene is sixteen, almost seventeen. I tell her not to worry because surely this thing will be over before he can be drafted. When I told her that, Jimmie looked at me like I was crazy because he believes the defeat of the Germans and Japanese will require three more years!

I'm reading a great deal now, something I never liked to do when I was in school. One day out of sheer boredom I wandered into the library near our apartment. The librarian recommended a new book by Agatha Christie *The Body in the Library.* Pretty good but I am a slow reader, so it is taking me forever. I also read magazines like *Life, Better Homes and Gardens, Photoplay,* and *Glamour.* And I scour the newspapers for war news to help Kathleen figure out where Walter's unit might be.

And I keep the radio on all day. I love "soap operas." People have started calling the stories this because soap manufacturers advertise to housewives who listen, and we use cleaning products.

My favorite is *The Guiding Light.* It is about a preacher Rev. Ruthledge, who advises characters that get into some pretty bad jams. He is the "guiding light" for them. His daughter was having a secret romance with her foster brother and married him in spite of the family's objections. The brother's real parents showed up, and the mother shot the father dead when she found out that he was trying to extort money from his own son. Presently, a character named Lucy is pregnant and not married. I'm sure to be home every day at 2:30, so I won't miss an episode.

Kathleen listens to this too, and we talk about it in letters. Or sometimes on the phone, but that gets too expensive if we talk very long. Mama says we are going to rot out our brains from that program, but it is a welcome distraction from war news.

The more I hear about the English and what they are going through, the more I feel so sad for them. That little island sitting just across the English Channel from France where the Germans have settled themselves in! After *The*

Guiding Light this afternoon, there was a special report about a speech by Prime Minister Winston Churchill celebrating an Allied victory over "the desert fox" Rommel in Egypt:

> *I have never promised anything but blood, tears, toil and sweat. We, however, have a new experience. We have victory - a remarkable and definite victory. The bright gleam has caught the helmets of our soldiers, and warmed and cheered all our hearts. Now this is not the end. It is not even the beginning of the end. But it is, perhaps, the end of the beginning. We mean to hold our own. I have not become the King's First Minister in order to preside over the liquidation of the British Empire.*

Brave and inspiring words. This victory happened because American soldiers joined in. I am calling Kathleen to be sure she heard that we are at the "end of the beginning."

1942 November 26
Ethel
Franklin

"Get your paws off that turkey, Eugene Fields Brantley!" I turn from the stove to see my baby boy pulling a strand of meat from our small bird.

"Sorry, Ma. It just smells so good!" He swoops down and hugs me around the waist with his long arms. With that mischievous grin I can never resist, he bounds out of the kitchen, but not before grabbing another bite of turkey.

The girls and I carry the dressing, vegetables, rolls, fried cornbread, and caramel cake to the table with the turkey as the centerpiece. Cake will be a hit because it will be adequately sweet since I saved up a month's worth of my sugar ration.

I know that Evelyn will not eat any turkey. When we bought him a few months ago to join our backyard chickens, Evelyn immediately gave him a name. Franklin, for the president, and she considered him her personal pet. While Gene helped me do the sorry deed of removing the life from Franklin, Evo ran from the house, tears erupting, and dashed up the hill to Edna's to find comfort. You should never name an animal you are going to eat.

Our table will be peopled by those I love: Evelyn, Gene, Kathleen, Buck and Polly, and Doris and Jimmie. I wonder how often they will be able to come from Columbia since gasoline rationing begins on December thirty-first. Missing is Roger who had to report to Bragg for his induction yesterday. And of course, Slover. The fact that he is in North Africa is heavy on our hearts. I wanted to invite some of the neighbors, especially the Kellys, but Franklin would only go so far.

I yell, "Y'all come," and everyone gathers around the table, eager to dig in. Buck holds up his palm and asks permission to return thanks. Hands drop to laps and heads bow.

"Father God, we come to you today with grateful hearts. Bless this food and our mama who prepared it. We are sad for those who are needy and make us mindful of how we can help them. We pray for your protection for Slover and all who are fighting to eliminate the evil that threatens our world. Help us to be the people you would have us be. In Jesus' name, amen."

My eyes fill with tears as Buck's voice reminds me so much of Wesley's, and I ache anew from the loss of him. Yet, I'm grateful for my children and how they all help and support each other. Perhaps by next Thanksgiving, this war will be over, and all our boys will be sitting at family tables.

We finish the meal, and there are some leftovers plus a significant hunk of the caramel cake. Evelyn suggests we take these to Janie's family. They probably had a very meager meal. The children just look at each other, and Gene says, "But Ma. We could have those great leftovers tonight!"

Buck speaks up. "Yes, but we have eaten our fill. We should share the rest." Without further words, everyone starts clearing the table. We wrap the food, and I put it in a basket. Evelyn and Buck take it down the street to Janie's.

When they return, Evelyn says that Buck slipped two whole dollars into the basket from his hard-earned wages from the drug store. "Mama. They were so happy, and Janie cried."

This might be a good time to bring out the Service Flag I made for our window. I unfold it and don't have words to surround the act. It bears three blue stars on a field of white surrounded by a red border in honor the service of Slover, Jimmie, and Roger.

197

Kathleen looks up and smiles then weeps softly. Doris hugs her Jimmie. Gene helps me hang the flag in the front window.

Unsaid, but in all our minds, is this: will stars for sweet, spiritual Buck, and young, vital Gene be added before this war ends? Will any of our boys be honored in death with a gold star?

1942 December 10
Kathleen
V-Mail

I am feeling pretty low today. Even the laughter and joking of Barbara could not cheer me at work. Truly, I can't fathom how she can be so jolly with her man in danger!

They got married about the time Walter and I did when her Carl was a student at Georgia Tech in Atlanta. Shortly after, he and other Tech students were drafted into the Army Corp of Engineers, and they came to Fort Bragg. The military figured these boys, with all the mechanical skills Tech offered, would be good candidates for officers in military support units.

So, Carl is a Lieutenant leading a unit of men that builds bridges in the dark before our soldiers go into an area. How difficult and scary that task must be. The engineers also do camouflage, vehicle maintenance, building construction, or whatever else troops need. Barbara has not gotten any letters from Carl after the "arrived at destination" one. She thinks he is in the North Africa campaign, but she doesn't know for sure.

Christmas is only fifteen days away, and the whole town is turning red, green, silver, and gold. There's a big tree in the bank lobby, complete with silver tinsel and red and green balls and bubble lights. It is lovely but only makes me sadder as I will not be spending Christmas with Walter. I am getting a box ready to send him, even though he said not to. Maybe it will eventually get to him.

When I get home, Evo and Mama are putting up our tree and ask me to help. "No, thanks. You two are doing a beautiful job." Mama is doing most of the decorating as Evo is sitting in the rocker trying to string popcorn with a needle and thread for garland. More goes into her mouth or on the floor than on the thread.

Mama has laid the mail on the phone table. The haul includes a card from Roger saying he is now at Ft. Slocum, New York, and expects to be there for a few months. He is getting medical training. Also, the sad news that he will only have Christmas day off and can't come home.

Underneath Roger's card is a small folded letter from Walter! I can't believe Mama did not call me at work and tell me! The address is printed and not in Walter's handwriting.

It scares me, and I imagine a slew of reasons someone else might have addressed the letter. Is he injured? Or worse? There is no envelope. It is just a single piece of paper folded over and addressed. Under that return address printed in red is "V-MAIL." There is some information printed on the outside, but I don't take time to read it and unfold the paper to get right to Walter's words. The print looks like a photograph:

> *My Darling Wife,*
> *There isn't much to say, the only thing is that I am up to my neck in mud and it is raining very hard. Otherwise I am okay and in the best of health and thinking of you all the time.*
> *Have you heard from Mother lately? Write and tell me all the news.*
> *Give your mother and all the rest my regards and tell them that I think of them very much.*
> *Well honey I will have to close. Remember honey I love you very much.*
> *Merry Christmas, Your husband*

Not much detail there. He was in mud and rain writing this. Maybe he was in a tent. I read the information on the outside of the letter:

V-Mail service is available to and from the personnel of our Armed Forces stationed at certain points outside the continental United States. If a message is addressed to or from a point where V-mail equipment is not in operation, it will be transmitted in its original form by the most expeditious means of transportation.

When transmitted by V-Mail Services, a miniature photographic negative of the message will be made and sent by the most expeditious form of transportation available. It is important that the message be written very plainly.

Then some more directions about how to fold the letter. I guess this is a way to censor a soldier's letters. Makes me feel funny to think that someone is reading Walter's words. I am mad to know more about where he is. I will just have to be content and be happy that I know he is ok.

1942 December 14
Evo
Drill Sergeant

We haven't seen Roger since before Thanksgiving when he had to go to Fort Bragg! I miss him so much!

Today we got a letter from him with this funny picture. I didn't understand what it meant, but everyone else in the house was falling over laughing. I must have looked puzzled because Kathleen explained that the big man was a drill sergeant who was being mean to the little guy who just joined up. I got it, but didn't like it because I don't like anyone being mean to Roger. Buck said that being mean to the recruits is a way of making them tough, and that soldiers must be tough to do their jobs. Ok, but I still hate the idea of anyone being mean to my big brother!

Roger is in New York for more training. He is going to be a medic. That is a doctor soldier. I hope that means he will be helping sick or injured soldiers and he won't be a fighting soldier.

Christmas is coming soon, and Kathleen has been buying things to send to Slover. Even though he said not to because he may not get the box, she is doing it anyway. She let me go shopping with her. She bought a little locket at Henebry's and put a picture of herself in it. At Woolworth's, she got Snickers Bars, handkerchiefs, foot powder, a razor and some blades, some comic books, and a *Life* magazine. She worried over each item because she didn't really know what he might need or want.

Mama baked a fruit cake. Kathleen said that Slover does not like fruit cake, but she didn't tell Mama because she didn't want to hurt her feelings.

I don't like it either. It tastes like a fruit brick. Kathleen made some biscuits and wrapped them real tight in waxed paper and then covered them with tape. Mama said they would be stale before he got them, but Kathleen wanted to try anyway. She also made cookies. And put in lots of pictures of herself and the family. I drew him a picture of Kathleen packing the box. The box was heavy when we took it to the post office.

When we were shopping, I saw a beautiful doll in the Capitol Department Store window that I would really, really, really like to have. It is called a Little Lady Ann Shirley doll and wears a coat, hat, and muff with velveteen trim. Her dress is blue, and she has white socks and black shoes with heels. Funny, but I hate wearing fancy clothes like that, but I like it on the doll.

I would also like to have a BB gun like Edna's, but there is no chance of Mama letting me get one. And I am sure the doll is way too expensive. Besides, there is a war on, and we all have to do our part by economizing. I'm not asking for anything. All I really want on my Christmas list is for the stupid war to end.

1942 December 25
Evo
Santa

I jump up, run to the window, and pull the blackout curtain back a little. Still dark. Kathleen raises her head and snaps, "Get back to bed right now, Evelyn Lou! It's still night!" Bah, humbug! I want to see what Santa has left for me.

I crawl back under the covers. I hear rain outside. No white Christmas. I wish I could turn on the light and read, but Kathleen would bite my head off.

So, I stare at the ceiling and think. Mama was talking yesterday about the new rationing that starts on December thirty-first. Gas, shoes, meat, butter, and cheese. Drat! I love cheese! And shoes! My school shoes are almost too tight. Will I have to walk around in my socks?

I made presents for everyone. I get a dime allowance every week, and I've been saving it since Halloween. I got a comic book for Gene and candy bars for everyone else except Mama. I snuck some leftover scraps from her fabric basket and some yarn. I cut two circles of scraps, balled up the yarn and put it between them, and sewed the whole thing together. A new pincushion. Mama loves green, so I chose green fabric pieces. The finished thing looked good. And I added some new needles from Woolworth's.

Finally! I hear Mama stirring in the kitchen, so I slip out of the bedroom and join her. "Evelyn, we won't open presents until after breakfast."

"I know, Mama. May I help you cook?" I hope I can speed her up a bit. Mama carefully mixes the biscuit dough, pats it into rounds, and sticks the sheet in the oven. While the coffee perks, she fries bacon and scrambles eggs.

When Kathleen, Doris, Jimmie, and Gene get to the table, Mama says a long, drawn out grace while my eyes are trying to sneak a peek under the tree.

Then we eat. "Stop bolting your food down, Evelyn Lou! You are going to choke," warns Doris.

Just then, there is a little knock at the door, and Buck and Polly arrive. And at long last, we head to the front room. I spot the white velveteen trim of a Little Lady Ann Shirley doll! The one I saw when Kathleen and I went shopping. Of course, I know that there really is no Santa Claus, and Kathleen is probably my Santa. But I pretend because the family thinks I don't know this.

I run to the doll and admire every inch of her. I didn't get a BB gun. I knew I wouldn't, so that is ok. In my stocking are some Hershey Kisses, a box of raisins, two pair of new socks (laced trim which I don't like because they will make me look like a baby), an orange, and a whole dollar.

We sit around and admire our gifts. Mama loves her pin cushion and new needles. It is a fun morning, but it is not exactly right. There are big empty places where Slover and Roger should be. I wonder if there will be more empty spaces next Christmas. Or maybe no empty spaces because everyone will be home from war.

Horace Purvis' banjo

Evo, age 10

Doris and Kathleen

February 8, 1942

Sgt. And Mrs. Slover

Rice shower

Wedding congratulations

Answers in the little window

Shelburn, Indiana visit

Walter and Mom.

Washing at the pump

Ninth Division Octofoil

Victory rolls hairstyle

Walter safe arrival overseas

V-Mail

Roger's induction cartoon

quilt from Grandma Coggins

Jimmie's training area

Jimmie, Columbia, SC

Grandpa, Grandma Coggins

1943 January 5
Kathleen
Scrapbook

January. Every day is grey, and I feel grey. I miss Walter. I'm moving in a daze.

At lunch, I go to the book store to buy a new novel to distract me. *Student Nurse* about a war nurse. No! *The Widow.* No! *The Fall of Paris.* Definitely not! I have no interest in reading about my city in the hands of the horrible Nazis! *A Bride Goes West.* She goes with her new husband to Montana to start a farm. OK.

At the cash register, I spot a shelf of scrapbooks for war memorabilia. Maybe I should start a collection of news and magazine articles about Walter's service. He said to keep the news for him to read when he gets home. I buy a book and some of the stick-on mounting corners. I have already saved some things. Yes, I will start tonight. *Victory Photo Record Book.*

Victory can't come soon enough.

1943 January 18
Ethel
Sliced Bread

The paper slaps the front porch steps. Frankie is getting pretty accurate tossing it from his bike. Since the paper is published in the afternoon, he gets it after school and makes his route.

Evo bursts in the door, carrying the folded paper. "I hate that Frankie Kelly. He tried to hit me!" She huffs off to the bedroom and slams the door so hard it shakes the dining room light fixture. At age eleven, she is starting to act like a teenager. Lord, I remember what Doris was like during those years. Not sure I am up to that again!

The paper's front page is all about the war. Fighting on Guadalcanal. Buck's friend Stan Applegate is a medic there. That must be a horrific job patching up all the wounded soldiers. Germans defeated in Tripoli. Hooray! Churchill and Roosevelt agree the war can end only with Germany's unconditional surrender.

A headline at the bottom reads, "No More Sliced Bread." It's now illegal to produce and sell it. Huh? With the need for scrap metal, parts for the slicing machines will no longer be made. That doesn't bother me much because we eat a lot of biscuits. But making sandwiches for lunches will be a bother. It's hard to slice through a whole loaf of soft white bread without it coming out all bunched up.

Kathleen came home in a tizzy. Slover's mama Verna and her two daughters Euleta and Maxine are coming for a visit tomorrow. She is in the front bedroom cleaning and rearranging. Our last roomers moved, and we haven't taken on more since we knew the Slovers were coming.

I wish she wasn't such a nervous Nelly. She worries about people liking her and making a good impression. She's embarrassed about our meager home. I told her to remember that the Slovers don't have indoor plumbing, so we are a step above in that area. That didn't seem to help. She worries about worn spots on the sofa and the fact that our yard has no grass. There is sure to be plenty of hair twirling while they are here.

1943 January 20
Kathleen
Grits

Mom, Euleta, and Maxine arrived yesterday by train to stay for a week. They were pretty tired and slept late this morning. We gave them the front bedroom room with the furniture Walter and I bought. I went back in with Doris and Evo. Evo offered me her bed and she slept on a pallet of quilts on the floor. She said it's like camping. That girl! She keeps us all laughing in these bad times. And she always manages to see the bright side of things.

I was nervous about Walter's family coming, but they are just as kind as when Walter and I visited them last year. Mom was very complimentary about our house and does not seem to notice our worn furniture and carpet. No one has said, but I bet they like not having to go to an outdoor toilet.

Mama and Mom got along immediately like they were old friends. They are digging through Mama's material box seeing what they might make for us girls during the visit. And cooking! They have planned a big meal tonight. Buck and Polly will join us.

Maxine and Euleta seem like my new sisters. Last night, we sat up late jabbering about movie stars and music and doing a little jitterbugging. They are good dancers. We are going shopping on Saturday, and I plan to take them to the Carolina Soda Shoppe so they can taste a real hot dog "all the way." The southern way: mustard, chili, onions, and coleslaw. They eat theirs in Indiana boring with just catsup.

Speaking of food, they sort of stuck their noses up at the grits Mama served for breakfast this morning. They did not know what they were and asked if they were a form of Cream of Wheat. Maxine took a tentative taste. She blurted out that they tasted like nothing and immediately

210

grabbed the sugar bowl and dumped about five or six big spoons of sugar in her bowl. I wanted to say that she was using up too much of the sugar ration, but I held my tongue.

Doris and Jimmie will come up from Columbia this weekend. We plan to take family pictures to send to Walter. Oh, how I wish he were here! There will be a space in those photographs even if everyone is bunched up close together. I will see his face, and my mind will put him right next to me. That is what I experience every time I see the shots we made at Christmas.

Life continues to chug along here. But without Walter at my side, there is an emptiness that at times paralyzes me. Sometimes, I don't hear what people say. A trance carries me away from the moment. Mama gets ill with me when she has to repeat something.

I picture Walter in Africa in the rain and mud he described in a December letter. He has not yet received my Christmas packages! How I wish he had them to enjoy. Hoping the cookies will not be stale. I put in some of his beloved biscuits which I know will be hard as dried mud, but I added them as a joke anyway. Maybe he and his men can play baseball with them!

In October and November, I missed my time of the month and was horrified thinking I could be pregnant!

Mama said I probably skipped due to stress. False alarm as "Miss Scarlett returned to Tara" and all is back to normal.

Now, I sort of wish I were in a family way. A little baby might help me take my mind off my fear and emptiness. Having Mom and the girls here is a little distraction. I want them to stay longer than a week.

1943 January 30
Evo
Girl Scouts

It's Saturday afternoon, and I'm going to Girl Scouts. Before I left, Kathleen wanted to take a picture with me for Slover. I made the Girl Scout salute with my hand over my brow and my fingers turned out. Kathleen used the regular military salute. I hope Slover will like the picture, and it will cheer him up. I know he misses us. I sure miss him!

I like my uniform with its belt, scarf, and beret. The beret has the Girl Scout trefold symbol for the three parts of the promise. I even have matching socks! Wearing my uniform makes me feel as if I am in the Army, which I wish was. We can only do projects to help the war effort: collecting scrap metal, selling War Bonds, helping our Moms with their victory gardens, and collecting old clothes for refugees. I want to help more.

When I get to the meeting, our leader Mrs. Waskey leads us in the Girl Scout Promise. I love the words:

On my honor, I will try: To do my duty to God and my country, to help people at all times, to obey the Girl Scout Laws.

We plop in the folding chairs, and Mrs. Waskey makes announcements. First, about cookie sales to begin in March. There will be no cookies next year because of the rationing! We will sell calendars instead. How boring!

Mrs. W. says Girls Scout troops are being set up in some of the Japanese internment camps! Oh, I hope there is one where Tomoko is living! I haven't had a letter from her. I would write, but I don't know where to send it.

1943 February 10
Doris
Economy Loaf

My days, or should I say nights, with Jimmie in
Columbia continue to be wonderful. The days are so boring
that I think I will go nuts waiting for him to get home. I
miss working at Verne's, and I have tried futilely to find
something here. There are so many wives of airmen
looking for jobs. By the time I answer an ad from the paper,
the job is always filled.

If we were in Mobile, Alabama, there are shipyards
hiring women. Also, California and Connecticut have
plants that manufacture and repair planes. I would be happy
to do that work. When I told Jimmie that, he laughed hard
and said I wouldn't last a day because I would mess up my
nails! Ha, ha. Jimmie says not to worry about it because he
is sure to be leaving the states soon. We have agreed that I
will go home to Fayetteville.

Jimmie and I have settled in to a comfortable
routine as husband and wife. Hardly any spats anymore. He
is such an attentive husband. He loves to cook! What a
surprise! Some nights he stops by the grocery on his way
home, buys ingredients, and makes some dishes that are
utterly delicious. He gets recipes from the cook in the mess
hall on base.

Last night he made ginger cream with orange jelly,
evaporated milk, some preserved ginger and water. It took
a long time to set up firm. While I was getting ready for
bed, Jimmie came in the bedroom carrying a tray with
bowls of the cream. He had a towel over his arm like a
waiter. He bowed. "Dessert is served, Mrs. Rice." We sat
on the side of the bed and slurped the cream down.
Scrumptious! Afterward, the moment was more
scrumptious as Jimmy put our empty dishes on the
nightstand and pulled me into bed!

One of his favorite dishes is called "Economy Loaf." It is a concoction of bread crumbs, peas, mashed potatoes, eggs, tomato soup, and a bit of seasonings and milk. Not my favorite but not too bad if you pretend it's meat. Jimmie can put down tons of it.

Yesterday's mail brought a letter from Roger who is now stationed in Camp Shanks, New York. It's a huge embarkation facility for soldiers to be shipped out overseas. Thank the good Lord, Roger is safe training in a hospital!

His superiors discovered how artistic he is, and now he paints signs. He did many for the hospital, and now they have him doing numbers and information on war equipment including tanks and airplanes. "My medical career may be coming to a close, and I am vying for chief painter for the US Army," he joked. The whole family is delighted that he is staying stateside and out of danger.

Kathleen called and read me a letter from Slover. It was dated January second, and he had just received six of her letters. He is in Algiers, North Africa, and says the country is pretty but not as pretty as Ireland. We now know he went to Ireland after Scotland before the invasion. Kathleen and I both thought Africa was all a hot desert, but maybe not. Slover says it is cold at night.

He has been in action but was not hurt. That revelation made Kathleen both happy and sad. Sad because it verified her fear that he has been in danger.

Included was a comment for Roger. "Tell him to always do as he is told, and he will have no trouble." Spoken like a true sergeant who commands men. Guess he thinks Roger could be a bit of a rebel. Well, he is right. Kat and I both know our big brother has a mind of his own. Slover did not know that Jimmie and I were married until he read her letters. He said he hoped that we would quit our fighting! He would be surprised to know how well we get along. Our physical relationship seems to smooth everything over.

Kathleen was very upset and cried because Slover still had not gotten his Christmas packages. The rest of the letter was a bunch of "lovey dovey" stuff about how much he loves and misses her. Soon, my life will be like Kat's: living through my absent husband's letters.

1943 February 25
Doris
Another Goodbye

Back where I started. I have returned to Fayetteville with the family.

Jimmy left last Friday. His parting words, "Ok, Mrs. Rice. Time to buck up and get this war over with. I am going to help do it. I will drop plenty of bombs on those Krauts, and they will be waving a white flag before we know it."

It was late afternoon when he got ready to board the train. Of course, I was crying and holding to him and generally acting like a fool. But I couldn't help myself. I wish Kathleen had been there to comfort me like I did her when Walter left. Or Mama.

His golden hair glistened in the sun just like it did the day he walked into Verne's and swept me off my feet. The last thing I saw, when he swung his duffle over his shoulder and turned to board the train, was that brilliant, remarkable smile, part charm and part mischief. And he was gone.

How will I survive this?

I will! I am going to wait, write letters, and fill myself with hope. And load the days with activity. I won't go back to Verne's because I would only think of our meeting there. Tomorrow, I will doll up and march myself down to Sears Roebuck and Company on Hay Street to answer the ad in the paper for an inventory clerk. I won't feel sorry for myself!

1943 March 10
Kathleen
First Anniversary

February 7, 1943

My Darling Wife,
Tomorrow we will be married a year. This has been the happiest year of my life, even though I have been away from you part of the time. Just to know that you are waiting for me and loving me all the time keeps me going. Honey, all the Jerrys can't keep me from coming back to you. I will get back some way if I have to whip the whole German Army! I got two v-mails from you and one letter with the picture of you in the snow. You look good enough to eat.

I am still in Africa. The locals speak Arab or French and I can't understand them at all. You can't buy a thing over here because the enemy got everything before we came in here. The only thing we have is what they issue us.

Sure glad to hear that you have some new duds, I sure would like to see you in them.

Well honey I have about run out of anything to say so I will have to close. I love you honey. Your husband, Slover

P.S. Have you ever got your money? let me know as soon as you get it.

Yes, Walter and I have been married for one year. Only half of it spent together. Our paper anniversary. Appropriate, I guess, since paper letters and newspapers are all I have of him now.

Maybe he will be home before we celebrate another anniversary. When I told that to Doris, she said I was a dreamer. She snipped at me, but I excused it. She has been on edge since Jimmie left.

Walter's folks in Indiana were the only ones who acknowledged our anniversary. Cards from Mom, Aunt Inez and Uncle Lawrence, and Aunt Teena, who included a note.

> *Dear Kathleen,*
> *Excuse this paper. (*She wrote on a piece of the back of an envelope. Some people are still in the save/use everything mindset from the Depression years.*) I just had to write you a little line. How are you? We are all well only worried and heartsick over our boys. I had a nice letter from Walter. I surely was glad. Wayne has been moved from Camp Wheeler to Fort Bragg. Maybe he can meet you and your family.*
> *I am sure hoping and praying that this war will soon be over. How is Doris? Is her husband still home? Give my regards to your mother and the rest of your family. When do you think you can come to visit us? Would love to have you.*
> *Honey, keep up the good prayers. They mean everything. And he will come back to you, I know with the faith you have. So chin up and I'm thinking of you always and hoping for your happiness. Love, Aunt Teena*

Hmm. Her optimism gives me credit for more faith than I have. I adored Aunt Teena when we visited last spring. We took to each other immediately. A kind woman with a great sense of humor.

Speaking of fun to be around, Barbara and I had supper together last night at the New York Café. She was all about the recent Academy Awards and Katharine Hepburn not winning for *Woman of the Year*. She idolizes

Katharine and is quite interested in her scandalous affair with Spencer Tracy. I don't admire her because of that. They keep it low key, but everyone knows. And he is married!

The way Barbara flirts with anything in pants, I wouldn't be surprised if she might cheat on Carl.

1943 March 22
Ethel
Train Wreck

Doris and Kathleen bust in the front door with Gene supported between them and hanging his head. What in the round world? "What's wrong with Eugene?!"

Both girls talk at once, as they ease their brother onto the sofa, recline him, and stretch out his legs. He says nothing and looks very pale.

"Stop, both of you! Doris, tell me what happened!"

"Kathleen," Doris orders. "Go get a wet rag to put on his head."

"Eugene, honey, what happened to you?" Then, I notice the big blue knot on his forehead. "Were you in a fight?" A ridiculous question as this boy is way too gentle to get into an altercation.

Doris holds up her hand. "No, Mama. As we were all coming from work, he tripped on the railroad track, took a tumble, and hit his head. He seems a little out of it. Mama, something real bad happened over on Hay Street, and I think he was distracted as we all were. A train hit a car! Didn't you hear the crash? It was awful."

"No! I had the radio pretty loud when I was cooking supper. Was anyone hurt?"

"I don't know. It looked like a terrible mess, but we didn't go over there since we needed to get Gene home."

Gene makes a little moan and rubs his head. "I need to get that last order of film developed before I go home, Mrs. Jordan."

He looks right at me and continues, "Mrs. Jordan, where is it? I can't find it anywhere. Are you hiding it so I will have to stay late?" Then his words become gibberish. He must think he is still at the photo shop.

Then, to Doris. "What am I doing here? Where am I? I need to go back to work." He starts to get up, but the girls push him back on the sofa. I am terrified that my son has gone round the bend!

Wondering if we should get him to the hospital as I am worried about the growing ugly forehead knot. We don't have a car to get him to the hospital because Doris' old one is about done for and won't start. "Ok, I am calling Dr. Monroe to see if he will come."

Gene throws up on himself and falls asleep. Worried for sure, I grab the phone and look up the number. Doctor will come.

While we are waiting, Mrs. Kelly comes over from next door to tell us about the wreck. Her husband was there on his way home from work. A woman didn't even stop although a train was coming. Horrible crash that mangled the car and threw debris everywhere. The ruined car was pushed all the way to the end of the depot platform as the train applied brakes and slowly screeched to a stop. A policeman told Mr. Kelly that they could not get the woman's body out of the car. What was left of her.

And the saddest thing. A little girl came walking by and saw her momma's car. She kept screaming, "Where's my momma? Where's my momma? She wanted me to go to the store with her, but I was too busy playing. Oh, oh! If I had been in the car, I might have seen the train coming! It's my fault!" Or maybe not. And there could have been two dead.

So much bad news from Europe, but we have our own tragedy right here in Fayetteville today.

Dr. Monroe examines my boy. Looks into his eyes with an instrument. Checks him all over for breaks and bruises. He thinks the knot will be ok, and Gene will soon come to his senses. "A good night's rest will help. Someone should stay awake and watch him. Wake him up every hour or two. If you can't wake him or he throws up again, call me immediately."

I sit by Gene's bed and wake him up from time to time. The first time, he just falls back asleep. The second time, he opens his deep brown eyes. "Hey, Mama. What are you doing in my room?"

"Just checking on you, my sweet boy. Just checking. Go back to sleep." He does.

I don't sleep a wink. When the light of day approaches, he sits up and stretches and says, "What is for breakfast, Mama?"

My boy is back.

1943 March 29
Evo
Chicken Fat

Back to school on a Monday. A cloud above me looks just like a bird with its wings spread. Tulip trees full of pink and white blossoms. The sweet scent of the blooms tempts me to skip school. No. Mama would whip me till I couldn't sit down. I force my feet to stay on the sidewalk and drag myself up the steps to my classroom. In my desk. I sit silently. Chatter fills the space around me, but I don't hear what anyone is saying. Day dreaming already, and I just got here. It's going to be a long day.

On the weekend, lots of stuff happened. Buck got his draft notice and is to report to Fort Bragg for his physical exam. I hope he fails it!

I don't want any more of the boys in our family to go. Aren't Slover, Roger, and Jimmie enough? Roger has been promoted to Private First Class, PFC. He said it stands for "Person for Commanding" because he still has to do whatever his superiors say. Ha, ha! Doris said that was a good one since Roger never likes to obey anyone. Kathleen reminded us what Slover said, "In the Army, you do what you are told, no questions asked."

Mama was in a tizzy because the government is now rationing meats, fats, and cheese. You can buy only two of pounds of beef each week. "I will have to wring more chicken necks!"

This made me ill as I do like to eat chicken, but there are a few out back that are my pets. Especially Henrietta, my favorite hen. Mama is sure to boil her for stock to get around the fat ration. She will let the fat rise to the top, scoop it off, and use it to boil vegetables.

Cheese is now rationed. But I love cheese! Sometimes I sneak a little slice off the big bar Mama buys at Gibson's. Just a little so she won't notice.

Yesterday, we went to the movies. I wanted to see *The Mummy's Tomb* starring the spooky Lon Chaney. Doris said it was way too bloodcurdling. Kathleen smiled at me behind Doris' back because she knows I love horror movies. She tried to persuade ol' boring Doris.

"Hey, Doris, maybe seeing something scary would help us stop worrying." Doris wasn't going for it. She decided that we were going to *For Me and My Gal,* which she said would be happy.

We tried to arrive after the newsreel, but we didn't and just got settled in our seats with our popcorn as it was starting. A scene in London and it was getting dark and people were trying to get to the "tube" which is what the English call their subway. They were pushing and stepping on and over each other to get to an air raid shelter. Sirens going off. Yelling and screaming. People hurt and lying on the pavement. And the narrator said, "One hundred and seventy-three people died in the crush in vain. It was a false alarm. No German planes in sight and no falling bombs."

Doris exclaimed, "This war is making monsters of everybody!" Kathleen was shaking and crying softly.

Then, the screen was filled with color and music. Thank goodness! *For Me and My Gal,* a musical starring Judy Garland and a new actor named Gene Kelly. A romantic story of Jo (Judy) and Harry (Gene) trying to get on Broadway and then planning to marry. The setting was during the Great War, and, of course, Harry got drafted. So much for Doris' idea that the movie would distract us from worry since the movie was all about war!

Harry smashed his hand, hoping the injury would keep him out of service. At that point Doris yelled out "boo, coward, chicken."

Then Jo learned her brother had been killed in the war. She was mad at Harry and left. Kathleen muttered, "Hooray for that girl!"

Then Harry tried to enlist to win Jo back, but his hand was crippled for good and they wouldn't take him. Next, he decided to help the war effort by entertaining troops. He was wounded when he tried to warn an ambulance convoy of a bombing on the way. And he got an award for bravery. Of course, as you might expect in a romance, Jo and Harry got back together.

Sappy ending. Give me Lon Chaney any day.

1943 April 13
Doris
Star Sapphire

A package today from Jimmie. A bracelet and locket from Egypt and a star sapphire ring from Sicily.

Wish I could be with you when you receive these things. I was intending on bringing them myself but am afraid I may lose them. Wishing you a very late Christmas and a very early birthday. I love you, Hon, Jimmie

I have been lucky to get many letters since my Jimmie left. He's been in North Africa like Walter. He does not mention missions, but I'm sure there have been many. I try not to think about it.

Other mail today for Kathleen was a certificate of commendation for Walter:

Staff Sgt. Walter C. Slover, Tunisia
Advanced by jeep through artillery fire to disabled half-truck vehicle, replaced the track amid falling shells and put vehicle back into action. His devotion to duty and courage was inspiring and are highly commendable.
M. S. Eddy Maj. Gen. US Army

Kathleen dissolved into tears. "Oh, Doris! He's putting himself in so much danger. He could have been killed."

"Yes, Kat, but we know this is his way. He strong and smart and will survive. I just know it."

1943 April 25
Kathleen
Easter Sunrise Service

At the cemetery I can feel the cold of the metal chair through my dress. I was stupid to wear my pink dress without a coat or sweater. I wanted everyone to see my dress. Vanity, vanity. Shiver, shiver.

It is six-thirty, and the horizon is pink and deep blue. The rays of the sun push up and spread across the sky.

I try to think of those women who, centuries ago, walked to the tomb of Jesus. What hopelessness they must have felt. A sea of tombstones lies before me, and Walter might be under one of them before this awful war is over or lie on a battlefield perished and alone.

Eight months since he left. An eternity. Sometimes I can't remember how his embrace felt. I might not even know him when he returns. And how he may have changed, and we will be strangers. If he returns.

Everyone stands for "Up from the Grave He Arose," but I'm too distracted to notice until Mama gently punches me with her elbow.

I try to take comfort in the belief that the dead will rise again, and that, even if Walter dies, he will live again. Well, I don't want to meet him again in whatever heaven is. I want him in this life.

The sun is high now and spreading bright sunshine across the greening landscape, Mama, Doris, Evo, and I pile in Doris' car and start home.

Back home, we prepare grits, eggs, sausage and biscuits. Gene is still sleeping but gets up when he smells the food. Why don't men cook for women? How nice it would have been if Gene had breakfast ready for us when we came in chilled and hungry.

1943 May 24
Ethel
Confederate Women

It's Decoration Day. Time to honor those who died in United States' wars. My family in Sanford always commemorated this day by visiting the cemetery and cleaning debris from the graves of the war dead and leaving flowers. Some Coggins men fought and perished in the Civil War and the last war with Germany.

None of my present family cares about this because they are not interested in old things and history. Or too busy to go. When Wesley was alive, the two of us went every Decoration Day to the old Cross Creek Cemetery on Cool Spring Street just past the Market House. It is a spooky place filled with low hanging trees dripping with Spanish moss and decaying, moldy tombstones. The air is heavy with the musty dampness of molds. Not a place I want to go without a man in tow.

I decide instead to visit the Confederate Women's Home and cemetery located on Fort Bragg Road, about two miles west of Roberson Street. Evelyn begs to go with me. I suspect her motive is to get out of school. But I let her go because I am glad for her company.

Most of the women who live in the home are daughters of Civil War soldiers, but there are a few widows in their nineties who lost their spouses in the "war for southern independence," as some folks call it. I think that war was a big embarrassment for our country, but I don't correct anyone about it. Some people still get their drawers in a wad about how the South was done in by the North. I want to honor the Confederate women because they were fighting their own "war" on the home front, just like me and my girls.

Right after lunch, Evelyn and I gather up some yard flowers, a few early zinnias, some forsythia branches. The walk is easy on Roberson Street but gets hard on the hill up to Haymont, and I am out of breath. Finally, the walking is easy again nearer the home.

Wish we had some cookies or cake to take the ladies, but we have already used up our sugar ration for this month.

The home is a crumbling brick building erected in 1915 according to the sign at the beginning of the sidewalk. We go out back first to the little cemetery whose entrance is marked by a metal archway supported by brick pillars. We look at the names on a few headstones. Most markers are very plain, with only the name and birth and death dates. A few have little verses: The Lord is my Shepherd. In Fond Remembrance. We don't leave any flowers. We are delivering them to the living inside the home.

Evelyn decides to look for the oldest person buried here. There are only about forty graves, so it does not take her long to accomplish her goal. "1845, 1860, 1832, 1862...1828! That has to be it." She scans the remaining graves. "Yep. That's it. Look Mama. Elizabeth McCaulley, born November 5, 1828, died December 25, 1916. She died on Christmas Day! That must have made her family sad every Christmas after. Wow! She lived to be eighty-eight. If she were alive today, she would be one hundred and fifteen." Evelyn is so quick with mathematics.

Evelyn says we ought to visit someone who is lonely. Most likely all of them are lonely. Evelyn spots a frail, white haired lady in a wheelchair by a window. She is turned toward the sunlight and lifts her face as if she is warming herself. Evelyn hops over to her and says, "Hello, ma'am, how are you this fine day? I am Evelyn, but you can call me Evo."

Slowly, the sun lady turns her face toward my beaming daughter and answers with a growing smile of her own, "Well, hello yourself, Evo! Aren't you a lovely girl?" I know that Evelyn is pleased to be called girl instead of child. "Have a seat on this ottoman, my lovely." Evelyn sits and hands her flowers. "Oh, thank you, my sweet. Forsythias are my favorite. They look like wands of sunlight. I am Mary Bailey Murphy Beamon, and I am ninety-three years old. How old are you, Evo?"

"I will be twelve in October."

Waving me over, Evelyn announces, "This is my mama Ethel Brantley." I move a little closer but let Evelyn enjoy her new friend without my interference.

"Ada Colvin!" Mary calls out to a large woman sitting at a table across the room. "Come meet lovely Evo and her mother Ethel." Ada gets up and waddles over, reaching for Evelyn's hand and then mine. Ada pulls up two chairs and motions for me to sit. We are a little club of three generations.

"How old are you, Miss Ada?" Evelyn blurts out. I give her a stern look for her rudeness, but Ada does not seem to mind.

"I have lived ninety years, and I am proud of each one. I never married, but I have many, many children. I was a teacher. I started teaching after my daddy died in the War Between the States and just kept on until I was seventy-five!"

"Miss Mary, did your father also die in that war?"

"No child, but my husband did. I married him in 1865 when I was only fifteen, and he went off to war and died, and I never saw him again."

I speak up. "My husband Wesley died in 1939 but not in war. He had leukemia. I know how it feels to lose your man. I miss him every day."

"Well, for me it wasn't so bad because I only knew him for a few months before we married and then he was gone. I am sure it is worse if you have a man a long time and then lose him. The hard thing was how we had to live. I lived on a farm, but all the men had gone to war and we women were left to do all the work.

230

"Some farms and plantations had slaves to help but not my family. We could handle many things like cow milking and chicken tending. But when it came to planting and harvesting the crops, the women folk could not keep up.

"It was hard to sell our crops because no one had money. We thought about selling grandmother's silver, but no one would pay much for it, so we buried it in the barn in case the Yankees came. We bartered for things and helped each other out, but we were hungry when we could not produce enough to last the winter. We were lucky because no Yankee soldiers ever came and took over our house and stole food from us like they did in some places. But, in the end, we survived and finally the war ended."

"Where are our manners, Mary?" says Ada. "Evo, tell us about you."

Evelyn hesitates and blushes. "Not much to tell about me. I am just a kid. Nothing exciting. I do like to read. I get my excitement from books."

"What are some of your favorite books?" asks Ada.

"I really like *The Adventures of Huckleberry Finn* and *Tom Sawyer*."

"Oh, yes! Two of my favorites also! Don't you just love the entertaining situations that Mark Twain gets his characters tangled up in?"

This conversation goes on until I interject, "We need to be getting on back home, so I can get some supper going."

"Please come again," Ada and Mary chirp, almost in unison.

"Oh, yes, thank you. We will," Evelyn answers back.

On the walk home, I think of these two survivors from an old war. Deprivation, fear, loss in a war that was being fought right where they lived. Suddenly, I am ashamed of my self-pity. Yes, my life is hard, but the actual war is far, far away.

Evelyn learned much more on this outing than she would have in a whole day of school.

On the way home, she begged me to take a little detour to see the ginkgo that Kathleen calls her tree. She and Slover liked to spend time there. It is full with new summer foliage. Truly lovely!

1943 June 8
Kathleen
Lysol

Dear Euleta,

When I got your letter, you can't imagine how glad I was. Letters are always welcome, especially when I am down in the dumps. I certainly am now since Walter has been gone almost nine months! So, keep writing, please.

I have been roasting all day. I wanted to go swimming, but I couldn't get anyone to go with me. Another handicap of being minus a husband.

How are you and Maxine getting along? I would be delighted if you two and Mom could come to visit again.

Mama and I went to church tonight for a service conducted by soldiers. A private sang "Ave Maria," and it was lovely. Boy, could he sing! The leader of the singing was a former Chicago choirmaster. So many men pulled from their former lives by war.

A girl I went to school with committed suicide Thursday night. They say it was accidental but she went to gargle with some Listerine but drank a bottle of Lysol. She must have been pretty drunk not to notice the awful taste. She had been unhappy ever since her parents would not acknowledge her marriage to a doctor's son and had it annulled. That could have been the reason.

So much sadness in this world. The war, of course, but also the miserable things that happen to people here. A woman died when her car hit a train. Sometimes I just can't stand it, and I just sit and stare at the wall. (Letter never sent.)

1943 July 11
Ethel
Anything, Anywhere, Anytime, Bar Nothing

The swing's rusty chain squeaks in time to the radio's gospel song flowing from the front room. The front door and windows are open. It is hotter than blue blazes. The children have gone to White Lake.

I doze in the heat until Lenna Kelly steps onto the porch. "Hey, Ethel. What cha'up to?"

I'm not in the mood for talk, but I invite her to sit. She starts in with a story she heard at church about the girl who died last month from drinking Lysol. "You know, Ethel, I heard she did it on purpose and that she was pregnant!"

"I don't know about that, Lenna. Why don't we just let the poor thing rest in peace. Bless her heart."

I change the subject. "We got a letter from Buck. He is in a tent city in Atlanta. He said he is living like an Indian! Ha, ha." I pull a photo out of my apron pocket. "Look what he sent us."

"He looks good, Ethel. His glasses are different and maybe he is a little heavier."

"Polly misses him so much. She has moved back in with her folks. Buck is training with the US Army Ordnance Corps."

"What in the heck is that, Ethel?"

"When he goes over yonder, he will supply combat troops with weapons and ammunition."

"That sounds pretty safe. No fighting."

"Well, maybe, but he'll still have to go to the battlefields to take supplies."

"What do you hear from the other boys?"

"Roger is still in medic school in New York. Jimmie is bombing in Sicily and Italy. Now that the Germans have given up in North Africa, Slover is in Sicily,

234

too. Got to get the Germans out of there too. They are just like nasty roaches, crawling from one place to the next!"

Pulling another picture from my pocket, "Look, Lenna. Kathleen got a picture of Walter's helmet. The Ninth Division's new commanding general Patty Flint painted this on his helmet, and now his soldiers are doing the same."

She squints at the picture. Three big A's separated by hyphens with a bar through them and a big O at the end.

"What do the markings mean, Ethel?"

"They stand for 'Anything, Anytime, Anywhere Bar, Nothing.' I reckon that is what all our boys are doing over there. As Slover said before he left, 'Whatever it takes.' So brave. And so scary, Lenna. What a sacrifice out boys are making."

1943 July 24
Evo
Leslie Howard

I'm at the Confederate Home to visit Ada and Mary. They want me to call them by their first names, but Mama says I should add "Miss."

"Oh, Evo. What a treat to see you!" Miss Ada struggles out of her chair and gives me a big hug that just goes on and on. "Oh, sorry, Mary is taking a nap. She has been doing right poorly. Come sit a spell."

She pulls *Life Magazine* into her lap and opens it to a dog-eared page. "Oh, Evo, look! Handsome Ashley Wilkes died today in a plane crash!" Miss Ada is going round the bend a little. This was old news about the actor Leslie Howard.

I don't correct her. "Yes, I know, Miss Ada. So sad."

"Oh, yes, he should have married Scarlett, and then she would not have ended up with that awful Rhett Butler! But instead, he became a spy. The Germans shot his plane down." She confuses the character and the actor.

I think the spy part may have been true because Leslie spoke out against the Germans and even went to Spain to try to convince them not to help the Germans.

I don't stay very long because Miss Ada nods off while I am telling her about *These Happy Golden Years,* the latest *Little House on the Prairie* book, and how Laura falls in love with Almanzo. I guess my summary is boring.

On my way home, I take a short cut by the hospital down Bradford to McGilvary Street.

I see something real strange! I see a girl and boy kissing on a bench under the big ginkgo tree. The girl turns her head my way. Holy cow! It is that Barbara girl who works with Kathleen! I want to snatch her up and jerk her baldheaded! Her husband is off in the war! I will tell Kathleen about it.

When I get home, the mail has just come, and Kathleen got two letters from Slover. She lets me read them! He is in Sicily now. I get out the map to see where it is. Near Italy where Jimmie is. Maybe they can meet up!

Slover asked Kathleen to send him a wrist watch. Not much other interesting stuff. Just how much he would like to have Mama's cooking and, of course, mushy stuff about Kathleen.

1943 August 20
Kathleen
Wounded

A letter from Mom brought the news:

Dear Kathleen, Walter is OK, but he has a been wounded. We got a telegram yesterday. He has a small wound in his leg but will recover fully. He must have thought it better to send to me than having a telegram arrive at your house.

She included the news article from the *Sullivan Times*:

Walter Slover Serves in Sicily; Is Wounded and Decorated

Word was received today that First Sgt. Walter Slover had been awarded the Purple Heart for valor after having suffered a shrapnel wound in the leg.
Sgt. Slover, the son of Mrs. Verna Slover of Shelburn and the late Ernest C. Slover, is serving with the United States Army in Sicily. He landed with the first forces in North Africa where he was sent from England. He enlisted as an infantry soldier in the Army three years before Pearl Harbor. Sgt. Slover attended Shelburn Schools and is twenty-three years of age. Most of his Army life before the war had been spent at Fort Bragg, N. C., where he married Kathleen Brantley. He is a brother of Miss Euleta Slover, Times advertising manager. August 17, 1943.

I know the news could have been worse, but I can't calm my shaking.

1943 September 11
Evo
Kewpie Doll

I just celebrated my twelfth birthday! It is Saturday, and I want to do something grown up. Mama is getting a little less strict with where I go and what I do. At last!

Edna came by around ten to bring me a present. She knows just what I like: *The Great Gatsby* by Mr. F. Scott Fitzgerald. My English teacher said it is trash and that F. Scott lived a scandalous life. Of course, this made me want to read it all the more!

Edna and I decide to go to town. I have birthday money from Doris and Kat, and it's burning a hole in my pocket. Mama's busy canning some late beans from the Victory Garden and is distracted in the kitchen, so I just yell, "Edna and I are going out." Her "be particular" floats into the front room, and we take off. She doesn't ask where we are going. She probably thinks we were going to Edna's. That's not a real lie.

On the way down Roberson street, I have an idea. "Edna, let's go by Janie Ringo's and ask if Abby can go with us." She is nine, and we like to play with her. Edna agrees, and we knock on Janie's door, and Abby answers.

"Hey, Edna. Hey, Evo. Would you girls like to come in and play?

"No, Abby," I say. "We were wondering if you would like to go to town with us?"

"Well, yes! But I will have to ask Mama." Janie comes out of the kitchen wiping her hands on her apron. Abby can't wait to ask her, "Mama, Mama, Mama! Edna and Evo want me to go to town with them!"

"Do your Mama's know you're going?"

I hesitate a bit but then decide to outright lie. "Oh, yes, Janie. I am twelve now, and Mama says I am big enough now to do things on my own. And Edna is almost thirteen, too." No, not a true lie because I just let Janie assume that I have permission. No harm in that.

"Happy birthday, child. You are getting to be a big girl, Miss Evelyn. Ok, Abigail, you can go but be on your best behavior and do what Miss Evelyn and Miss Edna tell you to. And look both ways when you cross a street. When you come back, I'll have a birthday cookie for you, Evo." I wonder how she always has a cookie or two since the family is so poor.

So off we go with Abby skipping happily beside us. When we get to the stores on Hay Street, we peer into windows and point out things we would like to have if we could afford them. Abby takes a shine to a little celluloid kewpie doll at Woolworth's. It is cute with its shy smile and little pointy head. We go in to see it, and it costs only twenty cents.

Abby picks it up to admire it and runs her hands all over it. "I wish I could take some scraps and make her a little dress, so she wouldn't be naked." Yes, she certainly could because she is very creative and has learned sewing from her mama.

Abby doesn't get toys except for maybe one at Christmas. I stick my hand in my pocket and feel the crisp, two folded dollar bills of my birthday money. Before I realize it, I say to Abby, "I want to buy that for you, Abby. I have money with me."

"Oh, no, Evo. I couldn't let you do that. You might need your money for something else."

"No, Abby. We are getting it." I pull out one of my dollars and hand it to the clerk. She hands me back a half dollar, a quarter, and a nickel and the kewpie in a little paper bag which I hand over to Abby.

The clerk makes a little frown and says, "Why are you buying that little pickaninny a toy?"

My face begins to feel warm, and I don't know what to say. I feel bad for Abby. I want to hit that clerk.

240

Edna rescues me. "Let's go, girls. We've got to get home for lunch." We can't get out of there fast enough. We don't look back, but I feel the wave of hate following us. The joy of the doll has been stolen from Abby, and she will think of the name calling every time she looks at it.

We keep walking by the stores but don't look in anymore. Abby looks like she might cry. I want to tell her what I read in the *Encyclopedia Britannica* about that word the clerk called her. It was a form of the word "pequenino" which means in Portuguese "small child." Some slave traders from Portugal used it. But I don't tell Abby about the word because it might make her feel even worse to think about slavery.

I have to do something to cheer her up. We are just outside the Carolina Soda Shoppe as an idea pops into my head. "Hey, girls, I am hungry. It is close to lunch time. Let's go in and get a sandwich and a Coca - Cola. I will pay."

"No, Evo," pleads Abby. "I am not really hungry, and I don't think that is a very good idea."

"Well, I do, and I can't think of a better way to celebrate my birthday and spend some of my birthday money than to have lunch with my two best friends."

Ignoring Abby's protests, Edna and I each take one of her hands and pull her into the Soda Shoppe. We walk up the counter and plop ourselves on three of the high red leather covered, silver-legged stools.

Then...I realize we have made a mistake. Immediately heads turn and eyes stare and the big, sweaty cook storms over from the grill and places his meaty hands on the counter in front of us.

He scowls and spits out, "What in the Sam Hill do you think you are doing?"

"Uhm...we just want to order some sandwiches and Coca - Colas."

He stares harder. "You two white girls can order. But the little nigger needs to get out. Now!" Glaring at Abby, "Get your little black butt off my stool."

Abby slides off her stool and backs out of the shop. Two teenagers spit at her and hiss. Big tears are sliding across her face. Edna and I jump off our stools.

The cook bellows at us. "You two can stay and eat and take something outside to the little nigger." He flicks his thumb toward Abby as she exits.

We're not hungry anymore. "No, thank you." We leave.

We catch up with Abby who is running hard. She is crying full out now. We are halfway home before we realize that she left her kewpie on the counter.

I want to run back to the Carolina Soda Shoppe and get the doll and tell that man that Abby is my friend and that I love her and how dare he talk to her like that. And I want to spit back at those teenagers. But I don't go back. Abby probably never wants to see another kewpie doll. I know I don't. And I will never go in the Carolina Soda Shoppe again even if they give away free milkshakes!

When we get back to Janie's, we have sucked in our tears, but Janie notices immediately that something is wrong. "Lord! What is wrong with you girls? You look like someone done stole your joy! Did some mean boys chase you? Come in the kitchen and tell me what happened?"

Over cookies which aren't real sweet thanks to rationing, we spill out our story, piece by piece.

Janie listens patiently. "Lord have mercy! You girls should know how things are. White people sell to Negroes, but they don't want to see us shopping with whites like we are equals. And no Negro can eat in a white restaurant."

"But, why, Janie? And why do people have to be so mean?"

"Not sure, Miss Evelyn. Maybe just because they can."

1943 October 1
Kathleen
War Souvenir

It's my birthday. I am nineteen years old. A good birthday present arrived. A letter from Walter reassuring me that he is OK after his wound.

> *My Darling Wife,*
> *I am fine after my little leg wound. A piece of shrapnel went in my leg bone. The doctors decided it could just stay there with no problem. Hey, I will always have a war souvenir with me!*
> *You remember Sgt. Darling from my unit? He was killed in the same battle where I was wounded. Damn, I miss him. So, I am pretty lucky.*
> *I am resting up in a tent hospital. I can walk fine but the doctors want the wound all healed and my leg working fine before I can get back into combat. I am itching to get back in the fight and finish this thing off in Sicily.*

I am overflowing with relief and fear at the same time. Fate gives one man a small wound, and another is killed. Just a matter of where the solider is standing as the bullets fly. Oh, God! How I wish Walter's injury would have sent him home!

1943 November 11
Kathleen
Armistice

There is a church service tonight to honor those who died in the last war since this is the anniversary of the day the Armistice was signed. Pastor Gaines wants to remember our men who are in war now and pray for them.

I asked Barbara to go with me. She wanted to go instead to the Broadway to see *Casablanca*. I shamed her into going to church by saying we should support our men.

Barbara seems to know everybody in town, especially men. We pause to chat with some. Barbara is flirty for a married woman. She makes me nervous, and the men look at me in a way that makes me more nervous. Some men were disqualified for service for health reasons. Like Tommy Bruce. I can't help but think of them as draft dodgers and cowards.

When we finally make it to the church, the service has started, and the choir is just finishing a hymn:

...Grant us wisdom, grant us courage,
For the facing of this hour,

Boy, do I need some of that courage. Walter has been gone over a year. He is going to England now that Sicily is over. I am mad that the Army is just fixing him up to send back for the next conflict. I can't get relief from the anxiety that makes me tense and my stomach churn. What will happen to him next? Buck and Roger believe there will be an invasion of France. The place of my dreams. Not the way I thought that beautiful country would impact my life.

Barbara's man is in Italy. She does not seem to worry at all about him. She actually dozed off during the sermon.

1943 December 24
Kathleen
I'll Be Home for Christmas

I'm staring at the Christmas tree in the dark. I can't sleep. The radio is low. Bing Crosby's "I'll Be Home for Christmas." Tears slip out of my eyes. My second Christmas without Walter.

I'm holding the little Christmas card he sent earlier in the month. Just a little V-Mail page with a smiling little cartoon solider. He's holding a paper that says, "Somewhere in Britain, December 25, 1943." I hold it to my nose hoping to drink the scent of Walter, but it just smells musty.

Doris got a card from Jimmie with a picture of a naked woman sitting on a bomb. We all got a little chuckle out of that, except for Mama who said it was scandalous.

I remember our first Christmas together when I sat on Walter's lap admiring my engagement ring. Everyone was jolly. Roger make a joke about how Walter will have the "old ball and chain" now. Evo sat beside Walter, her face shining with admiration. Walter gave her a little hug. That seems so long ago.

The padding of Mama's bedroom slippers intrudes on my thoughts. "Merry Christmas Eve, my sweet girl! Honey, let's go to the kitchen and start the biscuits. You need to practice so you will have them perfect when Walter gets home. I never saw a boy who could eat so many of them!"

Kathleen's scrapbook.

Maxine, Kathleen, Doris, Euleta

Kathleen and Mom Slover

Salutes for Walter

First Anniversary Card

Kathleen in snow

Buck in tent city in Atlanta

Walter's helmet
Anything, Anywhere, Anytime: Bar Nothing

The Brantley Family

Brothers in the service

Buck, Evo, and Roger

from Walter

from Jimmie

Mailing a letter to Walter

Roger

Bea Rogers and Ethel
By a roving photographer

247

1944 January 3
Kathleen
Little Moron Jokes

Another new year. So, what? I've nothing to celebrate. I try to find things to be happy about. I'm not doing very well. Just marking off the days.

I found no joy in Marj's latest letter. She's having a high time in school, partying, and ice skating! I resent her carefree life. She sent me some Little Moron jokes:

Why did the little moron take the hay to bed? He wanted to feed his nightmare.
Why did the little moron take his girl under the toadstool? He thought it was a mush room.

These are not funny! We started hearing them last year after a comic book called *The Little Moron* came out. It's heartless to make fun of a person of low intelligence. Our first sister Adele, who was not right, died two years before Daddy. She was always laughing when she wasn't supposed to, but she didn't know it wasn't right. Another part of Marj's letter made me even more depressed:

Lots more of our boys are being called to service. They take 'em right out of school if they aren't passing. Took a boy out of my class last Thursday. At Christmas, they took about one hundred and fifty out of Queen's University.

Oh, Lord have mercy! What if that happens here? But Gene makes good grades. Isn't it enough that we have given Walter, Jimmie, Roger and Buck to this mess?

1944 January 31
Doris
Sergeant Rice on the Beam

A long, exhausting day at Sears for monthly inventory. My feet are killing me as I walk home in the dark. Wish I had taken my car, but my gas ration ran out.

Evo is jumping up and down on the porch and waving the newspaper. "Look, look, look! Jimmie is in the paper!"

"Ok, girl. Let's get inside before you freeze your nose off."

Right on page two. There's my man! From the back. Just his helmet. And he is facing the plane's instrument panel:

Sergeant Rice On the Beam

Precision bombing two miles up, a B-25 Mitchell bombardment group reduces an enemy cruiser (the Tranato) in a Mediterranean port to a sunken hulk. Sergeant James C. Rice of Fayetteville participated in this effective pin point bombing mission. Mrs. Rice is with the local Sears-Roebuck store.

"We are winning, Doris! Jimmie is killing the enemy. I just know he will be home soon."

Evo pulls me and Kathleen off the sofa and starts dancing as "Boogie Woogie Bugle Boy" plays on the radio. Mama comes in from the kitchen, throws off her apron and dances with us!

A little moment of joy overtakes four war weary women.

1944 February 22
Ethel
The Wrong Side of the Road

Somewhere in England
412 February 1944

Dear Mama,

I received your two letters way over here in this country new to me. Hearing these people talk reminds me of my English class in high school. Reading those English stories. Can't quite grasp the feeling that I'm really over here. As I heard one guy say, I only thought things like this happened in movies.

Seeing the cars whiz by each other on the wrong side of the road to us. You think they're going to crash. I've seen some of the most beautiful country there is, I believe. Boy, if I had a camera, I could bring some real pictures back home. Maybe someday I can tell you all about it. Tell Kathleen that I'll be on the lookout for Slover. Love, Buck

Slover told Kathleen that he does not like England. Except that he can understand "some" of what the people say. I'm happy that these two boys are in a safe place for now.

I heard a woman in line at the grocery tell another, "The English say Americans stationed in their country are 'over sexed, over paid, and over here.'" Can't imagine this is true. Not good American boys.

1944 March 14
Kathleen
Somewhere in Limey Land

Walter writes of the constant rain and fog in England which he calls "Limey Land." We have misty weather here too which mirrors the fog in my head. My body aches, and my arms and legs feel like floppy noodles. A constant nagging pain in my lower back makes sitting uncomfortable. I cannot shake the sadness. Mama says maybe spring will help me feel better.

I told Walter of my suspicions about Barbara cheating. His reply:

> *Her husband is sure going to be hurt when he comes home to find that out after going through all the hell. But, honey, I hear men telling stories like that every day and I just think how lucky I am to have a wife like you waiting for me. That is the thing that either makes a soldier or breaks him. I have seen men go all to pieces when they get news like that from home.*

How can women do this to their husbands or boyfriends? I could never betray Walter. I hope I'm wrong about Barbara.

In a book of Edna St. Vincent Millay's love letters, I read this:

> *Where you used to be, there is a hole in the world, which I find myself constantly walking around in the daytime and falling in at night. I miss you like hell.*

Yes, Miss Millay, that is exactly the feeling. The big hole that's always there, and I can't get out.

251

1944 April 12
Kathleen
The Meet Up

Happy news from Buck!

Well, at last Sis I have found your long-lost husband. I spent two of the happiest hours tonight with him. I think he was as happy to see me as I was him. He looks good, I hardly recognized him. He is fleshier than I thought he used to be. Just as good looking as ever.

Had quite a time getting together. We met at the Red Cross in a small town. It is a long story, so I will tell you later. It is awful late now, and I am plum wore out. But I just had to write you and tell you not to worry about him. He is just the same nice fellow you let go to war.

I do feel better knowing that my husband and my brother were together. Good to be reassured.

I worry that Walter will be a different person when he comes home. I hear stories of returning soldiers being messed up in their minds.

I have trouble remembering his smile and the sound of his laughter. He has been gone far longer than the time I knew him before. What if we don't even like each other anymore?

1944 April 23
Evo
Crash Over Denmark

It's Sunday afternoon, and we have to sit around and visit. I'm usually bored to death. But not today!

Mrs. Todd from church came to tell us about her cousin who is a bombardier. Just like Jimmie. His plane took off from England to drop bombs on Berlin. But the plane was shot down and crashed in Denmark. The crew jumped out. Four died. Two were captured by Germans. Three others, including Mrs. Todd's cousin, landed on a farm.

Mrs. Todd jabbers on about her cousin when he was a little boy. And about his mama and sisters. I am on pins and needles to know what happened to her cousin.

Finally! She gets back to the story. A boy about my age rode his bike to the crash and found the men! They burned their parachutes, so the Germans could not find them. The boy had learned English in school, and his father who was a sheriff told the boy to help them. They were taking a big chance because there is a death penalty for helping Americans! The boy hid them in the woods. Then, he took them to a school where a teacher put them in the cellar.

Mrs. Todd gets off the subject again about another letter she got from the cousin's mother.

"But Mrs. Todd, what happened after the cellar?" Mama cuts her eyes at me. Children should never interrupt adults.

"Well, Evelyn. The resistance sneaked them off to Sweden. Then to England."

Wow! I wish I could go over there and work for the resistance. All this excitement. And I'm just collecting dang tin cans.

1944 May 6
Kathleen
Champagne

"What do you mean you aren't going?" Barbara can't believe I am not attending the party celebrating the bank's great first quarter of profits.

"No, I would just be a wet blanket, Barbara." The idea of circulating in the Prince Charles banquet room, making chit chat and watching the bosses pat each other on the back has no appeal for me. And there'll be lots of drinking and loose talk, and I don't drink. I would not go for love nor money.

"Come on, Kat. You need to stop your moping around and have a little fun."

I just don't know how Barbara can be so happy when her man is over there in England training for the invasion.

"I'm not taking no for answer. I will stop by your house at five o'clock. Fix yourself up nice."

"No, Barbara, I am NOT going."

Barbara knocks on the door at five sharp. "Surely, girl, that is not what you are wearing!" She makes her way in and drags me to the bedroom. I don't have the energy to argue with her. She picks out my pink Easter dress from last year, puts on my make up (too heavily), and pins my hair into fresh victory rolls.

Evo sits on the bed and watches my transformation. "You look so pretty, Kathleen."

The party isn't as bad as I thought. I get lots of compliments from men on my outfit. I hate to admit it, but I do enjoy it. It feels good to be in a gay place with lots of laughter. I relax for the first time in weeks.

Barbara keeps tabs on me as she whirls around the room, flirting and chatting louder as she drinks a glass of something pale yellow. "Come on, gal. Have a drink. You need to loosen up a bit."

She lifts a sparkling glass of champagne from the waiter's tray. *Ok, Kathleen, try it, Just this once. It might make you feel better.* The taste is sharp at first, but the more I drink, the better it tastes.

My head swirls a bit, and I start to feel good. Then, I have another glass. By the time the party is over, I have had three.

Tommy Bruce, who was invited to the party because he is a good bank customer, saunters over to Barbara and me. "Hey, girls. Let me take you home in my car. You look a little woozy. Wouldn't want you to stumble and fall on Hay Street."

"Thanks, Tom. But I am going out with a few of the cashiers before I go home." I hear Barbara through the haze that has taken me over.

"Well, how about you, Frenchwoman?" Tommy offers.

I don't remember saying yes, but before I know it, Tommy has his hand under my elbow and is escorting me to the parking lot.

How we end up sitting on the sofa in his apartment is a mystery. His arms are around me, and he is kissing me. It feels good to be held, and I give into the kisses.

"No! Stop that! I'm going home!" And I stand up, wobbling, as a wave of nausea sweeps over me. I throw up right in his lap.

"Whoa, girl! Maybe I better take you home."

"No, I will walk."

"You are in no condition to walk."

The next thing I know, I am home. I don't remember the car ride or going in the house or getting in bed with my clothes still on.

1944 May 8
Kathleen
Monday Morning

"So, girl, I heard you made quite a stir at Tom's!"

"Shhh, Barbara. Don't tell everyone in the bank! How do you know about it?"

"Tom came to the bar after he took you home and told me every detail. He said you are a pretty good kisser, even when you are drunk. You know, too bad you upchucked and ruined the evening. You could have had fun with Tom."

I stand up and put my arms under her elbows. "Look, Barbara. Last night was a big mistake. That is why alcohol is evil. It led me to do something I would have never done sober. I'm embarrassed and sorry, and nothing like this will ever happen again!"

She draws close to my ear. "Well, you missed a good time. After the bar, I went to his apartment and … Just use your imagination. He is a fabulous lover."

I pull back and stare in her laughing eyes. "Barbara. Listen carefully. I would never cheat on Walter. Stop trying to drag me into things. What you do is your own business, but you are on dangerous ground."

I turn, sit at my desk, and start typing. My temporary alcohol-induced feel good has left me even more sad and fearful. And my head is throbbing.

Last night I escaped discovery by Doris, Evo, and Mama. They were all long asleep when I slid into bed. I awoke with a start hours later and and changed into my nightgown.

I hope they never find out what I did. I'm afraid because you can't do anything in this town without gossip following you.

1944 June 6
Ethel
D-Day

I'm sweating over the ironing board and listening to *The Guiding Light* that Doris and Kathleen got me into. I'm about to start Evelyn's Girl Scout blouse as Rev. Ruthledge is warning a church member about the mortal sin she is committing by having an affair with a married man. A loud voice breaks in and interrupts the story:

> *Flash! Flash! Allied troops landed on the Normandy coast of France in tremendous strength by cloudy daylight today and stormed several miles inland with tanks and infantry in the grand assault which Gen. Dwight D. Eisenhower called it a crusade in which "we will accept nothing less than full victory." First reports of the invasion came through German sources but now the action has been confirmed by U. S. news services.*

Sweet Jesus! It has come at last. I give a little whoop before I think of the loss of life that will surely come. I fall to my knees and pray.

The front door flies open and Doris, Kathleen, and Evelyn rush in. "Mama, all the stores have closed, and school has let out and everyone is going to church to pray! Come with us!" Doris is flushed with excitement, but Kathleen is crying.

I wrap her up with my love. "Slover is strong and smart and brave. If he is with the invasion, he will fight and win and come back to you."

I turn off the iron, grab my purse, and we head to the church through growing crowds on the street. A car is clattering down Roberson Street on its rims! No new tires can be had thanks to rationing! The people inside waving a flag and blowing the horn. This war better be over soon, or we will all be riding on rims!

First Baptist sanctuary was filled to capacity with folks, some shouting and some crying. Pastor Gaines quiets the crowd and offers prayers for the success of the invasion, the safety of our men, and the French people.

When we get home, Rose Patterson calls me. "Oh, Ethel! Do you think this day means our boys will come home soon? We are wondering if my Willie Jane's fiancé was in the invasion. And how about Slover?"

"I pray that they are safe, Rose, and I'm excited that the Allies are moving in on the Germans in France. Maybe by Christmas …?"

I met the Patterson family at White Lake before Wesley passed. Wes and I had a rare day all to ourselves and we drove there in his Swift and Company truck for some relaxing.

We'd just laid our blanket under the pine trees when Rose and Lennie arrived and spread theirs in a nearby spot. They had their children Willie Jane, Bob, and baby John with them.

Rose smiled at me. "How're y'all doin' today?" She was so pretty and small. I felt like a giant when I walked over and exchanged greetings with her.

As we were finishing our lunch, Rose offered us some pound cake. We couldn't resist because it looked so good. Let me tell you, that was the best cake I'd ever tasted! Wish we had been able to share something with them, but all we brought was two baloney sandwiches.

We chatted while we rested before swimming. We didn't want anyone to get leg cramps and drown. Of course, I never go in the water myself. I just dangle my legs off the pier.

Lennie told us about his grocery store and Rose's cafe next door in Roseboro. What hard working folks they are! Rose is so sweet, and Lennie has a great sense of humor. He and my Wes really got along as Wes could be pretty funny himself.

When Wesley passed, they came to the house and brought us some of Rose's delicious food and returned for the funeral.

They guessed right that we were having a tough time financially with no man to earn money. They gave us food from the store several times after rationing began. I wish I had some way to pay them back, but they always said that it was their pleasure to share with friends. After the war is over, I will!

1944 June 28
Kathleen
Cherbourg

I am up early as usual to get the *Raleigh News and Observer* as soon as Frankie pitches it to our porch from his bicycle. Since *The Fayetteville Observer* publishes only an afternoon edition, and there were no invasion updates yesterday. I am mad to know where Walter's division is fighting in France.

I run to the porch swing, plop down, and quickly unroll the paper to the front page. The lead article:

Allies Continue Push into to Normandy: First Victory

The first decisive victory of the Allied invasion of Normandy came yesterday when Supreme Headquarters announced that General Omar Bradley's famous and tough Ninth Division has smashed its way across the neck of the Cherbourg peninsula and has massacred the German Seventy-Seventh Division that tried to break out of the steel trap.

My heart beats fast as I read this news of Walter's division! So now, at least, I know where he headed after landing on Utah Beach on June tenth. Other Allied forces are heading toward Paris.

Maybe this war will end soon, and my man will be home for Christmas!

My heart is wrapped around him. I wish I could touch him.

1944 July 10
Evo
Summertime and the Living is Hard

Sweat rolls off my neck and down between my shoulders as I pull butter beans from a bush in Grandma Coggins' big garden.

Mama and Doris left me here for a week to pick stuff and pull corn. Me and my cousins have to chase cows out of the cornfield, so they won't crunch ears right off the plant. Actually, it is pretty swell to watch them chew and see the white corn milk drip out of their jaws. When you shoo them away, they just move to another spot. Grandpa needs to put up more fences.

While I am working, I think of Slover over there in France and wonder if he will come home soon now that the Allies have invaded. He was in the paper for getting a medal for fighting in North Africa and Sicily. I bet he has shot a lot of Germans.

What would it feel like to kill somebody? I think I could do it if a Nazi was going to shoot me. I wish I could learn to shoot a real gun. Maybe Slover will teach me when he gets home.

Grandma rings the bell for dinner, and in my hurry to get there, I almost step on a snake curled up on the edge of my butter bean row. I jump but don't scream because the cousins would make fun of me. It's a good snake, probably a corn snake.

I am the first to the table and spy a big bowl of apples sitting to the side by a pie plate which grandma is most likely planning to use for an apple pie. I want one so bad. No one is looking, so I grab one. I start in and gobble the whole thing, skin, seeds, stem and core. I don't want to throw any part of it into the trashcan because Grandma might find it and be mad. What's one less apple in a pie?

But I get caught. Grandma spies juice dripping down my chin. She just laughs. "Evelyn Lou, you stay out of my cooking apples. You will get a smaller piece of pie."

I didn't get off so easy at home when I took sips from the Pepsi-Cola Gene had bought with his photo shop earnings and left in the ice box. I only took little sips, but he noticed the difference and yelled at me pretty good. Next time I will replace my swig with a little water.

After dinner, Grandma sends all the cousins down to the pond for a little swim before we pull some corn. The cool water feels so good in the heat. We splash and dive and float on our backs until Victor spots a water moccasin sliding off the bank and heading our way. We clamor out and lay down under the weeping willow tree.

My eyes are heavy, and I fall asleep until Grandma marches down the hill as the sun is falling lower and sends us off to the cornfield. Look out, cows, here we come!

1944 July 21
Doris
Hitler Assassination Attempt

Damn! Some German civilians and military officials failed in another attempt to kill the demon!

There were two bombs in a briefcase under Hitler's table, but the briefcase got moved under a heavy table leg. One bomb went off, but the other one did not and the blast was not enough to kill him or even injure him much. Had the plot been successful, maybe this nightmare would end, and my Jimmie would be home!

Kathleen and I continue to search every word of Slover and Jimmie's letters for some clue as to where they are. Jimmie gives me a bunch of description of the Italian countryside and some of the food he gets on leave that sounds delicious. But that is just about it.

Slover says they are beating the Germans back toward their own grounds and the war could be over soon. He is sending home a German flag he took in Cherbourg and will tell us the history behind it when he gets home.

I'm worried about Kathleen. She tries to be strong and positive, but sometimes her nervous side just takes over. Last night after we crawled into bed, she said, "Doris, I don't think I will see Walter again." And cried herself to sleep.

1944 July 31
Kathleen
Cpl. Ammirato

This was enclosed in Walter's last letter:

Cpl. Vincent Ammirato
c/o Dept. of patients
21ˢᵗ General Hospital
A.P.O. #700 U.S.

Hello Sgt. Slover,
I suppose you are surprised to receive this letter from me. I don't know how I got here but here I am being treated for injuries. I don't know how long I'll be here.
There is one thing about you that I'll never forget, Sgt. Slover. And that is the way you went over to pick up Lt. Robertson when he got hurt. You actually went to him under fire and risked your life to help him. While I stayed in my hole looking on. I'm so disgusted with myself for it.
But I envy you doubly so because you helped a man who unwittingly argued with you all the time. That is something very few people can do. I always admired you as a fine soldier, but now I'm more convinced. And finally, I must admit that sometimes I used to think you were unkind to the men and you did not have a heart. But after what I saw of you in action, you must have a heart for a helpful deed.
All I can say is that even though it is against your wishes that they make you an officer, I am positive you will go up the ladder so quickly that an extension of the ladder will have to be made for you to reach where you will go.

How is your wife? Have you received any mail? Give my regards to your wife, for after all I met her when she was at Fort Bragg on the day before we left.

Will you do me a favor, Sgt. Slover? Will you tell Franklin to send me my mail? And why not drop me a line?

Well, I'll close and wish you the best of luck and quick return, for I know your wife must need to see you again

Sincerely yours, Vincent

I'm so terrified to think of Walter doing something so foolhardy as going out of his fox hole under fire that I can't even be proud of his bravery. I feel ashamed of myself.

I also received a package today. A big Nazi flag with a note asking me to take good care of it because Walter shot it down from the city hall in Cherbourg when his unit helped free the city and open the port.

1944 August 1
Evo
Color Guard

School starts again next month, and I can't wait. I'm sick of this hot, hot summer. Nothing to do. Edna has gone with her family to the mountains, so I don't even have a friend to be miserable with me. Almost too hot to even read, and I can't find a cool place in the house to do it. Sweat, sweat and more sweat!

I'm going to try out for the color guard for the high school band. Yes, I will officially be in high school in September! I attended the informational meeting last Tuesday. Some of the older girls gave a demonstration. They had colorful flags that they whipped around while they were marching in step. Beautiful!

Tut McFarland, a senior, explained that we must be able to march to the rhythm and handle the flag without dropping it. And if we are serious about joining the guard, we should go home, make ourselves a flag and practice. I will do that. I can get a big stick from of one limbs of the chinaberry tree out back. Maybe Gene will help me to smooth the wood out, and Mama has plenty of leftover fabric scraps.

Tut said that there would also be positions for majorettes to twirl batons.

I raise my hand. "How can we make a baton? There is no extra metal anywhere." The last time Edna and I pulled the old red wagon through the neighborhood, Mrs. Loy added an old metal curtain rod that would have been perfect cut in half. Dang! Had I known then what I know now, I would have saved it. No, I wouldn't. That would be unpatriotic!

Tut, who is so smart and has ideas about everything, replied, "Well...I think we could use wooden broom handles, then put rubber balls on the ends and paint them silver."

I would never have thought of that.

I do so admire Tut. Her father died when she was very young, just like my Daddy. She is so independent, and nothing scares her. She volunteers at the USO and visits wounded soldiers at the Veterans Hospital just across the street from the cemetery. I guess if a soldier dies, they don't have far to go to bury him.

After the meeting, I run all the way home to look for color guard material.

1944 August 2
Ethel
Flag

I am cleaning up the lunch dishes and thinking about asking Bea Rogers if she can take me to Roseboro for lunch in Rose Patterson's café and a little shopping in Lennie's store. Seeing sweet Rose will give me a little cheer up.

Land o'Goshen! I look out the back window and see a flash of purple waving wildly and Evelyn's arms flaying a stick and legs dancing crazily across the yard! The chickens are squawking in fear. What in the Sam Hill is she doing and isn't that the purple cotton I just bought at Penny's to make Kathleen a cheer up dress?

I can't dash out the screen door fast enough. "What are you doing, girl, and why is my new cloth on that stick?"

She does not see or hear me, so I holler louder, "Stop!" She does and looks at me like I am crazy because I screamed so loud. "What in the world are you doing?"

"Practicing, Mama. I want to be in the color guard at school and march at the football games with the band. Tut told us if we really want to do this, we need to go home and make a flag and practice the steps."

"So, who gave you permission to use my cloth? I don't remember you asking me if you could have the purple."

"Oh, Mama, I was in a hurry to get started, so I looked through your scraps and found this." She waves the flag skyward. "Doesn't it look beautiful?"

"Evelyn Lou Brantley! That fabric is not a scrap. It is for Kathleen's new dress. And how dare you take it without asking!"

"Oh, Mama, I am sorry. I will put it back."

"Child, what were you thinking? Three yards of material is not a scrap. Let me see that thing."

The material will never be a dress. I spy the remainder of the cloth after she cut her flag out lying in the corner of the yard by the chicken coop. The flag is nailed to the stick, and there are holes and triangular shapes cut out of it.

"Evelyn, there is no way I can use this to sew a dress. Where was your mind when you did this? An almost thirteen-year-old girl should know better than to ruin a perfectly good piece of cloth with this foolishness. Go over to the forsythia bush and pull off a switch."

The girl saunters across the yard to the bush which has long ago lost its yellow blooms. She snaps off a branch and walks to me, head down, and tears starting.

"Turn around, girl." I trash her legs with the switch. She cries.

"Stop. Or I'll give you something to cry about! Now get in the house and go to your room! You will do extra chores until you work out the cost of the material."

"Oh, Mama, I am sorry. I so wanted to be in the color guard." She takes her tears into the house as the broken screen door bounces on its hinges.

1944 Aug 11
Ethel
Rose, Lennie, and Willie Jane

Bea Rogers is driving me to Roseboro to see Rose and Lennie Patterson.

Roseboro is not much of a town. Just one street of small businesses but bustling with activity today as it is Friday. Bea and I are to have lunch in the café, and then use some of our ration tickets to get some things in the store.

Rose comes right to the café door to greet us. Her big apron is dusted with flour. "I best not hug you, because I don't want to mess up your pretty frocks. Y'all come on in and sit, and Willie Jane will take your order."

Willie Jane is Rose's oldest at eighteen. Her sweetheart Ed Hyatt is overseas in the Navy. They plan to marry as soon as he gets home. Willie Jane is gorgeous with dark, reddish hair. She was named Willie after her grandmother Willie Ashley Pittman Floyd. I know she does not like that name, so I always try to remember to call her just Jane.

"Hello, Miss Ethel and Miss Bea. So good to see you here again." She hands us two menus.

"Oh, thank you, Will ... uh ... Jane. We are happy to see you. You get prettier all the time. What do you hear from your sweetie Ed?"

"Well, he took part in the invasion. He commanded an LST that carried troops ashore. I was so scared for him after I saw the newsreels of all the men who lost their lives just getting ashore and landing boats sinking. Oh, how I hope he'll be home for Christmas, and this horrible mess will be over."

"Oh, Jane, how terrible all this waiting for news is. We worry about Kathleen's Slover in France and our Doris's Jimmie flying in Italy. My Roger is in the US, thank goodness. He is in Nashville doing medical training.

Buck is in France providing supplies. We keep your Ed in our prayers along with our boys."

Rose's lunch is delicious. Baked chicken, dressing, green peas with pearl onions, and lemon chess pie. And sweet, sweet tea. Afterwards, we say good bye to Willie Jane and Rose and head next door to Patterson's Market.

Lennie is taking a phone order. "Well, hey there, Mrs. Dubose, you certainly do look stunning today. What can I get for you?"

This is Lennie's way, charming everyone with his banter and telling women he can't see how pretty they look. He hangs up and greets us. "Hello, ladies. You both look pretty as spring chicks."

We use ration tickets to purchase sugar, flour, some canned goods, and a little meat for stew which Lennie's son Bob wraps for us. Lennie advertises his meats as "tender as a mother's love" which they truly are.

Lennie continues to flatter us and make jokes while he gets our order ready.

"We best be on our way, Lennie. I need to get home and fix supper for my children who will be coming home from work and school soon."

"Y'all come back soon. It's always good to see you fine folks."

When I get home and unpack the bags, I discover that, in addition to what I ordered, there are some fresh late summer beans and peas, a few sticks of butter, and a jar of Rose's strawberry jam. What generous and kind people Lennie and Rose Patterson are.

I'm over the moon! The Allies have liberated Paris! The city I claimed as mine back in my high school days!

Now, perhaps I'll have a chance to visit after the war. Maybe Walter and I will vacation there, and it will be him, not the Frenchman of my childish daydreaming, who will glide with me down the Seine to dine in a quaint restaurant!

Of course, we would never have the money to make such a trip. That does not matter because the end of this nightmare is in sight! Perhaps after nearly two years apart, Walter and I will be together again.

With the help of the French resistance, Patton's Third Army, of which Walter's Ninth Division is a part, helped free the city. Maybe Walter is in Paris right now enjoying the celebration!

There are still some German snipers firing at groups of citizens, but many Germans have surrendered rather than die for Hitler. The Germans surrendered to the French, and General Charles de Gaulle has arrived to take control of the city. De Gaulle said that the enemy is "staggering, but he is not beaten yet. He remains on our soil. We will keep fighting until the final day, until the day of total and complete victory."

I can't wait to see the newsreels of the crowds along the Champs Elysees waving flags and cheering the passing jeeps filled with the victorious soldiers. Maybe I will spot Walter!

When I got to the bank this morning, Barbara grabbed and hugged me. "Oh, Kathleen! Paris is free! Our men will be coming home soon!"

"Yes, it is wonderful." I didn't want to squash her joy, but I doubt her expectations are true. The Germans still occupy other parts of France and Belgium. And Italy where Jimmie is. And then there is the fighting in the Pacific where our neighbor boy Billy Jennings is serving.

"Kat, don't you think that Hitler will just give up and surrender now?"

"Maybe so, Barbara, maybe so."

I settled in at my desk and started on the big stack of stenography notes to be transcribed into letters. Good to distract my mind from what may still lie ahead.

1944 September 11
Ethel
Danny Jennings

An unspeakable tragedy has struck one of our neighbor families. Worse even than the heartbreaking telegrams some of them have received about their solider boys.

A few weeks ago, the Jennings family was elated to receive news that their Danny was to be coming home from his service in the Pacific. Because of his long service, his medals earned, and his time in combat, he was eligible to come home before the war ends!

The newsreels have shown the horrors of the fighting and the cruelty of the Japanese. They knew that Danny was in the invasion of Guam earlier this year, but not much more about his whereabouts after. But all that mattered was that, finally, he was coming home!

The Jennings invited neighbors for a party to celebrate. They roasted hotdogs, and there was music and all of us were counting the days till Danny would return and we would have a bigger celebration. Mrs. Jennings was making a list of all Danny's favorite foods that she would prepare.

Danny's little brother William, who is Evelyn's age, was so excited that he could hardly contain himself. He had been walking up and down the streets and telling neighbors what he planned to do when Danny got home. Going to the high school field to toss the football. Building something in their father's woodworking shop. Asking Danny all about what it was like to be a soldier and if he killed any Japs. Going to the movies to see the new *Hopalong Cassidy* movie.

A telegram came saying he expected to arrive at the Fayetteville depot today. Mr. and Mrs. Jennings, along with William, waited to meet every train. Doris, Kathleen, and I went to the depot in the evening because we heard that Danny had not yet appeared. We thought we could help them pass the time, and we wanted to share their happiness

Finally, a train pulled into the station, and Danny stepped off with his duffle bag over his shoulder, looking so handsome in his marine uniform. William spotted him first and ran with open arms to his big brother. They all enveloped him in hugs.

But later, Mrs. Jennings said there was something strange about him. He just stood straight and did not respond. And when she looked into his familiar blue eyes, there was an emptiness as if he were looking at nothing. The light in him had gone out. She excused this to how tired he must have been.

Danny said he needed to stop in the restroom before they headed home, so we all sat down in the depot waiting room. He seemed to be taking a very long time. Finally, Mrs. Jennings told William to go check on his brother.

Just as William reached the door of the restroom, a loud crack shattered the air.

I thought a car had backfired or something was dropped from the unloading train.

No. William pushed open the door and screamed.

Heads turned to see William, mouth wide open, looking back at his mother. Then, sobs. Screams.

Mr. Jennings and a station attendant running to William.

The gaping door. On the floor, the beautiful boy Danny.

Next to his lifeless hand, a revolver. Blood.

I have no words to describe the scene. People crying or standing in silence or covering sobs with their hands or running outside. William, now on his knees, cradling the bloody head in his arms.

After a few minutes, police and ambulance attendants appeared.

What was once Danny, his parents' beloved son, the object of young Williams's worship, and a war hero, was gently lifted onto a stretcher and carried away.

A trail of blood followed.

I can't remember much about walking home or if we said anything on the way. Shock had numbed us.

Doris and Kathleen put their arms around each other and cried.

Why?

After all those days of danger when Danny could have been the successful target of a Japanese bullet or a bayonet? After he could have been captured and tortured? After he was safe in the arms of those who loved him?

Why?

1944 September 15
Kathleen
Closed Casket

Danny Jennings' funeral.

First Baptist Church full, even the balcony. The closed casket.

William trying to be stoic and honor his brother, but he wipes tears as he walks in behind the pallbearers.

Then to the cemetery. Soldiers around the casket fold the flag and present it to Mrs. Jennings. She breaks down.

And we all do.

This was not supposed to happen.

Danny was so young and vibrant. He was home and free to get on his life of promise. His own bullet ended that. Why?

Was war so awful that it ruined him, took his joy, and his ability to imagine a happy future?

I try to blot out the image of Walter running under fire when he rescued that lieutenant. Bullets whizzing. It would have been so easy for one to find him.

What if he comes home damaged like Danny and destroys himself?

My head spins, and my stomach churns, and my fog of despondency thickens.

1944 October 1
Kathleen
Ginkgo Return

It's my birthday, but I don't care. Walking home from work, my arms and legs are weak and tingly. I stumble over a crack in the sidewalk. My head aches.

I don't notice when I miss my turn on Roberson Street.

Before I realize it, I am at the hospital. And the ginkgo tree. I want to see its golden leaves and remember Walter and me there in the golden shower of tumbling leaves.

Too late. Early leaf fall. Only bare limbs against the empty, overcast sky.

Where is Walter and what trees can he see, if any? As far as I know, he is somewhere in Germany. That is all the detail his letters give. From the news, I think his unit might be in the Hurtgen Forest on the border with Belgium.

A forest. Images of dark fir trees on the newsreels. Soldiers, rifles in hand, plowing through the early snow.

As I stagger home, my mind goes to familiar fog.

After two years without Walter, it is hard to even remember his touch or his smile.

Like the ginkgo branches, I am empty.

1944 October 21
Doris
Rommel

Kathleen is in a state. Much worse than the time Slover wrote her that accusing letter when he was in South Carolina. At least then, she vented her emotions. She is in a distant place that I can't get into.

I dragged her to the movie this afternoon to see *To Have and To Have Not* with Bogart and Bacall. Hoped it would cheer her since it is set in France. Love affair between an American expatriate and a resistance leader.

She fell asleep. I didn't try to wake her. She hardly sleeps at night, so I figured she needed it more than the movie.

The newsreel had good news! German Field Marshall Erwin Rommel committed suicide. Slover's division fought him in North Africa. He was about to go on trial for plotting against Hitler.

The end of this thing has to be getting closer if Hitler's key men are faltering. Slover seems to think so. He writes from "somewhere in Germany" that he expects to be home soon, and he and Kat can take up their life where they left off. This news did not improve her mood.

1944 October 27
Kathleen
In a Family Way

I'm washing my hands in the ladies room.

The door flies open, and Barbara makes a bee line for the toilet. She throws up again and again. I hand her a wet paper towel, and she flushes the toilet. Probably another night out drinking. She wipes her face and straightens her blouse and skirt.

"Kathleen, I'm in a family way."

"No! Barbara, are you sure?"

"Yes. I went to a doctor in Raleigh. He can fix it."

"Who? Tommy?"

"Yes, I haven't been with anyone else."

I can't process this through my fog. I suspected she was fooling around with Tommy. Evo saw them kissing.

My indignation briefly turns to pity. I could be the one in this fix had I let myself go after the bank party. No, she should have known better!

"Barbara, you can't have an abortion! It is against the law and not safe. You could go away somewhere and put the baby up for adoption."

"Kathleen! Think! This baby will arrive in May. The war will surely be over before that, and Carl will be home. I can't keep this baby."

"Have you told Tommy?"

"Yes. He took me to that doctor, and he will pay for it. The doctor says it is perfectly safe. Or I might just do it myself."

"Oh, Barbara. There has to be another way. Give yourself some time to think."

"I can't wait, Kathleen. I will be showing, and everyone will know."

I hate Tommy Bruce, I hate Barbara's situation, and I hate this war. And the things that people do because of it.

1944 November 6
Kathleen
Barbara Missing

Barbara is not at work today.

I called her landlady who said she had not seen her all weekend. She went up and knocked on her door and got no answer.

She might have gone to that abortion doctor!

Where is she? Maybe she just went away somewhere to think and decide what to do about the baby.

Yes, that's it.

After work, I am on my way to her apartment. I struggle up McGilvary Street, and the tension in my arms and legs is worse than ever.

And my heart is sick with fear.

1944 November 6
Kathleen
The Bathtub

Two quilts cover me, but I can't stop shivering.

When I close my eyes, I see the blood pooling under Barbara's body.

Her skin is blue, and she does not move. An open coat hanger on the floor under her limp hand that hangs over the side of the tub.

Mama called Dr. Monroe who said I was in shock. I don't know about that, but I am so weak I can't get up and my heart is beating fast.

Doris sits by the bed. I don't speak but lean over the side of the bed and gag. Doris catches the vomit in a bowl and wipes my mouth.

Mama, wringing her hands, paces the room.

I sleep. I wake.

And the scene floods back. Barbara's landlady knocking on the door. No answer. More knocking and calling her name. The landlady's husband breaking down the door. More calling Barbara. Walking through the little sitting room and bedroom to the closed bathroom door. Pushing open the door.

Barbara.

The bathtub.

The blood.

My screaming.

I don't remember how I got home or who brought me here. I am helpless and sinking deeper and emptier into my bed of misery.

1944 November 10
Ethel
Natural Causes

Lord, what a week this has been!

On Monday evening a policeman brought Kathleen home after she discovered Barbara Emerson's body. She would not speak. The policeman helped me get her in bed, and then took me and Doris to the front room to tell us what happened.

I made Evelyn go into dining room, and I closed the double doors. Of course, she put her ear to the crack and heard every word. Explaining this to her was one of the hardest things I have ever had to do.

"Evelyn. Barbara died having a baby. The baby had just begun to grow, and something happened, and it died." I tried to be simple, but she had lots of questions.

"Mama, why was Barbara expecting a baby? How could it happen with her husband overseas? Why did the baby die? Why did Barbara die? What is an abortion?"

"That is enough, child. You don't need to know any more, and you will not tell anyone about this. If someone asks you, just say Barbara died of natural causes." That is what the paper reported:

Barbara Smith Emerson died on Monday of natural causes at her residence.

She was an employee of Fayetteville Industrial Bank.

She is survived by her parents, Mr. and Mrs. Herbert Smith of Atlanta and her husband Lieutenant Carl Emerson who is serving with the US Army in Italy.

Private services and burial will be in Atlanta.

That was all it said.

1944 December 17
Evo
Merry Xmas

Christmas in a week! I made paper chains and snowflakes. Doris bought bubble lights from Sears. She got a big discount since she works in the mail order department now. I love to watch them even though Mama won't let me keep them turned on very long.

Everyone is sad after the deaths of Danny and Barbara. I try to get Kathleen to laugh. But she won't even giggle during *Fibber McGee and Molly*. How can she keep a straight face when Fibber embarrasses the snooty Mrs. Abigail Uppington?

We've gotten Christmas cards, and I've lined them up on the telephone table. My favorites are the two Slover sent from Germany.

My Darling Wife,
Honey, I wish you a very happy Xmas and New Year. I pray that this thing will soon be over and we can be together for the next Xmas. I love you.
Your Husband, Slover

Mama and Doris didn't like spelling Christmas with an X. Mrs. Hall told us that the X stands for the Greek word for Christ. I like it. Merry Xmas!

The other card has a drawing of a soldier listing all the places he had served.

Some of the Japanese are being let go from the camps! Maybe Tomoko will be coming home! I am going to ask Mama if they can live with us when they come back.

1944 December 31
Kathleen
The Letter Box

New Year's Eve. My third one without Walter.

Some snappy swing music is playing, but it does nothing to improve my mood. I just want to go to bed and sleep, so at 7:30 I head for the bedroom.

I haven't heard from Walter lately. I pull out the box where I have saved all his previous ones and reread the one which that came a few days before Christmas:

Germany December1

My Darling Wife

Just a few lines to let you know I am okay. Miss you more all the time, love you more than ever.

Haven't received any mail from you in some time. I have never got any of my boxes yet but am expecting them any day.

Honey I am praying for the day I can hold you in my arms again.

Honey, I would like to have more pictures as soon as possible.

Well, honey, I am tired tonight so I will close. Remember my darling I love you.

Your husband, Slover

He repeats the same thing over and over, but I know he can't give any details of what he is doing in case the mail is intercepted by the enemy. It makes me so sad to think of him, probably in a cold, snowy foxhole without the treats I sent him. He must feel so alone. Me too.

I put away the box of letter, crawl under the covers, close my eyes, and try to sleep.

Kathleen, 1944
by roving photographer

sent to Walter

Doris working in Sears mail order

Jimmie in the news

Fayetteville train depot

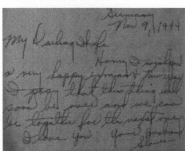

Christmas cards from Walter

Doris and Kathleen in the snow

Girls mailing letters to their soldiers

V for Victory

Easter

photo for Walter

Ethel

Lennie Patterson with
son Bob at White Lake.

Rose Patterson

1945 January 1
Ethel
Prayer Works

The beginning of the war's fourth year.

I prayed this morning that this will be the last. Slover, Jimmie, and Buck are all in the fight.

Doris, Kathleen, Evelyn, Polly, and me keeping the faith at home. Maybe we are fighting the war as much as our men. Newspapers and letters are all we have of them. Painful waiting. Making ends meet. Trying to find ways to help with rationing, scrap metal collecting, bandage rolling, buying war bonds even when we have little left at the end of the month.

So much hurt and fear in the faces of Doris and Kathleen. Especially Kathleen. I'm thinking of taking her to Sanford to our long-time family physician Dr. Morgan. He may know what to do to improve her mood. Some days she goes to work pretty upbeat, but others not so much. At home she sleeps too much and has little to say. And the constant, infernal twisting of her hair!

Evelyn, bless her heart, is our sole ray of light. Her antics keep us laughing, and she inspires us with her enthusiasm for supporting our men in uniform. Always the optimist, she expects her friend Tomoko to return to Fayetteville just as surely as she believes our boys will.

The paper published this Christmas card and prayer that General George Patton sent to his men.

Headquarters Third United States Army

To each officer and soldier in the Third United States Army, I wish you Merry Christmas. I have full confidence in your courage, devotion to duty, and skill in Battle. We march in our might to complete victory. May God's blessing rest upon each of you this Christmas Day.

288

Almighty and most merciful Father, we humbly beseech Thee, of Thy great goodness, to restrain these immoderate rains with which we have to contend. Grant us fair weather for Battle. Graciously hearken to us as soldiers who call upon Thee, that armed with Thy power, we may advance from victory to victory, and crush the oppression and wickedness of our enemies and establish Thy justice among men and nations. Amen

Well, the prayer for good weather worked! The Germans had taken advantage of bad weather, rain, snow, and freezing temperatures to counterattack and push the Allies west out of Germany. The weather improved, and the Third Army was able to break through at Bastogne, Belgium, on December twenty-sixth. The paper called this the "Battle of the Bulge."

Maybe, just maybe, this is the beginning of the end for that devil Hitler.

1945 January 9
Kathleen
Snow

When I got home from the bank today, there were two letters from Walter. Finally! Since I haven't heard anything since before Christmas, I have been desperate with worry.

There was also a letter from Buck with a picture of him standing in the snow in front of Notre Dame Cathedral in Paris! So glad he is safe in the liberated city and serving as a supply clerk. I wish Walter could have stayed there. My men are getting to see the city of my dreams.

The newsreel last week showed Patton's Army in the snows in Belgium trying to push back the German "bulge." The news says we are winning, and this is just Germany's last desperate push.

In December, they demanded that the Americans surrender! The gall to ask such a thing after we have freed France and pushed them almost all the way back to Germany. U. S. Brigadier General McAuliffe's answer to this stupid demand was, "Nuts!" That made us double over in laughter when Mama read it from the paper. For a moment, I felt better.

This has been one of the worse winters in Europe ever. I keep imagining Walter cold and wet and stuck in a foxhole. How long can these men live in a dirt hole at night and get up every day to fight Germans?

Walter's recent letter spoke of being in a bombed-out house, and someone was playing a violin. I was glad he was in a warm place but sad to think about what may have happened to the people who lived in that house.

We had some snow last night here, just about three inches which is a lot for Fayetteville. I had to walk to work this morning, of course, and my boots have a hole in the bottom patched with cardboard, so my socks got completely soaked. I put them near the heater in my office and put some dry cardboard under the hole before I started home, so it wasn't too bad. I remember how Daddy used to do this to our shoes during the Depression. He called them "TWB New and Better Shoes" by Thomas Wesley Brantley. I miss him so much.

Evo and I went out to take a picture of me to send Walter. She thought he would like it since he is in snow, too. I wore a pair of Gene's trousers and the jacket I've had since we got married.

Evo and Gene tried to get me into a snowball fight. I just turned and went back in. Too cold. Too dark. Like some of Europe, still covered in Nazi darkness.

My head tells me the war is coming to an end. But I have an awful sense that something will happen to Walter.

1945 January 22
Evo
Telegram

I'm home from school with a bad cold, lying on the sofa under one of Mama's quilts, and reading. A sharp knock on the front door startles me. I kick off the quilt, toss my book on the floor, and jump up from the sofa. It's too early for the mailman. I bounce across the floor and peer through the lacy curtain.

A short man, wearing a blue uniform and a hat, stands very stiff and still. He is staring at his shoes, and his face looks as if he would like to be anywhere other than 229 Robeson Street.

My hands shake as I open the door. The man holds out a small, brown envelope. My heart pauses, and I can't get my breath.

"Mrs. James Rice?" he says tentatively.

I intend to call Mama from her sewing, but instead, a scream escapes my mouth.

Mama comes running. Seeing the open door, the man with the envelope, and my white face, she makes a little drop with her knees.

With the two of us staring anxiously at him, he says for the second time, "Mrs. James Rice?"

"No," says Mama, "she is at work." She takes the envelope and thanks the delivery man who can't get off our porch fast enough.

Mama slumps down on the sofa, and I sit down beside her. I put my arm around her thin shoulders. "Open it, Mama."

Mama's hands begin to shake. She rips open the envelope. She reads to herself.

A big tear makes its way down her face.

1945 January 22
Doris
Lights Out

I didn't go right home after work. I went see *Bon Voyage* at the Carolina with a new girl from work. It was about a young Scottish RAF gunner prisoner who escaped

I pull up to the house, there are no lights inside.

Opening the door, I ask, "Why are the lights off?"

Mama says, "A fuse is out, honey. Gene's fixing it."

The room is filled with people, A party?

Candles burn.

I see Mama's face first. And her tears. And she envelops me in her arms.

The lights come on.

Mama hands me a telegram.

To: MRS. JAMES C. RICE
229 ROBERSON STREET
FAYETTEVILLE, NORTH CAROLINA

THE SECRETARY OF WAR DESIRES ME TO EXPRESS HIS DEEP REGRET THAT YOUR HUSBAND STAFF SERGEANT JAMES C. RICE WAS KILLED IN ACTION IN A PLANE CRASH ON 21 JANUARY IN ITALY. OFFICIAL LETTER FOLLOWS.

J. A. ULIO, ADJUTANT GENERAL

I freeze and stare about. Thinking of the escape in the movie, "No! I am sure Jimmie escaped the crash."

There is a scream somewhere.

It is mine.

1945 January 25
Doris
Disbelief

Three days. Just three days since I received the telegram. I have hardly slept, so it seems like forever, each day just slipping into the next.

I didn't cry at first. Just went into a haze of disbelief. Surely, this is a mistake. It was a plane crash. Maybe he jumped to safety and is wandering somewhere in Italy out of his head. Maybe he was captured by the Germans and was taken to a prison camp.

I read and reread the telegram. It did not say there were no survivors. Maybe there were, and he was one of them. So, I kept telling myself to wait for the letter that is to follow.

The worse thing was that I had to call Jimmie's parents in Kentucky because I am his person of record and all his official mail comes to me. I started to ask Mama to call for me, but that would be cruel to her. It is my responsibility. Mama sat with me and held my hand while I called.

I didn't know how to start, so I just blurted out when Mrs. Rice answered, "Jimmie was in a plane crash and died." She screamed, and her screams moved farther and farther from the phone.

Mr. Rice came on. He was calm and shared some of my feelings about the possibilities as to how Jimmie might have survived. He was so sweet and said he wished he was there to hug me and wait for the letter.

1945 February 7
Doris
The Letter

The letter arrived today. I hoped it would say it was all a mistake and that Jimmie is safe.

Dear Mrs. Rice,

St. Sgt. James Rice was a crew member on a B-25 Mitchell Bomber which took off from Alesani Airdome, island of Corsica, on 21 January 1945, on a mission to attack on a railroad bridge near San Michele, Italy. The plane dropped its bombs and was turning back to base when one of the other planes in the formation crashed into Sgt. Rice's plane. The plane was losing altitude before the crash and radioed in. That was the last heard of any of his crew. A thorough search through the ashes of the wreckage revealed nothing. The plane was completely burned. Sgt. Rice had completed forty-seven missions including the successful sinking of a German battleship in Spezia Harbor, Italy. He served his country honorably. I speak for all the members of his company who extend to you their deepest condolences.

I had to call the Rices again, and this time it was even worse.

I feel empty and despondent, but I will still hold to the possibility that Jimmie might have bailed out before the crash or somehow walked away.

There was no mention in the letter as to whether or not they found his dog tags in the wreckage, so how do they know for sure he was killed? I can feel the power of his strong personality. He can't be dead.

1945 February 18
Kathleen
Nazi Flag

Belgium
Jan. 4, 1945

My Darling Wife,
I love you more than anything in this world and I
miss you every second.
I received two very nice letters this week mailed in
early December. And also the box with sox and
bracelet. Thanks, honey.
You know, I have been away from you for three of
my birthdays, but I should be home for the next one.
I spent my birthday in a foxhole and also Christmas
and New Year's with snow on the ground. I was
thinking of you the whole time.
You asked me if I thought you have changed much.
Well, you are three years older, but I know you love
me even more now. As for me, I haven't changed
much only I have a moustache and my hair is cut
real short and I am a little heavier. I wish you could
send me more pictures. I have sent you a box with
the flag I took from Cherbourg and a German
helmet and bayonet. Did you get it? I want you to
take your picture with these things and send it. That
way, I can be reminded what I am fighting for. I
love you more than life. Walter

I did get the flag before Christmas. He must have
mailed it when he was in France. Evo took the picture for
me. I had to force a smile. Sitting with that Nazi stuff just
dragged me into a deeper sadness.

I hope Walter is in a warm place now that the Germans have been pushed back into their country. The war is winding down.

I should be able to hold to that thought and be hopeful, but I can't. After the news of Jimmie's death, I imagine the same thing happening to Walter. All this time, and he won't come back. I can't shake the blues, and they drag me down so that I can hardly move. Doris cries in bed at night, and I cry with her.

Mama has added Jimmie's gold star to the window. Doris is a gold star widow.

1945 February 28
Ethel
The Secret

Kathleen and I get up real early to walk all the way down to Person Street to catch the eight o'clock bus to Sanford.

This trip would have been easier if we could have gotten someone to drive us. Doris could not take us because she had to work. Most of our friends who have cars don't have decent tires or have used up their two gallon gas ration for the month.

Folks are thinking the war will be over soon and things will get better. I hope so. I am getting sick and tired of having to make do with rationing which seems to get stricter every few months.

Walking to the bus depot, Kathleen is so weakly and slow that I'm afraid we will miss our appointment. I just had to do something as she is so depressed and frets constantly over Slover. It is worse when she does not get a letter from him for a while. She assumes he is dead and jumps and bursts into tears when anyone knocks on the door, thinking it could be the Western Union man. She's worse since we got the news about Jimmie.

Our route to Sanford goes through the outskirts of Fort Bragg, and I hold my breath praying that seeing the barracks and supplies piled up won't set off one of Kathleen's crying fits. It doesn't because she is half asleep. She does not sleep at night, so she is drowsy all day. I wonder how she gets by at work.

The thirty-five miles takes about two hours and a half because of the stopping to pick up folks in Spring Lake and Tramway. We get there and, thank the good Lord, the doctor's drug store with office above it is only a block from the bus depot. I'm tired. I miss Wesley's strong and comforting ways at a time like this.

298

As we walk to the back of the drug store to the stairs, I am nervous to see Dr. Howard because of "the secret."

When I was growing up outside Sanford, I knew nothing about it. Only after Wesley and I had been married a few years did he tell me the secret and made me promise never to breathe a word about it. And I haven't, to this day.

The secret is about the doctor and Wesley's cousin George Bass's mama.

Once I commented on red-haired Betsey, the youngest of the eleven children in Bass family. All the other children had brown or blond hair, and I made a joke that maybe Betsey was fathered by the rural delivery mail carrier.

Wesley got a real serious look on his face. "No," he said right out, "Dr. Howard is her daddy."

At first I thought it was one of his jokes, but he looked down at his shoes and said, "Sweetie, I am saying the honest gospel truth."

You could have knocked me over with a feather! I didn't say anything for the longest time and neither did Wesley. Then I stammered, "What? How is that possible?"

"Well, in the usual way, Ethel.

"I played a lot at George's farm in the summertime. Sometimes the doctor would ride out to their place in the afternoon in his buggy and would say to us children playing in the yard, 'Came to check on your Ma since she has been right poorly. Where's your Daddy?' George's Daddy was never there. He always worked in the fields or took produce to market until six or seven in the evening.

"The doctor would tell us kids to go off and play in the woods, so it would be quiet as George's mamma needed to rest. Sometimes he would give us all a piece of candy from his store.

"This happened at least once a week one summer. I didn't know that George's mama was sick, but everybody took what Dr. Howard said as gospel. So, we did what he

299

said. We stayed away until we saw the dust cloud rising behind his buggy on the dirt road, often an hour or two after his arrival.

"Sometimes I would stay with George to eat supper, and we would find his mama in the kitchen cooking. We would ask if she felt better and she would say, 'The doctor knows just what to do for me.' That was strange because he never left her any medicine.

"The next May red haired Betsey was born. Yeah, the good doctor knew just what to do for her!"

"Wesley! What a thing to say! It is hard for me to imagine that stern, unsmiling woman enjoying sexual relations."

"Well, she must have, Ethel, or maybe since the doctor owned their house, this was rent payment. Maybe their Daddy even knew what was going on and allowed it as times were hard. He must have known about the visits because the kids must have mentioned them."

"Land o' Goshen, Wesley, I just can't take this in!"

"It's true, Ethel, but don't ever breathe a word of it. Most folks in Lee County probably know, but no one talks about it."

As Kathleen and I are climbing the stairs, I am thinking about the doctor's fire red hair.

1945 February 28
Kathleen
Burma Shave

I'm leaning against the bus window trying to get myself together before we reach Sanford. The dark clouds in my brain just won't let go. My whole body is weak and tight, and my stomach churns.

SHE KISSED THE HAIRBRUSH ...

The Burma Shave signs whiz by in the grimy window. I try to follow the sentence, but I can hardly concentrate.

BY MISTAKE ...

I have been just going through the motions at work. I hope no one notices.

SHE THOUGHT IT WAS ...

I thought the telegram was mine, and Walter had been killed.

HER HUSBAND JAKE ...

Jimmie's dead. I see Jimmie's beautiful hair and his handsome face dissolving into flames.

BURMA SHAVE.

I don't know how Doris has held up. She went to Kentucky for the funeral with his family and just came back and threw herself into her work at Sears, working longer hours or coming home very late. We never know where she goes after work. And we don't ask.

I am ashamed that I am the one who is a mess. Doris is too, but she keeps it in more. I hold it in at work; but when I come home, I let down and go to bed early and sleep. In sleep, I'm able to drop my burden of worry for Walter. I don't dream, or I don't remember if I do. But I usually wake after a few hours and just lie there and fret.

I wonder why Mama didn't take me to a doctor in Fayetteville. She has always gone back to Dr. Howard who was the Coggins family doctor when she was growing up. That's where she took Daddy when he got leukemia. A lot of good that did.

"Come on, Kathleen. We're in Sanford. We need to get off."

Her voice seems to come from far away. She reaches for my hand and leads me off the bus and to the to the office. I pray the doctor can help me as I need for this pain to go away.

1945 February 28
Kathleen
Electroshock

"Ethel, says you've been feeling poorly, Kathleen? Tell me what's wrong."

Twisting my hair, I try to find words. Mama pulls my hand from my neck.

"I just don't feel like myself."

"That so?" Dr. Howard pulls a big cigar from a polished wooden box and lights it with a fancy lighter. He leans back in his chair, and his big stomach rises above the desk. He takes a big draw on the cigar and exhales.

"So, what exactly are your symptoms, Kathleen?"

"Well... I'm weak and nervous. I only want to sleep, and that helps me stop thinking and worrying. But when I wake, the feelings are back. My stomach feels tight. In fact, your cigar smoke makes me nauseated ..."

"Sounds like you might be pregnant, dearie. You been stepping out on your brave husband who is fighting over in Europe? Huh...?"

"No!" There's a little lurch in my head, and it clears the dark clouds. "I have NOT been unfaithful to my husband! Not that there have not been offers because some men think a woman with a man away in service is easy prey."

"Well, let me examine you, just to be sure. You might have done something indiscrete and don't remember it."

"No! No! No! I have not! If there is nothing you can do for my depression, we are leaving."

"Settle down, little lady! If you aren't in a family way, we can send you to Chapel Hill for a little electroshock therapy. That seems to shake people out of their sadness and anxiety."

Mama, who has been silent the whole time, rises, picks up her purse, and puts on her coat and hat. "Thank you for your time, doctor. We'll be going now."

Dr. Morgan stands but says nothing.

Mama stamps down the stairs, and I follow. Out of the drug store. Onto the sidewalk to the depot.

Back on the bus, I am more alert and feeling better than I have in a long time.

Mama says, "The gall of that man, suggesting you are expecting! And the nerve to suggest a horrible treatment for you when he does not truly know what is wrong."

"I'll be ok, Mama. Maybe a little outrageous indignation is just what I needed."

The bus rolls out of Sanford and back to the highway. The next series of Burma Shave signs speaks my wish for that awful doctor.......

SPEED WAS HIGH...

WEATHER WAS HOT...

TIRES WERE THIN...

X MARKS THE SPOT...

BURMA SHAVE.

1945 March 3
Kathleen
Nero Decree

A brief wisp of warm breeze tosses my hair. Maybe we will have an early spring. I am walking slowly home from work.

"Hey, Mrs. Kelly. How are you this afternoon?" As I pass her house, she sits on her porch with her knitting.

"Well, hey there, Kathleen. Aren't you home from work a little early today?"

"Yes, I had no more letters to type, so Mr. Downing said I could go early." He has been so kind to me this winter. He knows how sad I have been even though I have tried so hard to cover it up.

I'm feeling more hopeful these days. Somehow the encounter with that nasty Dr. Howard shook me out of my fog. I feel stronger because I stood up to him. The paper is lying on the swing. I sit and read, and looky here! Right on the front page a little section about soldiers receiving medals:

First Sgt. Walter Slover of Fayetteville has been awarded the Bronze Star for meritorious service in Europe. Sgt. Slover was previously awarded the Silver Star for his gallantry in North Africa.

My man. I am filled with pride.

And, another frontpage article about Hitler destroying his government facilities that could fall into Allied hands as they go deeper into Germany. This is called Demolitions of Reich Territory Decree, but the Allies are calling it the "Nero Decree." Like Emperor Nero who supposedly started a great fire to destroy his failing empire to keep the enemy from getting treasures.

Evo comes skipping up the steps and settles in next to me. "Guess what, Evo? This war is about over. Hitler is getting soft."

She leans in and puts her arm across my chest and her head on my shoulder.

"I can't wait till Slover comes home. I have so much to tell him."

1945 March 11
Kathleen
Amazing Gift

Mama, Evo, and I went to church this morning. We left Doris sleeping. Since the news about Jimmie, she doesn't get up until lunch time on the weekends. One small comfort in her grief.

I'm ashamed that I haven't given her more support as I have struggled through my anxiety and depression.

I have low moments but am determined to pull myself up and hope for Walter's return. I've been getting outside more. Yesterday, I went to the ginkgo tree. It's putting out small leaves already.

We heard the most amazing thing at church. Pastor Gaines read a letter that Mrs. Inman received from her son who had been on the Belgium/German border in December. The same area where Walter was!

> *Dear Mama,*
>
> *I can now tell you about Christmas on the front. We spent the day in our foxholes. Surrounded by snow! Yes, we had a white Christmas. Mama, you are always wishing for a snowy Christmas, so I enjoyed one for you! We made snowballs. If a soldier stuck his head out, someone would let him have it! We got a chuckle when the lieutenant took one right in the face!*
>
> *We had a really good Christmas dinner. Delicious "GI Steak" known to you as Spam! And soggy crackers which were nicely soft. Delectable! You know that stuff isn't bad. Someone had two bottles of wine pilfered from a house on our march here. We passed them around and enjoyed a nice addition to our repast.*

Later in the day a strong breeze came along with some new snowfall. The ground got covered with fir branches. I pulled a few into my hole and pressed a little Christmas tree into the wall. The cracker can had a gold cast to it, so I cut a little star out of its roll back lid and put it on my tree! I am going to try to save it to put on our tree when I am home next Christmas.

I lined the borders of my hole with more branches. My buddy in the next hole started singing "Deck the Halls." Others joined in quietly as we didn't want to wake the enemy from their Christmas afternoon nap. They were probably dreaming about being home with their families, just as we were.

We're going to get this war wrapped up! Believe it! And next year I'll be home for Christmas, not in my dreams, but for real!
Love, Robert

There were plenty of tears in that sanctuary. Tears of hope. Tears of gratitude for our American boys who, like Robert, try to keep a positive attitude. Robert sent an amazing gift to his mother and to us by sharing this upbeat and funny story.

If the boys can be hopeful there, we have a responsibility to be the same on the home front. This war IS going to be over soon! And the boys will be coming home!

1945 March 16
Kathleen
A Letter from Mom

Dear Kathleen,

Just a few lines as I want to send the first boy that gets here to school this morning to mail this for me. I want you to get this as soon as possible. We haven't had any recent mail from Walter. Our last was dated January thirtieth. But, Kathleen, I am sure he is on his way home.

I drop the letter and scramble to pick it up!

Do you remember Joe Dig that was in Walter's company from here? Well, he wrote his mother and said, "Mom, Walter Slover is coming home and will come out to see you and tell you all about me." They live three miles east of here. Edward and me went out and read the letter. You remember me telling you of that lady in Illinois whose son was with Walter and was killed and Walter wrote to her? Well, I got another letter from her and she had gotten a letter from a Masonic service center in London and they said Walter was in there on February twenty-first and told them about her son being killed. She said I wonder if Walter is on his way home.

Get to the point, Mom! She knows how to drag out a story.

Well, you know if he was in London he is coming home for they would not take him back there for any other reason.

*Now, honey, now don't let this upset you and
get sick again.*

Why would she think this news would make me
depressed again? This is just the cure I needed!

*He will probably be in any day now and you
must be able to come on home with him. Let us just
pray for it all to be true and thank God for bringing
him safely home to us. I can't eat or sleep here.
I would have called you but was afraid to tell such a
thing over the phone.*

Oh, Mom! Why didn't you call? I could have
known this days ago!

*Rex got the telegram telling them Ralph was
killed. I could not tell them of Walter coming home.
I feel so sorry for them. And some of the boys from
here that had been reported missing have been
declared dead in the last few days.
Well, honey, I must close and get your
suitcase packed for I expect to see you soon. Since it
was nineteen days since he was in that service
center, it surely won't be long. All my love, Mom*

"Mama!" My shriek brings her out of the kitchen
with biscuit dough all over her hands. I grab her floury
hands and pull her into my dance across the room.
"Kathleen, have you lost your mind?"
"No, Mama. I have just found it. Walter is coming
home!"

310

1945 April 10
Kathleen
Coming Home

April 3, 1945

My Darling Wife,

I am on my way home, I still can't believe it.

You get your duds packed because we are going to head for home as soon as I get there.

One thing I want you to do is get that olive drab shirt and pants of mine cleaned and pressed. Have all the other things washed

My Darling I love you more than anything in the world and after all these months of dreaming of you, I will be able to take you in my arms again.

See you soon, Honey.

Don't write any more.

Your Husband, Slover

1945 April 13
Ethel
Warm Springs

The President died yesterday! He had a cerebral hemorrhage right there at Warm Springs, Georgia, where he went to rest up before going to a conference to help start the new United Nations.

What a shock!

He has been the president who got us out of the Depression and led us through war. Now that it is almost over, he does not get to see it through.

We were all so happy when he was elected for his fourth term. Things still looked bleak then and especially around Christmas with our boys fighting in Belgium and the Germans pushing back. Slover was in that. Now the Germans are on the run being pushed back into their country. And the horrors that the Allies are discovering! Jews held, starved, and murdered in camps like the one called Auschwitz. I wonder if Slover saw any of this. For years the Germans were trying to get rid of all Jews in these camps, and we never knew!

The President's body is traveling by train back from Georgia to Washington. The radio reported that thousands of people are standing elbow to elbow along the route. I wish his train was coming through Fayetteville. Evelyn was disappointed.

That child was absolutely inconsolable when I told her the news yesterday after she got home. She was the most upset for the first lady. She does not understand that the president and his wife were not particularly close and does not know of the rumors of his infidelities.

She loves Eleanor. "Will Mrs. Roosevelt be the president, now?"

"No, sweetie, Vice President Truman will assume the office. It's the Vice President's job serve if something happens to the president."

"Well," dabbing her tears, "she would be a better president than that stuffy old man.

"She is so nice and smart on the radio. When I grow up, I am going to run for president! And if I have babies, I'm naming them Franklin and Eleanor."

"I hope you will, my girl. You would be a wonderful president." I take her in my arms and smooth her hair.

1945 April 19
Evo
Good News Telegram

Slover's Mom called yesterday to tell us that she received a card from Slover letting her know he has arrived in the Port of New York.

Hooray! Yipee! He is coming home. I just knew he would. He is too smart and strong and handsome to get himself killed in Germany.

Kathleen and I are sitting in the swing after supper. Up the walk comes the short man in the blue uniform and hat. The same one that brought Doris' telegram. He holds out the brown envelope. "Mrs. Walter Slover?"

Kathleen takes it with a big smile and hands it to me. "Here, Evo. You should open it. Telegrams can bring good news."

I rip it open so fast that I tear a corner off the message. I read it out loud.

Arrived safely expect to see you soon don't attempt to contact or write me here.

Walter Slover

1945 April 20
Evo
I Just Can't Wait!

Walter is coming home!

I can't wait to hug him and tell him about all the things that happened while he was gone! The happy things: Doris' wedding. Kathleen getting well. Frankie's Bugs Bunny Bike. My learning to cook. Being in the color guard in the band. My Little Lady Ann Shirley Doll. Wonder Woman Comics.

And the sad things: Danny Jennings. Barbara. Jimmie. Our fort being destroyed by hobos. The president dying. Missing sugar. People being mean to Abby. Not ever hearing from Tomoko.

I want to see his scar where the bullet is.

Most of all, I just want to hug him.

1945 April 25
Kathleen
Salutes along Roberson Street

After Walter's telegram, I have heard nothing from him.

An excited but unsettled feeling in my stomach has become constant. Ecstatic, that my husband is coming home at last. Unsettled, as I'm afraid I won't know him after all these years.

It's hard to concentrate at work, and I have made mistakes in shorthand dictation from Mr. Downing. I try to pay attention, but Mr. Downing's words beat against the pulsing in my head. I sit at my typewriter and try to fill in the words I missed. Mr. Downing is sympathetic and gently asks me to make corrections when he sees the copy. His kindness brings me close to tears.

After supper, I sit in the swing. It's a gentle spring evening. Dogwoods bloom in full, and the air is newly fresh. I'm desperate for a telegram or a call. I know Walter disembarked in New York but have no idea when he will get to Fayetteville.

I have heard the horrific stories of returning soldiers having to find train rides or hitchhike to reach their homes. What if he is injured or killed by a robber? After all the danger he faced for almost two and a half years, what if he dies trying to come home? What if he has returned with the mindset of poor Danny Jennings?

Every day after work, I have met the arriving Atlantic Coastline trains and watched soldiers step off into the arms of family. No Walter. I'm a tangle of nerves.

The strains of Doris playing "I'll Fly Away" on our out-of-tune piano are irritating as is most every sound now. I don't ask my sister to stop since I know music is some shallow comfort after her Jimmie was killed.

Doris' music stops. It is quiet. The air is still and pleasantly warm. I hear the distant rhythm of yet another Atlantic Coastline train slow and slow and slow until the clacking stops.

I look down the street. The daylight is dying, bathing the houses in soft grey. My eyes focus past Gibson's Grocery toward the Ramsey Street and Roberson intersection.

Movement. A shapeless image darker than the evening air. Probably someone coming from work. Maybe Janie Ringo's Sam.

Neighbors, sitting on porches on this fine spring evening, begin to stand and salute.

My heart races and moves to my throat. I rise and step into the yard, my eyes fixed on the advancing image. A person. A man. And a bag over his shoulder.

I stumble over a tree root and almost fall. I begin to run as does the figure.

Walter.

Space between us diminishes until we are all arms and hands and kisses and tears.

Nazi Flag from Cherbourg Kathleen, February 1945 Buck at Notre Dame, Paris

Buck Roger Gene

Roger's drawing Evo and Kathleen Doris and Kathleen Ethel

Kathleen and Walter reunited, 1945

In the porch swing, 1946

Silk map of France carried by Walter
in the invasion

Walter's medals

1945 June 1
Evo
Baby

Hooray! School is out! No more pencil, no more books, no more teacher's dirty looks!

Edna and I are planning to use the summer to work on our "look." We read every page of Doris' *Glamour Magazine* and a new one just for teenagers called *Seventeen*. Mama won't let me wear lipstick, but Edna and I plan to buy some and put it on after we leave for school. And then, rub it off on the way home. What Mama doesn't know won't hurt her.

But the most exciting thing is that Kathleen and Slover are expecting a little baby in January! I believe it will be a girl, and I keep suggesting names. Scarlett, Eleanor, Elizabeth. They are living in Indiana now, so I write to Kathleen and tell her my choices.

And, Roger is stationed at a hospital in Hawaii! Wow! Would I ever love to be there with all the pineapple, grass skirts, and beach!

It is so swell that the awful war is over. Well, the German part is. We can forget all the bad things. Like Jimmie Rice being killed in a plane crash and Danny Jennings killing himself. I just will never understand why he did that. Mama said it was because he was sad about things he saw in the war. But he was home and safe and could just forget that old war.

That old history that doesn't concern us now.

1945 September 15
Doris
Beer

My Jimmie made it almost to the end. At Christmas he wrote that he would be coming home soon.

I still believe he is alive somewhere, captured, or rescued and wandering around looking for a way home. He is going to show up one day.

None of the family knows this, but after work, I have been going to a little bar on Hay Street with some other war widows. There are four of us. They drink beers, and I order one too but just sip a little because it tastes awful. Mama would keel over with apoplexy if she knew I even let a trace of liquor cross my lips.

We widows cry and tell each other our feelings and then laugh when the beers start to kick in. This may be wrong, and I would die if anyone I know saw me going into the bar. But I need this. Being with these women is my only comfort.

No one else understands. People say things like, "You must be proud to know your man died serving his country" or "You are so young, and you will find someone else." No, I am not proud that Jimmie died, nor do I want to find someone else. These people are well-intentioned, but none of this talk is helpful.

Just leave me alone! I am sad beyond words, angry, and empty. I would give all that I have or ever will have just to put my arms around Jimmie one more time and tell him how much I love him. We used to fight a lot, but I can't remember why.

Kat writes me from Indiana that Slover is not like she remembers him before. He is sometimes distracted and does not respond when she talks to him. And angry. Upset when she doesn't keep their room neat. He grits his teeth and speaks sharply, but not loudly. She knows he doesn't want his family to hear. Around them, he is all sweetness and light.

He doesn't talk about things from the war. But during the night, he will awake and mutter nonsense, or his body will jump and startles her awake.

War. It took my life and joy. It may have broken Slover. Yes, it is over but festering wounds remain. Will they ever heal?

1946 April 4
Ethel
Normal

It's been over for a year now. Normal life is coming back, little by little.

No more rationing. I think we all are getting a little fatter because I make plenty of sweet cakes and cookies! We go more places since gas is available, especially to Sanford to the farm to see Mama and Daddy. There is a lightness among the neighbors on Roberson Street. More laughter, more freedom.

Roger is in Japan working at a hospital. They treat Japanese children there, many of them survivors from the atomic bombs. Heartbreaking that we had to use bombs to make the Japs surrender.

When Roger's service time is over, he is going back to Washington state and marry Dee. I haven't even met her! He's head over heels for her. He has moved from one girl to another so often that I can't quite take in his settling on one.

Buck is back home. He was never directly in combat but was in danger with the Ordnance Division as he delivered arms and supplies to the soldiers on the front. He got his old job back at the drugstore. They let go the woman who took his place. Too bad for her, but our returning men have to come first.

My sweet baby boy Eugene, drafted near the end, is in Germany with the occupation forces. Even though the Germans were soundly whipped, we have to keep an eye on them and help them rebuild. Funny that we help them, but I know there are innocent German citizens who suffered under the Nazi craziness. Those Nazis even made boys as young as ten fight near the end.

Evo is happy as a lark. Busy in high school, she has a boyfriend! And believe it or not, it's Frankie Kelly from next door! After all those years of fighting and pestering each other! He took her to a Valentine dance. She looked so pretty in the rose-colored taffeta dress I made her.

Doris continues to believe Jimmy will come home, but she is strong and plunges ahead. She has been promoted to accounts at Sears Roebuck. Last Sunday, she invited Charlie Johnson, who works in the tire department, to dinner. He served during the war in medical supply in Oregon. Real nice, very gentle and mannerly. Hmm. I wonder if anything will come of that?

And Kathleen. She got pregnant immediately after Slover got home. He wanted to go back to Indiana to live, so off they went. He works in Turner's Store. It just broke my heart when their little daughter Cheryl Dean was stillborn in January and buried in Little Flock Cemetery in Shelburn. There were not enough tears to wash away the pain of losing my first grandchild.

Kathleen wrote that Slover thought that the baby died because he was being punished for all the lives he took during the war! War. In its wake, it leaves continuing pain and suffering.

Now, Kathleen is pregnant again! Praise Jesus! They are moving back here for a fresh start. Slover hopes to get a Civil Service job at Fort Bragg and use his GI Bill to buy a house before the baby comes.

I wonder about all the boys who came to our house before we got into the war. Are they buried under war-torn soil or are they home with their families? Doris has never heard from Horace Purvis who had the big fight with Jimmie and left his banjo in her care. It is lying on top of our piano, gathering dust.

Life moves ahead. But we are changed. I don't think I will ever feel completely safe in the world or be able to erase images of the awful things done to innocent people in Europe. But in the end, things were set right.

1946 October 20
Kathleen
Ginkgo Survivors

"Walter, look." We are swaying leisurely in the swing. He is staring into space. "Honey, look what's in the paper!" I read:

Extreme examples of the ginkgo's tenacity may be seen in Hiroshima, Japan, where six trees growing between 1–2 kilometers from the 1945 atomic bomb blast were among the few living things in the area to survive. Although almost all other plants (and animals) in the area were killed, the ginkgoes, though charred, survived and were soon healthy again.

"Just think. The ginkgo is a survivor! Just like us. Let's go see our tree."

"If you want to." We walk in silence. I try to draw him into talk about his new job as a Civil Service clerk at Fort Bragg, but he has nothing to share except, "It's fine."

His distance began when I asked if he saw any of the Jewish concentration camps. His face contorted and darkened. "Yes, we wasted those German guards." End of discussion. How I wish I had never asked. What he must have seen! The photos in *Life Magazine* were beyond belief skeletons in ditches and emaciated, ghost-like survivors.

Mama says Walter is trying to make sense of the awful things he saw in the war and will be better as time goes on. I hope so. Maybe when our little baby comes in February, he will snap out it.

The tree is just beginning to drop leaves, but they are not golden. Thanks to an almost rainless, hot summer, they are dull, brown, and brittle.

1954 August 10
Sherry
The Porch

The concrete porch, shedding its gray paint, is cool against my legs; a contrast to the humidity of the August dog days evening. My bare feet sprawl on red brick steps, where my pals and I played "Mother, may I" before the setting sun and anxious parents called us home. I am seven years old.

There is no tv or air conditioning to lure me inside. It is cool on the porch. My mother is inside by a window fan working crossword puzzles. Street lights illuminate neighbors' houses where a few are perched on their porches. Fireflies blink in little flashes and tempt me to capture them in a jar with holes poked in the lid.

Post-chase, I sit next to my father. He wears a sleeveless tee shirt and khaki shorts. He smokes a cigarette and flicks glowing embers into the darkness like little earthbound shooting stars. A symphony of crickets and cicadas rises and falls in an electric buzz. Mosquitoes nip bare arms and legs. We swat and keep sitting.

It never occurred to my childish mind to engage him in conversation or to ask what he was thinking.

But today, I know there must have been a panorama of terrifying memories playing in his head. A mere ten years earlier he had been smoking his cigarettes in Europe, plunging on through France and Germany, liberating Jews from Nazi death camps, eliminating a monster.

Those nights we sat in silence, he was hurting. Perhaps he was trying to come to terms with horrific things he had seen and done.

My father did not try to banish the demons of war by talking to his family, a therapist, or anyone. He just sucked up his hurt and went on with life.

Yet, today, too late to help him, I realize that he was racked by guilt of deeds he was forced to commit in the name of liberty. He sought peace in his religion that offered the miracle of forgiveness, but I don't think he ever was able to forgive himself.

Two souls, sitting on a porch, witnesses to a summer night. If only I could have offered him solace. Maybe I did, just by being his child, sitting sentinel to his thoughts.

Acknowledgements

My gratitude to:

My mother Kathleen Brantley Slover, who left me artifacts that grew into this book: stories, high school yearbooks, diaries, postcards, family letters, scrapbooks, pictures, magazines, and newspapers. And her most precious gifts: my dad's helmet, dog tags, and his canteen cup on which he embossed the names of all the places he served (Scotland, Ireland, Algeria, Tunisia, Sicily, England, France, Belgium, and Germany), a silk map he carried in the invasion, and his letters.

Members of the "Greatest Generation" who granted me interviews: Evelyn Kelly, Frank Kelly, Doris Johnson, Tut McFarland, Billie and Hershel Osborne, Emily Middleton, Lois Robinson, Stanley Applegate, Maureen Hedrick, Jean Manly, Frances and Winfred Bryant, and Marylou Hobgood.

Those who shared memories from their relatives or friends, diaries, documents, and ideas: Clay Johnson, Linda Brantley, Jackie Dickey, Cindy Ray, Mike White, Jim Todd, and Robert Downing. Tomoko Sugano Little who allowed me to borrow her name. Weeks Parker for the postcard of White Lake and locations of some landmarks and buildings in Fayetteville in the 1940's. Bob Applegate who suggested the title. Trevor Ledford who created the beautiful cover.

The World War II class at First United Methodist Church in Dalton, Georgia, led by Ralph Williams, that set me on a path to learn about the places my father served, along with *Eight Stars to Victory: The History of the Ninth Division* (compiled and written by Captain Joseph B. Mittelman, Battery Press, Nashville. 1948.)

My friends in the Lesche Women's Club of Dalton, Georgia, who brought some chapters to life in a dramatic reading and helped me see the story in a whole new way: Glenda Rizer, Martha Waskey, Mary Etta Sanders, and Virgelia Meek.

My Beta readers who edited: Stanley Applegate, Elizabeth Avett, Martha Waskey, Susan Brigman, Sherrian Hall, and Rob Thompson. The Dalton Area Writers Group for their encouragement. Jamie Patterson and Pam Rogers for layout assistance.

My patient husband Jim Patterson, my anchor throughout the birthing and completion of this novel ... and in life. Thank you for getting me a new laptop. And accompanying me to Normandy and standing in awe with me on those beaches.

My father First Sergeant Walter C. Slover, 3rd Army, 39th Infantry, Company K. European African Middle Eastern Campaign, Bronze Star (4th highest award for bravery), Silver Star (3rd highest combat decoration for conspicuous valor in the face of the enemy), Victory Medal World War II, Efficiency Honor Fidelity (Good Conduct.) And Purple Heart. And a piece of German shrapnel in his leg.

About the author

Sherry Slover Patterson, a graduate of the University of North Carolina at Greensboro and the University of West Georgia, is a retired high school English teacher, having taught a variety of literature and grammar courses, English as a second language, and creative writing

She has been writing poetry and short pieces all her adult life, but *Under the Ginkgo Tree* is her first book.

She was born in North Carolina and has lived in the South and the Northeast.

Currently living in Dalton, Georgia, with her husband and cat, she plays a mountain dulcimer, directs a group of folk musicians, volunteers in community and church, and is an avid reader, lover of nature, and traveler.

Made in the USA
Monee, IL
28 April 2020

27078574R00196